CHARLEY SUNDAY'S TEXAS OUTFIT
DEADFALL

CHARLEY SUNDAY'S TEXAS OUTFIT
DEADFALL

STEPHEN LODGE

PINNACLE BOOKS
Kensington Publishing Corp.
www.kensingtonbooks.com

PINNACLE BOOKS are published by

Kensington Publishing Corp.
119 West 40th Street
New York, NY 10018

ISBN-13: 978-0-7860-3391-1
ISBN-10: 0-7860-3391-6

First printing: May 2015

10 9 8 7 6 5 4 3 2 1

Printed in the United States of America

First electronic edition: May 2015

ISBN-13: 978-0-7860-3392-8
ISBN-10: 0-7860-3392-4

Prologue

1961

Marshmallows were bubbling like lava, with tiny clumps dropping into the remains of a glowing charcoal fire, as the Pritchard family prepared their individual desserts—putting a cap to a wonderful Memorial Day backyard picnic.

Everyone giggled and laughed as the burned and gooey, sugar-laden globs were pulled from the straightened wire coat-hangers, then sandwiched between chocolate-covered graham crackers.

The entire family was there: Noel, the youngest; Caleb, the middle child; Josh, the oldest—the only teenager; their mom, Evie; and their great-grandfather, Hank. As for the children's father—he was the main reason they were celebrating.

"I'd like to say a few words about your father, if you don't mind," said the old man, Hank.

Everything came to a stop while the members of the Pritchard family found places to sit—in folding chairs and at a redwood picnic table—before they gave the older man their full attention.

"Captain Henry E. Pritchard III . . . husband, father, and grandson to one of the members of this gathering, was lost over California's high desert a few years back, while test-flying a newer version of a United States top-secret reconnaissance airplane," said Grampa Hank. "As you all know, that is the only information the government would release to us at the time."

All around the neighborhood other families were also bowing their heads in remembrance of their own personal never-to-be-forgotten loved ones.

Hank's words about his grandson brought tears to everyone's eyes, especially Evie, mother of the honored man's three children. Hank summed it all up by asking Noel to lead them in The Lord's Prayer.

Later on, as darkness began to fall, Evie asked her late husband's grandfather if he would mind sharing with her and the children the story about his parents being abducted in a city along the Mexican border, then spirited away, leaving no trace. And how his personal experience of losing his parents—even though it was only for a short period of time—might compare with the feelings her children had about their own father's disappearance.

"That's the God's truth," said Hank. "I was with my folks when it happened. I witnessed the whole thing."

"Then tell us the story," said Noel. "Will you, Grampa?"

"Yeah, Grampa Hank," said Josh, "you never mentioned anything about your parents being abducted before."

"If you were there, why weren't you abducted, too?" added Caleb.

"Well, since it's a holiday and all that," said Hank, "I

suppose you all won't mind staying up a little later than usual."

Noel said, "School doesn't start until nine thirty for me, Grampa Hank. And since today was a holiday, it'll be a special school day honoring Memorial Day. Mommy already told me I could stay up later than usual tonight, if I wanted to."

"Well, if that's the case," said Hank, "I better get started because sometimes this story can be a long one . . . depending."

"Depending on what?" asked the three children almost in unison.

"Depending on whether I want to make it a short one," said the old man. "Now let me think a minute. Let's see how I want to start this thing off this time . . ."

CHAPTER ONE

1900

Eleven-year-old Henry Ellis Pritchard sat quietly between his parents in a hired, open-top carriage, as they traveled down Main Street in Brownsville, Texas.

He was dressed in his Sunday best—from his blue, four-in-hand tie, his suit coat and knickers, with their knee-high stockings, to his brand-new, lace-up, ankle-high shoes. His light brown hair, slicked backed when the journey began, was now blowing gently in the gulf breeze. His ever-present smile shone bright as always—just as his mother had taught him to do at all times.

Sitting across from the family was a well-dressed Mexican gentleman, a security officer employed by the man they were going to visit. The security officer's name was Jose "Roca" Fuerte—and he would smile at Henry Ellis every so often.

Henry Ellis studied the man. In Austin, where he came from, one seldom saw a Mexican anymore. But here in Brownsville—directly across the river from Matamoros, a thriving Mexican city of its own—they were plentiful. He'd seen a few Mexicans during his visits to his grandfather's the previous summer, when he stayed with him on his old ranch in Juanita, Texas. But Juanita was much closer to the international border than Austin.

Jose Roca Fuerte wore a large *sombrero*—not one of those with a very high crown, and extremely wide brim, that Henry Ellis had seen in one of his history books, but a much tamer version, made from beaver pelts, as most American-made hats were constructed. His once black, now going to white, mustache, had been trimmed neatly above his upper lip. And he wore his sideburns and hair—also white—quite long, to cover some smallpox scarring he had on his neck and both cheeks. Henry Ellis knew that was what it was because he'd seen the same scars on several of his classmates back in Austin.

Betty Jean, the boy's mother, held a bouquet of long-stem roses in her lap.

"I am glad you are enjoying the flowers, Mrs. Pritchard," said Fuerte. "They were gathered from the personal gardens of Don Roberto."

Henry Ellis watched as Fuerte spoke, the man's eyes shifting from one direction to another—always on the alert for trouble. At the same time the boy listened to the sounds of the border city—especially those made by the hooves of the two-horse matching team that pulled the carriage. The Mexican driver was taking them to the border bridge crossing at the far end of the well-traversed, cobblestone boulevard.

Other carriages, buggies, and freight wagons, plus men of all dress on horseback, packed the wide thoroughfare, moving in both directions, as the carriage made its way toward the gated, international boundary.

"Now, son," said the boy's father, Kent, "I know you've been to Mexico with me several times before . . . and I know you've always enjoyed those outings we've had together below the border. I just want to remind you again that this trip isn't going to be just like it was on those other occasions. This visit is primarily for business reasons—though there will be a social side to it.

"As you already know," he went on, "our family has been selected by my company to be the guests of Don Roberto Acosta y Castro . . . the owner of one of the major trading firms with which we do business. The Don is also a younger brother to the commanding general of the Mexican army. We will be staying at the Don's *hacienda*, on his *rancho* on the other side of Matamoros, Brownsville's sister city across the Rio Grande. Señor Fuerte has been assigned to accompany us for our protection. There are some people in Mexico, we've recently discovered, who would do us harm just because I work for a company that does business with Don Roberto."

The boy looked again at the security man sitting across from him.

"Does the Don keep any horses on his *rancho*?" the boy asked.

"The Don?" said Fuerte. "I am sure that he does. *Sí*."

"Now don't you let me catch you begging Don Roberto for a horseback ride, young man," said his mother, Betty Jean, "or anything else. If you do, I'll paddle your little butt so hard you won't be able to sit down for all the time we're in Mexico, plus what it takes for us to get back home to Austin."

"Sorry, Mother," said Henry Ellis, feeling somewhat uncomfortable. "I'll try not to embarrass you if you try not to embarrass me. I'm almost twelve years old, Mother."

"Don't you crack wise with me, young man," said Betty Jean.

"He wasn't making a joke of it, darlin'," said Kent.

"Henry Ellis will fit in just fine during our stay with Don Roberto."

"I am sure that he will," said Fuerte.

The boy's attention had been drawn to a small plaza up ahead where a freight wagon appeared to have broken down. Several men wearing colorful *ponchos* and large *sombreros* were attempting to remove a broken wheel, while the anxious mules balked at the imposition. Others had gathered around to observe.

The driver slowed the carriage as they prepared to pass the damaged wagon near the fountain in the center of the plaza.

"Señor Pritchard," said Fuerte to Henry Ellis's father, "this is not a place for an accident . . . This is a place for an . . . ambush."

"I knew we should have gone another way," said Betty Jean.

"There is no other way," said Fuerte.

He reached inside his waistcoat and pulled a small .32-caliber, four-barrel pepperbox pocket gun, handing it to Kent, who seemed reluctant to take it. Fuerte turned to Betty Jean and the boy.

"You two must get down . . . at once," he said.

Fuerte helped Betty Jean and Henry Ellis kneel down onto the floorboards of the carriage.

By then the plaza had filled with more curious onlookers. In Spanish, Fuerte told the driver that he should back the team up and find another route.

Fuerte finally shoved the small gun into Kent's hand and drew his own sidearm—a .44-caliber Smith & Wesson Russian model double-action revolver.

The two-horse team was urged to back up—pushing the rear end of the carriage into a two-wheel handcart that someone had purposely rolled into the vehicle's path.

Suddenly a large Mexican man in the street stepped onto the running board of the coach and pulled Fuerte out of the carriage, sending them both sprawling onto the cobblestones.

In the meantime the carriage driver was able to find an opening in the crowd. He whipped at the horses, moving the coach farther on up the street.

Still on the ground, Fuerte swung at the man with whom he was fighting, using his pistol as a club. The attacker's blood splattered onto several people nearby.

Fuerte turned to run after the carriage. Even so, the bloodied man reached out, grabbing for his boot.

Without hesitation, Fuerte whirled and fired his weapon point-blank at the man. The bullet found its target between the attacker's eyes.

Fuerte stumbled on, continuing his pursuit of the coach.

Up ahead in the carriage, the boy watched his father fire the small pepperbox pocket gun Fuerte had given him, twice—with both slugs hitting their mark. One of the attackers took a bullet to the shoulder, with the second projectile clipping the other man's earlobe. It was then the boy's father realized he only had two cartridges left, and that he wasn't going to do much damage with the small pistol he had against the number of men who were surrounding them. In moments, Henry Ellis's father was completely overpowered, face-to-face with the large number of armed Mexicans who were now climbing onto the running boards on each side of the carriage. Henry Ellis continued to watch as their driver was attacked by two men from each side and his throat slit. The driver's body was then dumped onto the cobblestones, where it fell like a rag doll. One of the ambushers took his place behind the reins.

Henry Ellis was watching all of this from the floorboards

as his father continued to defend his mother and himself from the swarm of aggressors with his fists.

His father looked down and shouted to the boy:

"Forget about your mother and me for now, Henry Ellis. Just get out of here . . . *at once* . . . and please, my son . . . Trust no one!"

He reached over to the handle of the opposite door and opened it for the boy.

Henry Ellis jumped . . . right through the tangle of Mexican legs crowded together on the narrow running board.

The boy rolled several times on the cobblestones before he was able to sit up.

As the carriage carrying both his mother and father disappeared into the throngs of people, Henry Ellis could still see his father as he handed over the pepperbox pocket gun to one of the Mexican men who had been assaulting them.

A tear began to form in one of the boy's eyes. He blinked several times to shake it free . . . and when he could see clearly again, Roca Fuerte was standing over him, the smoking Smith & Wesson still in his hand.

"Come with me at once, Henry Ellis," he said. "We must leave the city immediately. It is of no use for us to follow them. Those men appear only to want your father for now, not us. It is better that we report what has happened to Don Roberto as soon as we can."

"What about the police?" said Henry Ellis. "Shouldn't we contact the police?"

"No *policía*," replied Fuerte firmly. "We do not want the authorities involved. It is much better that we let Don Roberto handle this situation using his own militia."

Henry Ellis jerked away from the security man. He turned immediately, then ran into the crowd, disappearing completely from Fuerte's sight.

His father's words, *Trust no one*, rang over and over in his ears.

Don Roberto Acosta y Castro was riding in from surveying another seventy-five thousand hectares of grazing land he had recently inherited from a deceased cousin. The newly acquired property was adjacent to his own estate, which was part of an old Spanish land grant shared by him and the rest of the Acosta family.

The Don galloped through the entrance gates leading to his *hacienda*. He was followed by his foreman and eight Acosta *vaqueros*.

As the assemblage reined up in front of the main house, Tomás, his number one houseman, came running down the steps holding a small envelope in his hand.

"Don Roberto," he called out. "Something terrible has happened. A messenger was just here. He left this note for you. He said it was very important."

When he reached Don Roberto, Tomás handed him the envelope. The Don took a few moments to open, then read the short message before turning to his foreman, Luis Hernandez.

"Luis," he said, "this message is from Roca Fuerte. The Americans he was bringing to visit me have been abducted . . . and Roca thinks the Armendariz gang had something to do with it."

"*Sí*, Don Roberto," said Luis. "Shall I contact your brother in Veracruz?"

"No," said Don Roberto. "Not yet. For now I would like to keep the army out of this. I think we should be able to handle it ourselves. I will send him a message when we know more about what is going on."

"*Si, mi jefe*," said the foreman.

"I want you to do whatever you can to find them, Luis. It is my responsibility to locate that American family and bring those who took part in their abduction to justice. Choose the best gunmen in my employ; they will know how to handle Armendariz and his people."

"But where do we start looking, Don Roberto?" asked Hernandez. "This is a big country. Where do we start?"

"I will be with you, Luis, and I do not care where we start," said Don Roberto. "And I also do not care about how many men we must kill to find them. Just as long as we find those Americans and bring them here to my *hacienda*."

"I will gather up a few more men—"

"You will take the chosen members of my militia, plus all of my *vaqueros*, if need be," said Don Roberto. "This is an embarrassment for me. And it will bring me a much larger humiliation if anything happens to that American family."

Chapter Two

Charley Sunday was smiling.

He stood reminiscing beside his favorite horse, Dice, the handsome paint with one blue eye he'd taken to Colorado and ridden during the Colorado-to-Texas longhorn cattle drive nearly a year earlier.

Charley's brown, leathery hands stroked the horse's neck. His just as tanned and deeply furrowed countenance wrinkled even more as he squinted in the afternoon sun's fading rays. For a moment, he hitched his thumbs under his lime-green suspenders and gave his pants a tug, pulling them up half an inch or so to keep them in their proper position.

Man and horse were resting in the shade of an old pepper tree at the top of a low hillock overlooking Charley's Juanita, Texas, ranch.

Charley had been casually watching a distant object nearly three-quarters of a mile away, something that had momentarily perked his interest.

A familiar old wagon was lurching down the recently graded farm-to-market road that passed the entrance to his ranch. The slow-moving vehicle was also weaving—

zigzagging slowly—as if the driver might be having trouble with the steering mechanism, or with his team. Or possibly, God forbid, the driver had been drinking.

Charley continued to observe the wagon as it finally pulled over and came to a standstill at the side of the road. A single passenger was discharged before the old wagon pulled out onto the thoroughfare again. The driver put his horses into a wide U-turn, then headed off back in the direction from which he had come.

It had been a while since Charley and his brave little band of dedicated cowhands had driven the herd of Texas longhorns down from Colorado. The three hundred head of longhorn cattle had belonged to an old transplanted Texan who, years earlier, had sixty-four longhorns delivered to his new homestead—a large ranch near Denver, Colorado.

When the old man died a year ago, his family put the entire herd—which had grown to three hundred—on the auction block. By doing this—bidding on the entire herd, then driving them back home to Texas—Charley Sunday had earned for himself, to keep as his own, ten percent of the entire herd.

Flora Mae Huckabee—the local hotel, bar, and poolroom owner—had been Charley's special lady-friend on and off since their childhood years, and was also the financial backer of the Colorado to Texas cattle venture. She had allowed Charley three whole days by himself to pick and choose his way through the longhorns. Charley had spent many an hour separating out from the others the stock he wished to keep for his own. That comprised a fair amount of breeding-age heifers. It also included the only bull in the bunch—a smaller than normal-size male he called Blue Bell. Charley's friend Feather Martin had given the bull that name early on because of the animal's sweet and peaceful disposition.

Charley chewed on his pipe stem. He sucked every now and then on the stale tobacco taste that lingered in the old hand-carved bowl. He was thinking about the cattle he now owned, and how his small herd of thirty had grown by nine or so calves since he and his outfit had arrived back in Juanita ten months earlier—thanks to Blue Bell, of course, and to his personal intuition, which allowed him to look a heifer in the eye and tell if she was with calf or not.

Those same eyes were now following the narrow dirt wagon path that wound its way up from the main entrance, past the holding pens, and to the ranch house itself. The figure of the person who had been discharged from the wagon was now making his way on foot, up the path toward the corrals.

He's too slight to be a full-grown man, Charley was thinking to himself. *He appears to be either a woman wearing men's trousers . . . or a half-grown boy.*

After another good look down the path, Charley shook his head—then he looked once again.

By golly, he thought, *that sure looks an awful lot like my grandson, Henry Ellis.*

He squinted, then he spoke out loud:

"It *is* Henry Ellis," and again to himself, *I wonder what he's doing way down here all by himself?*

Charley stepped into the stirrup of Dice's saddle, swung his other leg over, then spurred out down the hill toward the approaching boy.

About then, Charley's lifelong friend and partner, Roscoe Baskin, who was just a little bit overweight and near Charley's age, happened to look out the kitchen window. He saw his partner dismount, then sweep the boy up into his arms where the two remained hugging until the horse nudged Charley from behind.

Charley lifted his grandson up and into the saddle. With reins in hand, he began leading both horse and boy up the remainder of the path toward the ranch house.

"My mother and father have been abducted, Grampa," said Henry Ellis.

Charley stopped in his tracks. He turned and looked up at his grandson.

"Abducted?" said Charley. "My daughter? My Betty Jean? . . . and Kent? Where? . . . and by who?"

"Brownsville," answered Henry Ellis. "I think they were bandits."

"What in tarnation were the three of you doing in Brownsville?" asked Charley.

"My father was going to Mexico on business . . . he was taking Mother and me along because the invitation had said for him to bring us with him."

Roscoe had been in the process of cooking a chicken dish for that evening's supper. He just happened to look out the window again as he set a freshly baked pie on the sill to cool. He adjusted his wire-rimmed glasses so he could see better.

Charley was now leading Dice, with the boy in the saddle, and the two were talking. Roscoe knew the new arrival was Henry Ellis right off, by the way Charley helped the boy dismount in front of the house. Then Charley took him into his arms, swinging the just under five-foot-three boy around at least three times, before letting him go so he could stand back to get a better look at his only grandson.

The next hug contained a few kisses—several on the boy's forehead administered by Charley, and more than the usual amount planted on Charley's cheeks from the overly animated Henry Ellis.

"It's a long story, Grampa," said the boy, as the two of them entered the ranch house through the rear screen door.

"As soon as Roscoe gets some nourishment down you, I want to hear the rest of the story," said Charley.

"Well, look who's showed up out a' the blue," said Roscoe as he met the two of them at the kitchen door.

"Give Henry Ellis some room," said Charley, leading the new arrival over to the kitchen table, where he let him sit. "He's been on the road for a while without anything to eat. Can't you see he's starved, Roscoe?"

Roscoe, who had been preparing supper for Charley and himself anyway, grabbed a plate and dished up some of his chicken casserole. He used a fork to put a sweet potato onto the platter along with it. After adding some biscuits and gravy, he set the plate down in front of the boy.

Roscoe moved to the icebox, where he found a pitcher of buttermilk. Taking a clean glass from the cupboard, he filled the container to the brim before setting the chunky liquid down on the table beside Henry Ellis's plate.

"Dig in, sonny boy," said Roscoe. "There's always more where that came from."

A short time later, right after Henry Ellis had sopped up what remained on his plate with one of Roscoe's special-made sourdough biscuits, Charley urged him once again to continue his story.

"So, you were in Brownsville, with your parents, on your way to visit someone in Mexico, when you were attacked by a gang of Mexican thugs on the street? Is that right?"

"At first none of us knew what was happening," said the boy. "Then Señor Fuerte said something about an ambush."

"Fuerte?" said Charley. "Who is Señor Fuerte?"

"He's an undercover security man who works for the gentleman we were going to visit in Mexico. He was supposed to be a bodyguard for us. He met the three of us at the train depot with a rented carriage and said he was not to let us out of his sight during our entire stay with Don Roberto," said the boy. "When it was all over I almost went with him, then I remembered my father's last words to me.

"And what were those words, son?"

"My father said, 'Trust no one.' And he meant it, Grampa. I know he did."

"So instead of going off with this . . . bodyguard, you—"

"I saw that there were still a lot of people standing around, so I just ran, hoping the crowd would help block his view of me, while I made my way back across town to the train station."

"So, you got back on the train and then came here?" said Roscoe.

"I wasn't going to go all the way back to Austin," said Henry Ellis. "There's no one there I can depend on. Plus, Grampa Charley's the only person I thought of when I knew I had to find someone I trusted."

He leaned in closer to Roscoe. "You too, Uncle Roscoe . . . I trust you almost as much as I trust Grampa."

"Let's get back to your story, Henry Ellis," said Charley. "How did you ever manage to buy a seat on the train with no money?"

"That was as easy as pie," said the boy. "When we travel, my father always pins a brand-new one-hundred-dollar bill inside my coat sleeve . . . just for emergencies. Well, I figured that the abduction of my parents was an emergency, so I bought a ticket and got here to Juanita as quick as the train could get me here. It was getting from the depot to your ranch that had me stumped, Grampa. The folks that run the passenger wagon at the depot only go as far as Juanita's Main Street. I thought finding someone who would take me on to your ranch might be a problem until an old man offered his services. That's how I got here."

"So, Feather Martin brung ya, did he?" said Roscoe.

"I thought that man looked an awful lot like Feather," said Henry Ellis, "but he was really dirty . . . and smelly . . . and he never said he was Feather . . . plus he had a full beard that covered most of his face. I think he had fleas, too, the way he was always scratching himself. I'm sure I would have recognized Feather if that was him . . . don't you think?" he added.

"I'd say that under the circumstances it was up to Feather to recognize you, son," said Charley . . . "Unless he's gone and lost his memory, too, this time."

"It wasn't Feather," said the boy. "Why I'd know Feather anywhere."

Charley shook his head. "Not anymore you wouldn't, I'm afraid," he said. "I don't think Feather Martin has drawn a sober breath . . . or taken a bath . . . since summer, when we got the longhorn herd back here to Juanita."

"He's become a barrel-boarder, Henry Ellis. A bum. A drunken sot. Plus the fame kinda went to his head, you might say," added Roscoe.

"It was the lack of fame for Feather if you ask me," said Charley. "Now let's get back to *your* problem, Henry Ellis . . . enough about Feather Martin."

Charley stood and walked over to the kitchen sink, where he turned on the faucet and filled a glass with some water for himself.

"What do you think, son?" he asked the boy. "In case you didn't notice, we got inside plumbing these days, too."

"And that includes an indoor privy," said Roscoe. "I won't be havin' ta clear the ol' two-holer out back of spiders and their webs fer ya anymore, kid."

"And we finally got electricity for the whole house," said Charley.

"Which means we got e-lectric fans everywhere," added Roscoe. "Lots a' e-lectric fans. So we don't have ta live out there on that back porch all summer long anymore."

The three of them sat on the back porch steps together, finishing up their pie and watching the sun go down. Charley puffed on his pipe while Roscoe collected the forks and plates, stacking them on a tray on the step beside him. He finally got to his feet, picked up the tray of dishes, then excused himself.

"I'll be back," he said as the screen door slammed behind him. "Want me ta turn on the porch light fer ya?"

He flicked the switch on without thinking.

The porch light glowed bright in its new fixture beside the door.

"No . . . shut it off, will you, Roscoe?" said Charley. "Me and Henry Ellis want to watch the sun go down over the horizon together, don't we, boy?"

"Yes, Grampa," said Henry Ellis. "We sure do."

The light went out, and the sound of Roscoe's old boots faded as he clomped across the unvarnished floorboards into the kitchen.

Charley turned to his grandson.

"It's times like this when I miss that old dog," he said.

Henry Ellis looked up.

"We got your letter telling us Buster had passed on,

Grampa. I'm sorry, I was really sad when I heard about Buster."

The boy's eyes began to well up.

"I cried, Grampa," Henry Ellis continued, "I really did. I loved ol' Buster like he was a . . . human being . . . or a horse."

"Sometimes dogs are wiser than us humans," said Charley. "Buster was wiser than most. I raised that ol' dog from a pup, you know. Did I ever tell you that story, bub?"

"You told me, Grampa," said the boy. "As a matter of fact, you told me that story more than once. But I'd still like to hear it again, if you don't mind telling it again."

"I don't mind telling it, Henry Ellis, you know that."

He turned some so he was facing the boy. Then he began.

"Roscoe, me, and Feather was sleeping out on the open range one night a long time ago. This was when we were working cattle for a living, not during our Ranger years, mind you. It was my turn to nighthawk . . . a warm night. The reason I remember it being warm is because there aren't that many warm nights in west Texas during the Fall.

"Anyway, I snapped around at the sound of something growling and yipping like I'd never heard the likes of before in my life. It hadn't woke up Roscoe or Feather yet, and the cattle I was watching weren't bothered by it none . . . so I decided I'd get up for a look-see and find out what was causing such a ruckus.

"Thank God I made sure I took my rifle with me when I set out following that terrible noise," Charley went on. "Finally, I come around a big rock . . . maybe it was a big bush . . . I don't rightly recollect which one it was after all these years. So, I come around whatever it was there blocking my view, and I seen Buster for the first time in either one of our lives. He was the one doing all the growling and yipping. Directly across from that little dog was this good-sized panther. That little squirt of a pup had that mountain lion backed up against a rock, so all it could do was swat with one of its big ol' paws—with its claws extended, slicing through the air in front of it.

"Little Buster kept that cat pinned against that boulder just long enough for me to put a 44-40 slug between its eyes. Right then, that little pup shut its mouth, and there wasn't another sound came out of it until Feather and Roscoe showed up a-running 'round that rock . . . or bush . . . or whatever it was. Buster started right off, growling and yipping at those two, just like he was doing at that cougar.

"Wasn't long before Feather found the pup's mother and her other pups . . . they had all been killed dead by that panther. All of 'em except for little Buster. That little booger had scared the bejezus out of that cat, at least just enough to keep it from making supper out of Buster's family."

Charley leaned back against a support post.

"Anyhow," he said, "we buried his mother and the rest of the pups and I took Buster home with me. After a while he decided he liked me enough to stick around for . . . for, well . . . for the rest of his life."

Henry Ellis watched his grandfather as he stared off into the coming darkness—just long enough for a tear to begin to form in one of the old man's eyes.

Charley stood up abruptly, shaking his head.

"C'mon, boy," he said gruffly. "It's about time for the two of us to go on inside."

* * *

Later on that evening the three of them were gathered around the kitchen table with a map of Old Mexico spread out before them.

"Since that security guard your father's company's friend sent to protect you didn't appear to want the law involved," said Charley, "maybe we ought not report your parents' disappearance to the U.S. or the Mexican authorities . . . not just yet, at least. But in the meantime"—he nudged Roscoe—"there's nothing keeping us old Rangers from doing a little investigating ourselves, is there?"

"You're not thinkin' 'bout the three of us goin' inta Mexico after that gang who took the boy's parents, are ya, C.A.?" said Roscoe.

"No," said Charley. "I was thinking more of going into Mexico after them abductors with a meaningful number of guns backing us up."

"Just like you did in the old days," said Henry Ellis. "Wow!" he shouted, banging his fist on the table and grinning.

"And you can start, Roscoe Baskin, by first finding, then sobering up, Feather Martin. I need to go into town myself . . . I still got me a lot more thinking to do on this matter."

"Mercy," said Roscoe, "sober up Feather Martin? May God have mercy on us all."

"And that's a fact!" added Charley.

Chapter Three

Later on that night, Charley tied Dice to onc of the fancy hitching posts in front of Flora Mae's Palace Hotel. A large sign above the front entrance was illuminated by a row of electric lightbulbs. Charley walked past the hotel's main entrance and on around the building to another access. The swinging doors took him right on into the bar and pool hall, which were located in a section of the structure that had once been freestanding until the hotel was built around it thirteen years earlier.

The entire establishment was owned by his longtime friend, and many times more-than-friend, Flora Mae Huckabee, a lively woman of Charley's generation whom hc had known for what seemed like forever.

Flora Mae had been the only one of his close friends who had taken a chance on Charley a year earlier when the old cowboy had come up with a wonderful idea of how to get back on his feet financially. He had been down on his luck, and too broke to carry out the scheme himself.

Flora Mae had given him the money he needed, so he, Henry Ellis, and Charley's other friends could take the train to Denver, Colorado, where Charley participated in a longhorn cattle auction.

Through a fluke, Charley ended up with the entire herd of three hundred longhorns.

Flora Mae had also made sure Charley had enough support and capital coming his way to drive that herd all the way back to Juanita, Texas, when a local Denver meatpacker did everything in his power to prevent Charley from shipping the longhorns by rail.

"Well, I'll be hanged," the red-haired Flora Mae said softly to herself as Charley entered the place. "Elmer," she called out to the bartender, "get out a bottle of my special whiskey and two glasses. Can't you see Charley Sunday's come to town?"

She moved past the several customers who were still in her establishment—one at the bar, the other playing a game of solitary pool—and sat at a table in the far corner. She beckoned for Charley to join her.

The bartender was just serving her the special-blend whiskey bottle and two shot glasses when Charley arrived and slid into the chair opposite the woman.

"Elmer," she asked the bartender, "why don't you order us a couple of beef-steak sandwiches from the kitchen and I'll—"

"Not hungry," said Charley in a somber tone, pulling off his riding gloves one finger at a time. "I already had my supper."

Flora Mae leaned in closer, trying to humor him.

"That's a good one, Charley Sunday. I've never known you to turn down a free meal in my entire lifetime."

Charley looked up at her from under the brim of his Stetson.

"Not hungry, Flora Mae," he repeated. "I've had my

supper. I'm just here to do some serious thinking, like always."

"I 'spose you also came in here for a little expert counseling, too," she said.

"I only need your advice when my own brain don't give me the right answers. You know that, Flora Mae."

"Well, right now," said the woman, "you look like you left your brain somewhere between here an' Del Rio."

Charley grumbled.

"Well, maybe I did," he said. "Maybe I did."

He raised his eyes and made total contact with her.

"Henry Ellis's parents got themselves abducted," he told her in a whisper.

Those words quickly got her attention.

"Kent and Betty Jean? How long ago, and where?" she asked.

"Yesterday morning, in Brownsville," he said. "More'n likely they're in Mexico by now . . . but don't ask me why they were taken . . . because I . . . don't . . . know . . . why."

"Thank God Henry Ellis wasn't with 'em," she said.

"Oh, he was with 'em, all right," said Charley. "But he got away. He had some money, so he was able to buy a ticket on the overnight train. He showed up at my place late this afternoon."

"And you want me to tell you that I think it's all right for you to go after the people who abducted his parents, is that what you want?" she said.

"No," said Charley. "I just need to borrow some cash money to buy some supplies for the men I intend to take with me into Mexico to find the scum-suckers that took my daughter and Henry Ellis's daddy. And I'm afraid whoever it was is going to have a well-armed gang of thugs behind 'em, Flora Mae, so I'll be taking some expert man-hunters with me."

"Some of your old Ranger friends, you mean."

"Roscoe and Feather Martin for starters," he said. "Roscoe's trying to sober up Feather right now, as we speak."

"I don't know if sobering up Feather Martin again is possible, Charley," she told him. "I've seen plenty of men with a love for the bottle, like Feather, try to dry out over and over again, but most of 'em only had a certain amount of tries in 'em."

"You're saying Feather might not have another—"

"I'm saying if Feather goes cold turkey one more time, it could damn well kill him."

Charley reached for Flora Mae's special bottle and filled both glasses again. He raised his shot glass to his lips and threw back his head.

"I don't want Feather dying on me," he said. "Do you think you might have a better solution?"

Flora Mae tossed down the contents of her own shot glass.

"Just let him keep on drinking . . . only have someone watch over him at all times to make sure he paces his drinks. Taper him off."

"And that'll get him sober?" Charley asked.

"No," said Flora Mae, "of course it won't get him sober. But it'll keep him in a state where he might be able to do you some good."

"I've seen Feather shoot a gun when he's drunker'n a skunk from his boot-toes up to his hat," said Charley. "He's a better shot drunk than most men are sober . . . and that's a fact," he added.

"I'll keep in mind what you've told me, darlin'," he continued. "Now, I figure I'll need about seven hundred dollars to get me those supplies."

"Here ya go, Charley," said Flora Mae, reaching down the front of her bodice.

She handed him two five-hundred-dollar bills.

Charley took the neatly folded pieces of paper money like they were hot pieces of coal. He fumbled with them, then he put them into his shirt pocket.

"I ain't got no change, Flora Mae," said Charley, "but I'm grateful this loan don't have no strings attached like last one did."

"If you mean that dance we done together at the end of the cattle drive 'cause you lost a bet . . . that didn't have nothin' to do with strings attached, Charley Sunday. That was because we like each other."

"Still and all, Flora Mae," he said, "I just don't think there should be strings attached to this one. Now I gotta go."

"You just hold on one more minute there, my good friend, because I never told you there weren't no strings attached this time . . . it was you who said that."

Charley drew in a deep breath, then expelled it.

"So what do you want from me, Flora Mae?" he asked.

"I don't want ta be tellin' you that right now, Charley . . . but when this thing of yours is all done and over with, you'll find out. Oh, will you find out," she mumbled under her breath.

"Feather Martin, is that you?" Roscoe called out into the darkness of an alleyway behind Ben Cobb's Funeral Parlor.

There was no answer.

"I know yer' there, little man," he said, "'cause I can smell ya a half-a-mile away."

"G-geezes G-god," came a shaky voice from behind

a rainwater barrel. "R-roscoe? I-is that you c-come a c-callin'?"

It was Feather's voice.

Roscoe went right to him.

Feather Martin—raggedy beard, dirt, stink, mud and all—was lying on his back with his head propped up on several discarded funeral preparation pillows. In his hand, a near-empty bottle of rotgut whiskey, with not more than one swallow left in it.

As Roscoe leaned down to attend to his old friend, Feather took that one last swig, then he let the empty bottle slide onto his chest. He drew in a deep breath, which caused the container to roll off his chest and land in some horse muck by his side.

Roscoe lit a match, holding it up to see his friend's face.

Feather's eyes fluttered and closed again because of the brightness of the flame. His puffy, reddened face was smeared with the alleyway's sludge.

"C-cut that out," the little cowboy sputtered through chalky lips. "T-turn out that lamp. L-leave me alone."

Roscoe shook the matchstick to extinguish the flame.

"How would you feel about going on another manhunt?" asked Roscoe.

Feather's eyes opened one more time.

"You know I'd give up everythin' I got ta be huntin' outlaws with you an' Charley Sunday again," he said, "but I h-h-h-hocked my gun last week ta b-buy this hooter I'm on."

His eyes rolled back and he went wobbly.

Roscoe caught him before his head fell back.

"We can get yer shootin' iron back for ya, Feather," whispered Roscoe. "I just hope we can get *you* back together . . . all in one piece.

* * *

Charley and Flora Mae were finishing up a game of pool when Roscoe entered, dragging the inebriated Feather along with him.

They were both in Flora Mae's eye line as she sighted in on her final shot, so she was the first to acknowledge the two men.

"Oh, Lordy," she gasped, taking her shot and missing the eight ball completely.

"What's the matter, darlin'?" said Charley, moving quickly to her side.

He put an arm around her shoulders to keep her from falling in case she was going to faint. It was then when he saw both Roscoe and Feather stumbling toward them. Actually, it was Feather doing most of the stumbling—Roscoe was just weak-kneed from carrying half of Feather's weight across the street and into the bar.

"Can you give ol' Feather here a nip a' whiskey, Flora Mae?" Roscoe asked politely. "I was gonna buy him a bottle myself so's I could wean him off some, but I left my billfold back at the ranch."

"Put him in that chair over there," said Flora Mae, "'til I can get some hot coffee goin'."

"It ain't coffee he needs, Flora Mae," said Charley, who was now giving Roscoe some help settling the drunken man into a chair. "Like you just said," he continued, "Feather needs some whiskey. I'll even buy," he added.

Charley reached into his pants pocket, pulled out the contents, and handed the woman a crumpled bill.

"The cheapest you got . . . that's what his body's bound to be used to."

Flora Mae took the money and went over to the bar. She put it on the counter.

"Gimme a bottle of Old Indian whiskey, Elmer," she said to the bartender. "Charley wants it so he can help sober up that little booze rat over there by the pool table who's about ta throw up in his hat or pass out cold."

"Yes, ma'am," said the bartender. "Old Indian it is." He reached for a full bottle behind him on the back-bar, handing it to his employer.

Flora Mae rushed back to the table where the others had made Feather as comfortable as they could. She handed the bottle to Charley who immediately popped the cork and splashed some of its contents onto the little wrangler's face.

Charley had made sure that some of the fiery liquid had gotten to the cowboy's lips, so it wasn't long before Feather began showing some signs of life.

"Lemme have some more," choked Feather, reaching blindly for the bottle he couldn't see.

"Not until you sit up, my friend, and give me your full attention," said Charley.

He held the bottle up like a carrot to a mule.

Feather did his best to reposition himself in the chair until, with a little assistance from Roscoe, he was able to sit upright facing Charley eye-to-eye once again.

"C-can I have a itty-bitty s-swallow now, B-boss?" he asked.

"Only if you can promise me to be bright-eyed and bushy-tailed come morning . . ."

Feather nodded, then he reached out to where he thought the bottle should be.

". . . and," Charley went on, "I want you to take the Pledge for the whole time we're on the trail of those men who abducted my daughter and her husband, down in Mexico."

Feather nodded profusely, even though he hadn't a clue as to what Charley was talking about. He was desperate.

"Y-yes, yes, y-yes, and double y-yes," he said. "Now g-gimme that drink, will ya?"

Charley handed him the bottle.

Feather took it in his trembling hands, lifting it to his lips. He gurgled some down.

He only had a chance for the one swallow before Charley took it back from him.

Charley handed the bottle to Roscoe.

"Roscoe here is going to be your whiskey monitor, Feather," said Charley. "He's going to dole it out to you one swallow at a time . . . until you start to get your senses back. After that, he'll wean you down to nearly nothing. We can't be working with you, Feather, if you're going to stay roostered all the time. You know that."

This time Feather's nod was a sincere nod.

"I p-promise I'll do whatever it takes, Boss. H-honest . . . I promise," said Feather. "N-now can we start that one shot at a time b-business before my head explodes?"

Chapter Four

The following morning, after Roscoe had brought Feather to the ranch, barely conscious, slung over the saddle of the little man's own horse, Charley and Henry Ellis saddled up to go in search of several others who might find chasing down members of an international abduction ring a whole lot more interesting than living out the rest of their lives with little or no excitement at all.

"But first," said Charley, "we need to stop at the telegraph office out at the train station. There're a couple of old friends of mine I'd like to contact, and I'm pretty sure they're still living where they were living the last time I heard from them. Plus I need to wait for an answer to the telegram I'm going to be sending to the governor."

"I didn't think you liked the governor all that well," said Henry Ellis.

"That's true . . . I don't. And I don't know him that well, either, Henry Ellis, but he sure knows me. After all the free advertising we gave the great state of Texas last year during the cattle drive . . . he owes me plenty."

* * *

Charley and Henry Ellis had ridden for a mile or so since stopping for Charley to send off his telegrams. They were reminiscing—while their horses trod slowly along the road—about last year's cattle drive, and how proud Henry Ellis's mother and father had been when they were finally able to find Charley and their son after the celebration parade.

The parents were both proudly telling anyone and everyone they passed by on the street that day that Henry Ellis was their son, and how pleased they were for him—his mother conveniently forgetting that if there had been no newspaper coverage or world fame for *The Texas Outfit* at all, she would have been chewing out her father right then and there for allowing her son to be exposed to such a perilous situation.

Farther on down the road, then four miles east on another rutted thoroughfare, they came upon a small ranch that stood out from the others they'd been passing by on their short journey.

The little white ranch house looked as if it had been freshly painted. The light blue trim added a definite feminine touch to the door and open shutters. Red carnations sprouted from the window boxes. The ranch yard itself was surrounded by a white picket fence with wild flowers growing at pleasing angles at its base. There were two gardens—one for vegetables, the other for flowers—with a recently planted row of fruit trees in the side yard near the clothesline. And the corrals—also painted white—contained mustang ponies, not cattle.

In the ranch yard itself, near the barn, a man lay on his backside under a buggy, working. It appeared he was trying to fix a mechanical malfunction of some sort. When the man heard the riders approaching, he began to slither his way out from under the front wheels.

"Rod," yelled Henry Ellis, when he recognized the mechanic was Rod Lightfoot.

Rod—a dark-skinned American Indian, Cuban war veteran, with long black hair down to his shoulders—was a want-to-be attorney, who had helped Charley during the previous year's cattle drive in more ways than one by just advising him on matters of the law.

The boy turned to his grandfather.

"You never said we were coming to see Rod."

"There's someone else you'll be happy to see, too," said Charley.

He indicated the porch of the house where a young woman in her late twenties was just stepping through the front door.

"Kelly," yelled the boy. "It's Kelly King!"

"She's Kelly Lightfoot now, son," whispered Charley. "They were married last winter."

Henry Ellis dismounted, then he ran toward his two friends, intercepting them both and diving into their open arms.

"Wow," said Henry Ellis, "it sure is good to see you two."

Kelly finished pouring lemonade into the tall glasses she had set up on the table in the shade of the front-porch roof, where everyone was gathered.

"Thank you, Kelly," said Henry Ellis.

The others chimed in, thanking her as the boy had done.

When Kelly had finished pouring the lemonade, she took her seat between Henry Ellis and her husband, Rod, directly across from Charley.

"Mexico is it?" she said to Charley. "And you're not sure yet just where in Mexico? . . . just that it's Mexico?"

"My daughter . . . Henry Ellis's mother . . . and her husband, Kent, have been abducted, Miss Kelly," said Charley. "This could turn into a very solemn situation. That's why we rode out here today to ask Rod if he'd like to ride along with a bunch of ex–Texas Rangers and see if we can track down the bad *hombres* who are responsible for this dreadful act."

"Why were they taken?" asked Kelly.

"Why . . . ?" said Charley. "Hell, I don't rightly know why. Henry Ellis here just showed up on my doorstep and told me all about it. I don't know any more than that."

She turned to the boy.

"Do you know why your parents were abducted, Henry Ellis?" she asked. "Do you think they knew who the men were that abducted them?"

Henry Ellis shook his head.

"No," he said. "My mother and father were just as surprised as the rest of us when those men started jumping onto the side of the coach."

"How did you manage to get away?" she asked.

"My dad told me to jump out of the carriage," said the boy. "So I jumped."

"Then, it appears to be obvious that they weren't after you. Just your parents."

"I really don't know," said the boy. "Señor Fuerte told me that—"

"Who is Señor Fuerte?" asked Rod, cutting him off. He moved in closer.

"He's a bodyguard," said Charley. "Henry Ellis's father's company hired him to protect all three of 'em while they were in Mexico."

"He certainly wasn't very good at his job, was he?" said Kelly.

"Tell me more about this special bodyguard," said Rod.

"I don't know anything more," said the boy, "except that he wanted to take me to Don Roberto Acosta's *hacienda* right then, instead of going to the Brownsville authorities."

"Don Roberto Acosta," repeated Kelly. "I've heard that name before. Rod," she said, motioning for her husband to follow her.

Rod got up and followed his wife, while Charley and Henry Ellis watched. The couple stopped to discuss something of importance near the front door.

When they were done talking, they both returned to the table and took their seats.

"Rod's going to go along with you, Charley," she told him. ". . . And so am I."

Her words made Charley a little bit uncomfortable. He squirmed.

"I can't be taking a woman into Mexico, Miss Kelly. This'll be a lot different than the cattle drive. There could be shooting."

"There was shooting on the cattle drive, too, Charley Sunday, or have you forgotten that?"

"No . . . no," said Charley, "and I haven't forgotten that you're a pretty fair hand with a gun yourself. But you were with us on the cattle drive to do a job . . . your newspaper reporter job. There won't be any daily reports sent from where we're going, young lady. And besides," he added, "I thought you quit that newspaper business when you married Rod?"

"The news syndicate where I worked left it open for me to submit whatever stories I thought might be of interest to the public . . . and a bunch of ex–Texas Rangers getting together to rescue an abducted husband and wife from a brutal Mexican bandit gang, below the border, sounds pretty interesting to me. In fact," she continued, "this story could also be turned into a book, more than a newspaper series like I did with the cattle drive. Plus, I won't have to tell anyone where I'll be going, or what I'm writing about, since I'll be submitting the manuscript way after we get back from Mexico . . . after the story's been written."

Charley turned to Rod.

"How do *you* feel about your wife coming along with us?"

Rod shrugged.

"Are you going to argue with her, Charley?"

Charley looked away. Henry Ellis was overjoyed.

"That's what I thought," said Rod.

He turned to Kelly beside him.

"Well, Mrs. Lightfoot, you'd better get to packing. I'm sure these two gentlemen have other places they need to be."

Charley and Henry Ellis rode along again, with the boy just as unsure of where they were going this time as he was before their stop at the Lightfoot ranch.

"Is Rod still studying to be a lawyer?" Henry Ellis asked his grandfather.

"Better than that," said Charley. "Rod's working on his law degree by mail order. Seems these days it's possible for a man . . . or a woman, I suppose . . . to go to college by mail. And that's what Rod's doing."

How about that, thought the boy. *And no one will know if he's an Indian or not if they're dealing with him through the mail*. That had been one of Rod's previous problems in his quest to obtain a law degree—certain people's prejudice against Indians.

"We don't have much farther to go, son," said Charley. "I just wanted to see if we could find Plunker Holliday where he said he was going to be."

"That's great," said the boy. "I always did like ol' Plunker."

"Besides still being as good with a gun as he is at his age," said Charley, "Holliday is also a person I feel I can trust, even though he's not family."

"What about Rod, Kelly, Roscoe, and Feather?" said the boy. "They're no relation to us."

"Maybe there aren't any blood ties between us and them four, Henry Ellis," said Charley, "but, they're family, by God."

Charley and Henry Ellis rode down the one-sided Main Street of Spofford, Texas, with Charley checking out the signs on the storefronts until they came to an alleyway with its own sign directing them to:

SPOFFORD SHOOTING RANGE, ONE BLOCK SOUTH

The two reined their mounts in between two storefronts before continuing on.

It wasn't much of an alley. Just the backsides of a few more establishments, spread out here and there along the way. But it was definitely not another street.

They hadn't gone that far when they heard the sound of gunshots.

"That'd be Holliday, I suspect," said Charley.

They came to a rather large, man-made mound of dirt and stopped. Charley motioned for the boy to follow him as he rode around to the other side.

It wasn't Holliday doing the shooting. It was one of Holliday's customers. He was a man dressed in a three-piece business suit who appeared to be quite good with the six-shooter in his hand.

The man had been reloading from a box of cartridges on a bench beside him when Charley and the boy rode up. When he was ready, the man snapped the gate closed, quite professionally, and began firing at several ragged targets about thirty feet away. When the man had gone through his six bullets and was about to reload again, Charley called over to him.

"Excuse me, mister. Is there a man called Holliday working here?"

The businessman continued to eject brass while he nodded.

"Holliday's my instructor. He's right over there," he said.

His nod took their attention to the porch of a small wooden shack nearby where the figure of a man dressed in all black was slumped back in a large overstuffed chair, snoring away.

"Sometimes it's hard to think of Plunker Holliday as an instructor," said the man. "Especially when he's napping, like that. But he's training me to be a real fine shootist, just like he is . . . in spite of that bad eye of his."

"That's him," said Charley. "Thanks, mister."

"It's 'Thank you, Mr. Mayor,'" cut in Holliday, who was by then standing up and taking off his coat.

Charley tipped his hat to the man.

"Your Honor," he said.

Charley and the boy dismounted, tied off their horses, and walked across an open area to where Holliday was just starting off toward them. The three of them stopped and shook hands.

"Mighty good ta see you two, Mr. Sunday . . . Henry Ellis," he said.

Charley answered, "Mighty good to see you, too, Holliday."

"You thinkin' about puttin' together another cattle drive,

are ya?" said the Wild West show sure shot. Because I'm gettin' pretty bored with this teachin' job."

"Not quite," said Charley. "I can't offer you another cattle drive, but we got something that offers a little more excitement this time around."

Holliday cocked his head. He stared at Charley with his one good eye.

"And just what might that be?"

"Have you ever been to Mexico, Plunker Holliday?" asked Charley.

Holliday took a moment to study Charley's eyes, then he looked over to the boy. When he realized the two were dead serious about taking him to Mexico he answered:

"Nope, I've somehow managed to keep myself on this side of the border all these years. But now I get the feelin' I'll be wearin' itchy wool *ponchos* and ten-gallon *sombreros* for a spell. Who're ya goin' after?" he asked.

"Henry Ellis's parents were abducted a few days ago," said Charley. "We don't have much time, I'm afraid."

"I might be a little rusty," said Holliday. "I don't shoot people that much anymore. I just teach people ta shoot people nowadays. Lemme get my possibles together. Then I'll meet you two up at the sandwich shop on Main Street. Best we get somethin' under our belt buckles before we head down inta Mexico, don't ya think?"

Charley shook his head.

"No," said Charley. "There'll be more than three of us when we go. No, you go on and eat. Me and Henry Ellis have another fella we need to talk to within riding distance from here. Suppose you just take your time packing up and eating. Just be at my ranch in Juanita tomorrow, before noon."

Chapter Five

Jagged strands of blazing white lightning zigzagged across the darkened sky, while thunder rolled repeatedly. Heavy rain came down in sheets, pounding the rigid buildings and barbed-wire-covered walls that made up the Texas State Penitentiary at Huntsville.

Inside one of the squalid cellblocks, a uniformed prisoner's ruddy fist slammed into the defiant face of Mitchell Pennell who, like the others surrounding him, was dressed in lackluster prison garb.

"You're a pig, Mitch Pennell," said the convict who was administering the beating. "A cheatin', rotten, lyin', stupid, low-life pig!"

Several other long-timers were holding Pennell securely from behind, making it impossible for the man to defend himself.

"I agree with every word you just said about me, except stupid," said Pennell. "The *sucker* in a con game is the stupid one, Belford, not the instigator. That means . . . you must be the stupid one," he added.

Another hamlike fist wiped the grin off Pennell's face and he slumped, still in the other two jailbirds' grasp.

"Now you men hold him good," said the convict called Belford. "I wanna make sure he never cheats another man in this crummy joint . . . ever again."

As Belford drew back his fist to strike Pennell one more time, a voice called out:

"Hey! What's going on over there?"

It was a guard's voice.

The convicts who'd been observing the one-sided exchange broke up the gathering and went their separate ways. The two men holding Pennell let go of him and he stumbled over to a wall where he leaned, huffing.

Belford was trying his best to remove the blood spatter from his knuckles when he heard the click of a switchblade knife.

The guard called out again:

"Number three four six eight . . . Mitchell Pennell. The warden wants to see you in his office . . . On the double!"

Mitch Pennell's lopsided smile, showing bloodied teeth, was one of triumph—at least for the moment. He started forward—then he stopped as he looked Belford in the eyes. The bully's face was one of awkward surprise. Pennell reached out and pulled his switchblade knife from Belford's chest, where his swift throw had buried the blade to its hilt.

Belford crumbled to the ground with his heart pumping its contents into a widening pool of blood on the sandstone floor. Belford's eyes were still locked on to Pennell's. Pennell bent down and wiped the blade clean on the wounded prisoner's own sleeve, then he closed the blade and returned the knife to his pocket.

For a moment the two men stared at one another, then Pennell turned away. He stared at the other two prisoners.

He spat a bloody glob onto the floor beside them. It splatted at their feet.

* * *

With a prison guard on either side of him, Mitch Pennell stood facing Warden F. Q. Dobbs, who was sitting stuffily behind his oversized desk.

"That's what I said, Pennell . . . a temporary reprieve," Dobbs told him.

He held up an official looking document for Pennell to peruse.

"It came all the way from Austin by special messenger," said Dobbs. "Signed by the governor of Texas, personally."

He handed the document to Pennell, then he shook his head.

"Do you want to know something else, Pennell?" he went on. "In all my years of experience with the Texas state prison system, this is the first one of these things I've ever handed out to a prisoner who's doing ninety-nine years and a day."

"Do you wanna know somethin', too, Warden?" said Pennell. "In all my years of experience with the Texas state prison system, this is the first and only time I ever got one of these things . . . let alone seen one."

Warden Dobbs leaned forward, getting to his feet.

He ordered the two guards: "Get him out of here. There's a government wagon out front waiting to take him to the train station."

The warden held another piece of paper in his hand; he passed it to Pennell.

"Here's your train ticket. It was delivered with your temporary reprieve . . . It's to a little town out west called Juanita. I've been advised that someone you know will be meeting you there."

* * *

A two-horse U.S. Army wagon rolled into Charley Sunday's ranch yard late that night, with two glowing oil lamps hanging from nails driven into both front corners of the wagon's bed. Behind the reins sat the driver. The man sitting beside him wore a U.S. Army field uniform with master sergeant's stripes sewn to the sleeves. As he began to climb down from his perch, his silhouette showed him to be imposing in both physical size and color—muscular and black.

The sergeant moved around to the wagon's tailgate where he found, placed one beside the other, three olive-drab, padlocked, metal cases with his name and rank neatly stenciled on each.

Charley, Henry Ellis, and Roscoe stepped out onto the back porch, turning on the electric porch light as they passed the switch. All three were in their nightshirts and slippers.

"Is that you, Captain Sunday?" said Sergeant Stone from across the yard.

Charley nodded as he came down the steps, with Roscoe and Henry Ellis following close behind.

"It is," Charley called out. "And that must be you, Sergeant Stone?"

"Master Sergeant Tobias P. Stone reporting for duty, Captain," said the large black man, saluting. He was now standing at his full height.

"I know Fort Clark is less than a few miles away from here, Captain," said the sergeant. "But after you and your grandson left me today, I was given a lot of paperwork to fill out . . . plus gettin' my toolboxes off the post proved to be more difficult than I had expected. I finally found a friend with a wagon, and we searched around for a delivery gate that was unattended, plus we waited for night. We used that gate, Captain Sunday. But we still took a roundabout way to get here, just in case someone might have spotted us. Is it really Armendariz?" he added.

"Like I told you this afternoon, Sergeant, I don't know of anyone else who would be crazy enough to abduct two American citizens in broad daylight, then scurry them off into Mexico without a ransom demand."

"I'll be damned," said Stone. "And here I thought you Rangers had put the last nail in Armendariz's coffin, years ago."

"Well, that ain't true," said Charley.

About then the wagon's driver whipped up the team, turning the wagon.

"I gotta be gettin' back, Sarge," said the man.

Sergeant Stone nodded, and the wagon moved out of the ranch yard, disappearing down the path and into the night.

Roscoe took a step closer.

"I'm Roscoe Baskin, Sergeant," he said, "Charley's pardner. I reckon you got to know Henry Ellis this afternoon. But I don't think the two of us have met before."

"Sergeant Stone an' me met one another during the War between the North and South, Roscoe," said Charley. "I reckon I never got around to telling you that story. Sergeant Stone was wearing blue like he is now, fighting for the Yanks. And I was wearing gray, leading a patrol for the Confederacy. One night I came across some of my men using Sergeant Stone for bayonet practice. I put a stop to it."

"Nearly killed one of 'em, he did, savin' my life," said the sergeant. "I owe Captain Sunday a lot for what he done for me that night. That's why I'm here. I'm on a thirty-day administrative leave stamped by the Department of War."

He looked over to the olive-drab boxes, now on the ground where the wagon once stood.

"And I got my tools, Charley. That's all that matters."

Chapter Six

Kent Pritchard and his wife, Betty Jean—the parents of Henry Ellis—sat watching as a middle-aged Mexican man dressed in a haphazard collection of mismatched uniform pieces, plus a jumble of glittering gold medals pinned to his chest, had breakfast prepared for, and served, to his two *guests* by several camp followers.

A long, wooden table had been set up on the front porch of the abandoned adobe building that was temporarily serving as the colonel's headquarters. There were rooms inside where he and his officers slept, plus similar accommodations on the second floor where he kept his prisoners.

The Pritchards appeared to be somewhat uneasy in the colonel's presence. Since their abduction several days earlier, neither of them had been allowed any food at all—until this morning. They had been given only water to drink while they were brought overland in the same coach in which they'd been captured. It had taken them some time to get there. Upon arrival they'd been locked in a small second-story room inside the adobe building, which looked as if it had been a bedroom at one time. Now, the following morning, both of them were wondering why they were suddenly being offered this special treatment.

"You will find that while you are the personal guests of Colonel Alfonso Natividad Armendariz, that starting now, you will always eat well and be treated like royalty."

"And just what exactly is that supposed to mean?" asked Kent.

"Exactly what it sounds like, señor," said Armendariz. "I have just received orders that you should be treated as guests, and not prisoners, from now on."

"Why did your men let my boy go when they took us?" asked Betty Jean.

"My men did not let your boy go," said Armendariz. "He escaped. A small mistake was made by one of my men that allowed your son to get away. They are searching for him now."

"You must be speaking of Señor Fuerte when you talk of a man who mistakenly allowed my son to get away," said Kent.

"No, no, señor," said Armendariz. "Señor Fuerte is who he presented himself to be . . . a security official hired by Don Roberto Acosta. Señor Fuerte most certainly does not work for me."

Betty Jean interrupted.

"Do you have any milk, Colonel?" she asked.

"I do," said Armendariz, reaching for a goatskin bota that hung from a branch nearby. "I have milk and it is cold, señora. My women brought it from the creek just for you."

Betty Jean took the leather pouch and poured some milk into one of the glasses that sat on the table in front of her. When she was done pouring, she picked up the glass and drank. The sour taste turned her stomach.

"Oh, my Lord," she said, almost gagging, "what is this?"

"It is milk from the goat, señora," said the colonel. "I am

sorry if you prefer milk from the cow . . . but we have no cows."

"No, thank you," said Betty Jean, waving the bota away. "I am finished with my breakfast."

Armendariz waved his hand and the two peon women moved in quickly, taking her utensils before scurrying away.

Kent spoke: "We are not your 'personal' guests, Colonel Armendariz . . . nor are we royalty," he began. "We are your prisoners . . . there's no doubt about that. We are also United States citizens, who have been forcibly abducted and taken against our will across an international border. That's a punishable crime in my country, mister. And . . . let me tell you something more, Colonel, the state of Texas, and my government in Washington, D.C., still do not pay ransom."

"Is that what you are thinking, señor?" said Armendariz. "Do you still think that my employer has ordered your abduction to collect a ransom?"

"Not one red cent, Colonel," said Kent, "that's what you and your employer will get. Not one red cent."

Both Pennell and Holliday had joined up with the rest of Charley's little outfit, which, besides Charley, Henry Ellis, Roscoe, and Feather, now included those two, plus Sergeant Stone, Rod, and Kelly as well.

The outfit, now astride their horses, with two newly acquired mules pulling Roscoe's makeshift chuckwagon—a vehicle that carried food for them and their horses, plus supplies and Sergeant Stone's mysterious toolboxes—were headed for the Juanita train station. That was because Charley had decided they'd travel by rail—as they had done a year earlier to get to Denver. As before, this was being done to save time. Once they were in Brownsville,

Charley hoped they might be able to pick up the trail of the boy's parents and their abductors. The faster they got there, he felt, any clues, or witnesses to the abduction who were still there, would be much easier to find.

The chuckwagon had once been Charley's two-seat buckboard, but due to the cost of purchasing a brand-new chuckwagon for last year's cattle drive, Charley had decided that by adding a used undercarriage with sturdier wheels and all, plus a cook's box, fly, and canvas top, the old buckboard would serve them just as well as a store-bought chuckwagon—and it had.

Don Roberto Acosta y Castro and his foreman, Luis Hernandez, leading thirty-two members of the Don's most trusted militia men plus eighteen of his best *vaqueros*, had stopped on the Mexican side of the Brownsville/Matamoros border bridge, and were in deep conversation with Roca Fuerte.

"You said in your message that you have no idea of which direction they took after crossing into Mexico?" said Don Roberto.

"Only that when I was finally able to get to this side of the bridge, their trail appeared to go north . . . along the river. Now those tracks have been trampled many times over by the regular border traffic."

"Immediately, I am thinking that a trail north is a tactic to send us off in the wrong direction," said the Don.

"I am sorry, Don Roberto," said Fuerte. "I wish that I could have gotten here sooner after the incident, but I thought searching for the boy should take precedence."

"You made the proper choice, Roca," said Don Roberto, "and I thank you sincerely. I will lead my *vaqueros* and follow the trail leading north . . ."

He turned in his saddle.

"Luis," he called out, "choose eight *vaqueros* who are experts with a sidearm, and bring them with us. We are following the trail leading north. The rest of you men will head west. Before you go, I will split you up into separate groups. Each unit will spread out along the way and report back to me every other day at sundown."

"I would very much like to go with you," said Fuerte. "I still feel as if the abduction and the boy's escape were my fault—"

"No, Roca. I need for you to stay in Brownsville. Find out if the authorities know anything about what happened yesterday . . . or if the boy might have gone to them after he ran off."

"*Sí*, Don Roberto," said Fuerte, "as you wish."

"And report to me, by messenger if need be, of what you find out."

"I will do the best I can, Don Roberto," said Fuerte. "And I apologize for letting yesterday's incident happen in the first place."

"Roca," said the Don, "my friend Roca. I told you that what took place yesterday could have happened to any number of men. It was an ambush . . . You were attacked by superior forces unexpectedly. Please do not keep blaming yourself, Roca. It was in no way your doing."

"Then I will make it up to you, Don Roberto," said Fuerte. "I will find the boy. And when I do, I will take him to your *hacienda*. Then I will begin to search for his parents, as you are."

"What you do, Roca, is up to you. Just stop blaming yourself."

Fuerte nodded his head.

Don Roberto smiled. He turned to his foreman.

"Whenever you're ready, Luis. Split up the men, then I will give the order to move out.

It took almost a full day and part of the night to get from Juanita to Brownsville by rail—most of the time—unless something unexpected came up along the way. *Unexpected* usually meant things like a hot box, an unscheduled oncoming train, a derailing, or a dysfunctional brake or two—things like that. But on the day Charley's outfit was making their journey to Brownsville, *unexpected* meant the train was attacked by a gang of border-crossing Mexican marauders.

At first Charley figured he wouldn't even need to draw his pistol. But when a bullet smashed its way through the glass directly above his grandson's head, he pushed Henry Ellis to the floor beside his feet while at the same time drawing his old Walker Colt from his boot.

Most of the other passengers—besides those members of the outfit traveling along with Charley—were greenhorn army infantrymen who would surely begin firing back with their own carbines, Charley figured. But when another stray outlaw bullet shattered the pane of window glass two seats in front of Charley, showering several soldiers with jagged shards of glass, more than a few of the new recruits began acting foolish. Some dropped their rifles and began to shout, while others started running up and down the aisles like headless chickens. All the while the bandits, who rode their galloping horses parallel to the train, kept firing.

Even though it appeared the attackers were only a few yards from the passenger car, many Mexican bullets went wide of their intended targets.

By then, Roscoe, Feather, Holliday, Rod, Kelly, Sergeant

Stone, and Mitch Pennell were firing back at the bandits through the train car's shattered windows.

One of the attacking Mexicans decided to show off for his companions; he rode up very close to the train's clattering wheels. From there he transferred from saddle to coach in one swift and easy motion, quickly climbing the several steps to the back platform before kicking in the rear door of the passenger car and entering with his two pistols blazing.

Holy Moses, thought Charley as he shoved Henry Ellis's curious head back down below the seat again. Then he watched as the remaining soldiers dove for cover beneath their own wooden seats, pawing for safety, paralyzed by fear.

I reckon I'm going to have to get myself involved in this silly ruckus anyhow, thought Charley.

With the onboard Mexican's bullets ricocheting all around every which way, Charley stood up, raised his pistol, and sighted carefully. He triggered one single shot. The daring bandit's eyes bulged wide as the flat of his belly intercepted the old Colt's swirling ball of lead, setting him back a step. His face showed absolute bewilderment. In his haste, the bandit had not seen the older cowboy in the gray coat, with the oversize Stetson, among the many American soldiers. Now the wounded bandit could only stand silent trying to hold in his leaking intestines. His two weapons dangled useless at the ends of his crossed arms.

The members of Charley's outfit kept on firing out the windows while the soldiers took all the time they needed to rise up from behind their seats, aim their carbines in unison, and shoot the intruding bandit twenty-three more times. The soldiers may have been frightened their first time under fire, but when push came to shove, they were all crackerjack shooters. Every single bullet they fired hit its mark. The recruits' primary volley cut the lone invader in half, his upper torso falling one way while the pelvic region and legs toppled the other. A second volley followed shortly, blasting the man's head into a thousand pieces before what remained of it hit the floor like a half-eaten apple core.

It was close to midnight when the train pulled into the Brownsville station. Several depot workers, plus a single newspaper reporter, were there to welcome Charley and his outfit. That was so reports of the incident would greet the citizens of Brownsville over their morning coffee. Charley refused to talk to the reporter. He let Kelly speak for all of them while he and the rest of the outfit began to unload the chuckwagon and the livestock.

An hour later Charley and the others had the horses, mules, and the chuckwagon off the train and were saddled and ready for cross-country travel.

"That reporter must have returned to his office by now to write his story about the bandit raid," said Charley.

"That'd be a good bet," said Kelly.

"Did you tell him why we were here?" asked Charley.

"Only that we're a for-hire cattle outfit from up Amarillo way, come to Brownsville to pick up a herd to drive north," she said.

"Good girl," he told her. "Beforc we mount up," he said to the rest of them, "I'll bet there's a few of you who could use something to eat."

He turned to his grandson.

"Henry Ellis . . . why don't you give Roscoe a hand unpacking some of our vittles. Nothing that needs any cooking, mind you. Ham sandwiches, jerky, and cold beans ought to do it. A campfire would just draw attention to us anyway. After that, we can all catch up on a little shut-eye before we head out. But I don't want us anywhere near this depot when the sun comes up. The local folks might not like waking up to a well-intentioned, well-armed posse camped so close to their city."

"You will be safe wherever you are," came a heavily accented reply from the shadows . . . as long as I am with you."

Guns were quickly drawn as everyone turned to the sound of the voice.

"Step out here into some light," said Charley, cocking his Walker Colt. "Show yourself."

Roca Fuerte followed Charley's order and moved out of the shadows and into a shaft of moonlight.

"It's Señor Fuerte," said Henry Ellis. "Don't shoot. I know him."

The boy moved through the little group, then past his grandfather, who still had his large revolver pointed at Fuerte. He stopped, facing the man.

"I thought you were one of them," said the boy. "But you wouldn't be here now if you were."

"The man who hired me has communicated with the man who runs your father's company," said Fuerte to the boy. "When he mentioned that your grandfather was the famous Texas Ranger, Charley Sunday, I knew that must have been where you went."

"And if I'd known I was famous," said Charley, moving over to Fuerte and Henry Ellis, "I'd have found another way to approach Brownsville."

With that, Charley uncocked his pistol.

Both men broke into laughter, throwing their arms around one another.

"Roca Fuerte, you old bushwhacker," said Charley.

"Charley Sunday, *mi amigo*," said Fuerte.

"Do you two know each other?" asked Henry Ellis, who was still standing nearby, confused.

"You bet we do," said Charley. "When I was a Ranger and Señor Fuerte worked for the Guardia Rural, the *Rurales* . . . for the Mexican government, mind you . . . I depended on him for information about what was going on . . . or about to go on . . . along the river. Both sides of the river. But that was a long time ago, Roca."

"*Sí*," said Fuerte, "a very long time ago."

"My grandson tells me you wanted to take him some place after he jumped from the carriage," said Charley.

"All I wanted to do was get him away from those who wanted to do him harm," said Fuerte. "Obviously he had the same idea, but he chose his own direction. But now he has brought you back with him . . . and by the size of your party, I surmise you are expecting to participate in one very big *shoot-out*."

"Some of the *old-timers* where I come from call that a Texas fandango," said Charley.

"*Sí*," Fuerte continued. "I am familiar with that expression."

A shot rang out—the single bullet ricocheted off the bell of a nearby locomotive, producing an eerie retort.

Everyone drew their weapons, including Charley and Fuerte. But whoever had fired the shot had already disappeared into the night. The sound of galloping hoofbeats faded into the distance.

"A warning shot?" asked Charley.

"A coward's shot," said Fuerte. "He was probably told to kill one or more of us if he could . . . but he either missed or lost his nerve at the final moment."

"Well," said Charley, "at least they know we're here now."

"I am sure they knew you would be coming after them before they attacked your family," said Fuerte.

"Would that mean they let Henry Ellis get away on purpose?"

"Not necessarily, Señor Charley," said Fuerte. "Perhaps they were going to send you a ransom note . . . but when the boy escaped, they knew he would go directly to you."

"Are you thinking they're interested in me instead, and all this abduction stuff was just a ruse to get me off my ranch and down here to Mexico?" said Charley.

"Don't flatter yourself, *mi amigo*. They want you here in Mexico because it is easier to keep an eye on you if you are in Mexico. We both know we are all under surveillance as we speak."

"The gunshot proved that, don't you think?" said Charley.

"*Sí*," said Fuerte. "The gunshot proved someone knows you are here."

"Do ya think it's still safe for us ta camp here for a few hours?" said Roscoe, who had moved in beside the two.

"Just as safe as we were before that gunshot," said Fuerte. "Wherever we go they will know where we are. We may as well bed down right here like we had planned to earlier. Just post another guard or two."

"Besides, we'll be long gone before the sun rises," said Charley.

"With that I must agree," said Fuerte.

"Pennell, Roscoe, and Sergeant Stone'll take first watch for an hour. Rod, Fuerte, Holliday," said Charley, "you three are on second watch. After that, it'll be time to get moving anyway."

Henry Ellis slept uncomfortably during the first hour, knowing that his grandfather and his friends had been in

Brownsville for only a short time before someone had taken a shot at them.

The boy would later tell his grandfather it hadn't been that long after the second watch had begun that he had first heard the noises.

It sounds like an animal, was his first reaction, though by the next time, it sounded more like a human child whimpering to him.

The boy slipped out of his bedroll and stood up. Everyone else appeared to be sleeping soundly, except for the three men on guard duty. That trio had taken up positions with two of them at the east end of the tiny camp while Holliday stood by the chuckwagon, facing south. Their backs were all to Henry Ellis.

There it was—that whimpering again. *Someone could really be hurt or dying*, thought the boy. *Maybe I ought to go and see if I can help.*

Henry Ellis cocked his head until he heard the soft whining one more time, then he turned and started off slowly into the darkness in search of whom, or whatever, it was making that sound.

Time had passed quickly yet Charley awoke from his deep sleep as if he had gotten a full eight hours. He checked his gold pocket watch, which he had placed on the portion of his bedroll he wasn't using—the Roman numerals told him it was 3:47 in the morning. He sat up, then he nudged Roscoe who was sleeping beside him.

When Roscoe was half-awake, Charley spoke to him in a rough whisper.

"'Bout time to put the coffee on, Roscoe," said Charley. "I'll wake the others as soon as I get my boots on."

* * *

Within fifteen minutes the entire outfit was dressed and ready. They were standing around complaining about the cold coffee left over from the night before. Those had been Charley's orders—he'd asked Roscoe to find a well-hidden location between the empty cattle and passenger cars, where he could boil up more coffee than usual. The steaming liquid was then poured into several extra cooking pots to be used when the outfit woke up in the wee hours. This was done in order to keep the camp a cold one.

When the horses had been fed and saddled, and all were aboard their mounts, and just before Charley gave the signal to move out, he sensed something was wrong.

"Where's Henry Ellis?" he called out. "Where has my grandson run off to now?"

There was some commotion near the rear of the column. Henry Ellis rode to the front to join his grandfather.

"Where have you been, son?" asked Charley. "We darn near left without you."

Henry Ellis looked up, smiling.

"I heard some noise in the night while I was trying to sleep," he told his grandfather. "I didn't go far . . . just far enough to find this."

He reached behind and opened the buckled strap on his left saddlebag.

Charley glanced over.

The wet nose and glistening brown eyes of a mongrel puppy's face pushed itself up from under the open flap. The young dog looked over at Charley.

"Why, I'll be," said Charley. "A pup."

"I've already given him a name, Grampa," said the boy. "I call him Buster Number Two."

CHAPTER SEVEN

1961

"Henry Ellis found a puppy to replace old Buster. Isn't that neat?" said Noel.

"Only I wouldn't have called him Buster Number Two," said Caleb. "I'd have called him Blackie, or Spot . . . you know, after whatever color his coat was."

"Well," said Hank, "Buster Number Two seemed like the right thing to call him at the time. The main reason was that Charley had just lost Buster number one. I would imagine that Henry Ellis was thinking of how sad his grampa must have felt over losing the old Buster, and that's why he named the puppy Buster Number Two."

"Can I have another root beer, Mom?" called out Josh, the older one.

"They're in the ice chest, sweetheart," said Evie. "Who was your servant last year?"

Grumbling, Josh got to his feet and stumbled over to the ice chest. He rummaged through the slush until he found his root beer, then he brushed off the melting ice that was still clinging to the can. "Where'd you put the opener, Caleb," he hollered.

"I didn't use it last," said Caleb. "Grampa Hank did."

Hank held out the rusty old bottle opener, and Josh took it from him.

"Thanks, Grampa Hank," he said as he put a V-shaped hole near the lip of his soft drink can with a single flick of the wrist.

"I'll be needing that opener back, son," said Hank. "It's my personal opener. Grampa Charley gave it to me when I turned twenty-one. He said a man . . . especially a Texas man . . . had always better have his own church key."

"Is that what they called one of those things back then, Grampa?" asked Noel.

"People still call it a church key today," said Caleb, moving over to the ice chest for his own can of soda.

Hank lent him the opener so he could expose the contents of his container. Caleb opened the can, then handed the opener back to his great-grandfather.

"You can open both cans and bottles with my opener," said Hank. "Look at both ends . . . one for cans, one for bottle caps."

"I bought one of those new pop-tab cola cans the other day," said Josh. "It was real cool. You pull the attached tab off the top, and the opening you drink from is right there on top of the container for you. I hear that pretty soon they're going to have bottle caps you can open with your thumb, too."

"I'd like to see that," said Hank.

"Plus, screw-off caps," said Evie, the children's mother. "They're making things so easy for us these days, I wouldn't be surprised if they came up with an easy-opening ketchup bottle next. One that you didn't have to pound on the bottom to get the last drop out."

"How about if they made a ketchup bottle out of plastic, and all you had to do was squeeze it instead of having to shake it until your ears fell off," said Josh.

"Toss me one of those soda cans while you're over there, will you, Caleb?" said Hank.

"What flavor do you want, Grampa?" asked the boy.

"Doesn't matter," answered Hank. "But if there's a cream soda in there, I'll take it."

Caleb rummaged through the slush again and pulled out a cream soda can.

"I found one, Grampa," he said, tossing the container to his great-grandfather. "Catch!"

Hank didn't get his hands up fast enough and the can bounced straight down, hitting the ground beside him. He quickly retrieved the can and opened it up. Cream soda sprayed every which way.

"Aw, geez," said Hank, shaking his hands, one at a time, then wiping them on his trousers. "I just reckon I ain't as fast as I used to be." He took a large swig.

"Now let me think," he said to his family. I just gotta remember where I was in my story . . ."

Chapter Eight

1900

The outfit rode north in the darkness for at least two hours, putting them several miles beyond the border bridge before Charley figured it was safe to cross.

Taking Fuerte's word for it, Charley led them into the chilly waters of the Rio Grande. The former *Rurale* had chosen a shallow route for the horses so nothing would happen to delay the mission, and hopefully they would be able to slip into old Mexico without being seen or heard.

Bright rays of sunlight bounced off the glittering sand and reflective rocks that surrounded them, which, like the abundant cactus plants dotting the land, had been a familiar part of the northern Mexican landscape for centuries.

Charley, Henry Ellis, and the others rode in twos, like the military, keeping themselves bunched together so there would be no chance of stragglers.

After a few moments, one of the riders broke away and galloped up to the front of the column where Charley and his grandson were leading. As the rider got closer, Henry Ellis recognized her as Kelly.

She reined in beside the boy, making eye contact with Charley, who rode on his grandson's other side.

"Charley," she began, "do you, or anyone else, know where we're going, for heaven's sake? Or are you just guessing at which trail the attackers might have taken? We've been paralleling the river heading north for quite a while . . . are you sure that's the right direction?"

Charley smiled at the woman's concern.

"If it was just me," he said, "I would be guessing. But this time I decided to leave it all up to Señor Roca Fuerte."

He indicated the Mexican gentleman riding directly behind them.

". . . He's not only real familiar with this territory, Miss Kelly, he's also got a pretty good idea about where those men took my daughter and her husband. And for now, the trail heads north."

Fuerte spurred ahead joining the others.

"When we were attacked back in Brownsville, I was able to recognize several of the abductors," he told her. "They are only faithful to one man . . . an ex–Mexican army officer who has participated in these types of abductions before . . . mostly political kidnappings . . . and always for a price."

Charley picked up the conversation.

"What Señor Fuerte means is that this ex–Mexican army officer, Armendariz is his name, does not do these abductions for himself alone; he is always hired by someone else."

Charley went on, "Señor Fuerte also thinks that tracking Armendariz to wherever his present location might be will eventually lead us to the person, or persons, who ordered my family's abduction in the first place . . . and, whether he is still keeping them as prisoners, or has sent them on ahead to whoever is paying him."

"Thank you both for bringing me up to date," said Kelly. "We've all been riding since before sunup, Charley. Don't you think it's about time we stopped for something to eat?"

"Now, why didn't I think of that?" said Charley.

He turned in his saddle.

"Roscoe," he called out, "how about fixing us up a noon meal?"

"Can I build me a fire this time, C.A.?"

"I suppose so . . . it should be all right now."

Fuerte nodded.

"Then I'll start with the coffee," said Roscoe. "Hot . . . *hot* . . . coffee."

"Not too hot for me," said Fuerte, as he circled back, moving in beside Roscoe. "If you take in a deeper breath than normal, you'll realize that today is going to be even warmer than yesterday."

Holliday moved in beside Charley and the others. He carried his frockcoat folded neatly under his arm. Perspiration had already begun to stain portions of his frilly fronted dress shirt.

"Hell," he said, "it's already hotter'n a skillet full a' fryin' bacon."

"Now ain't that funny," said Roscoe. "That's exactly what I was about ta whip up for your noon meal, Holliday. Along with some of those tins of Mexican *free-holies.*"

Sergeant Stone and Pennell were already stretched out on their bedrolls. Rod and Kelly were doing the same a few feet away. The sergeant's three toolboxes remained tied to the chuckwagon nearby.

"What do you have in those boxes of yours, Sergeant?" asked Rod. "Looks to me like a couple of those cases might contain M1895 Colt-Browning machine guns."

The sergeant whipped around, ready to fight if need be. "Have you been snooping around my boxes, Indian?"

"Calm down, Sergeant," said Rod. "I saw a couple of those automatic Colts in action during the Cuban campaign. That's all."

"Then you must have been one of Roosevelt's team."

"That's right," said Rod. "During the battle for San Juan Heights, I was one of the first to make it to the crest at Kettle Hill."

"And he was one of the first to make it back down to the bottom of that hill, too," said Kelly, cutting in. "His boot heel was shot out from under him just as he reached the summit."

"It was definitely a rock-hard tumble . . . all the way down, I remember," said Rod. "Lead was flying in every direction, but not one bullet found a piece of me."

"You're lucky," said the sergeant.

"More than that," said Rod. "I'm blessed."

The puppy was playing in the dirt—its neck attached to Henry Ellis's wrist by a long piece of rawhide.

"Lookit them feet," said Roscoe, who was putting away his supplies and tying several frying pans to one side of the chuckwagon. "He's gonna grow up ta be as big as Buster was."

"Bigger," said Charley, who stood nearby. "I remember the old Buster at this one's age. He wasn't that big at all."

"How old do you think he is, Grampa?" asked Henry Ellis.

"Not more than three or four months, I reckon," said Charley.

"What should I feed him?" the boy wanted to know.

"Buster ate table scraps and whatever he could find in the chicken yard," said Roscoe.

"Oh, no, no, no," interrupted Kelly, who was near enough to have heard Roscoe's remark. "You can't feed a puppy table scraps. It's not good for them."

"I've been eating food that makes table scraps all my life," said Charley, ". . . and the first Buster ate my table scraps. It never hurt neither one of us none," he went on.

"The only time ya ever got sick after eatin' a meal, you blamed it on my cookin'," said Roscoe. "An' it turned out ta be the opossum meat in the stew that was spoilt."

"That was raccoon meat, Roscoe, and it wasn't spoiled. You know I'm allergic to raccoon."

"Well maybe it's time to change Mr. Sunday's way of thinking about food," said Kelly. "'Specially dog food."

"Pardon me, Miss Kelly," said Charley. "But don't you think I should know something about what to feed animals by now? I've been raising all kinds of 'em since I was a tad younger than Henry Ellis here. Birds and tortoises, too," he added. "I've raised 'em all."

"Just promise," said Kelly, "to cut off the fat if you feed him meat . . . and mix him up some gravy and rice to go with it."

"That won't be no problem, ma'am," said Roscoe, "seein's how it's me who does all the cookin'."

It was late in the afternoon when they arrived at what remained of Colonel Armendariz's camp. Of course they found it to be abandoned. Several local peons were all that remained, and even they ran off into the surrounding foliage before Fuerte could question them.

A search was made of the adobe building that had been built on the land, plus the area nearby, and it was agreed upon that nothing had been found to support the fact that Henry Ellis's parents had even been there. That was until Henry Ellis, himself, found something in one of the old building's second-floor bedrooms.

"Grampa! Grampa!" he called out.

Charley and some of the others who were close by came running, finding the boy in one of the smaller upstairs sleeping quarters.

The boy was on his knees in a corner with his back to Charley when the old man entered.

"What do you have there, son?" said Charley as he advanced closer to his grandson.

Henry Ellis turned around slow and easy. In his hand a single red rose, faded, with a broken stem.

"They were here, Grampa," said the boy. "Señor Fuerte brought Mother a bouquet of red roses as a welcoming gift from Don Roberto when we arrived in Brownsville that day."

An hour later the outfit had made camp and Feather was bedding down the horses and other livestock. The horses had been unsaddled and were now tied in a string beside the adobe.

The rest of the outfit had spread their bedrolls in a wide circle surrounding the chuckwagon and the campfire. Roscoe was cooking the evening meal over the flames, while at the same time he was making sourdough bread in a Dutch oven he'd remembered to bring along.

Charley sat on the adobe's porch steps with Henry Ellis and Roca Fuerte on either side of him—they were going over some maps. The rest of the outfit was either sitting or laid back on their bedrolls. They were watching what their leader was doing on the porch and waiting for their orders.

"The Armendariz gang is not as large as I first thought they were," said Fuerte. "He has no more than ten or twelve men riding with him . . . plus several female camp followers. It appears they all left this place at around the same time . . . shortly before noon . . . and they left in a hurry, I suspect, by the condition in which they left this place."

"Well," said Charley, "then it shouldn't be that hard to find them, should it?"

Fuerte raised a finger, hoping to get a word in.

"There is only one problem, Señor Charley," he said. "They have now split up into smaller groups of twos and threes and are headed out in many different directions."

"We can handle that," said Charley. "We'll just do the same thing. Fuerte, you will ride with me. Henry Ellis will go along with Rod and Kelly. Roscoe, you, Holliday, and Feather can partner up. Pennell, you and Sergeant Stone can ride together. Does that suit everyone?" he added.

They all nodded, agreeing.

"So, everyone get some take-along grub from Roscoe," Charley continued. "He'll also supply you with extra ammunition in case you happen to run across Armendariz and his gang. If you find any clues that could possibly help lead us to them, then stop who you're following in their tracks. But don't kill them. Question them about where Armendariz is headed, and make sure you find out where they're taking my daughter and her husband. By the time we all meet up again, just maybe we'll know where they're going."

"So, where shall we meet?" asked Kelly.

Fuerte answered for all to hear: "Upriver from Laredo about three miles, then inland around six miles, there's an old, deserted Mexican army fort. It has not been in use since the 1860s. You can find it by following the river road, then turning inland at a small Indian village called Borrego Springs. The fort is six miles due east of that village."

"Let's all plan on meeting at that fort in, let's say, three days," said Charley. "In the meantime we'll just hope one of us can find out more information about where Armendariz is taking my daughter . . . my grandson's parents," he corrected himself. "For now, it's getting too late to do anything but eat and get a good night's rest. I want everyone up by dawn, packed and ready to travel."

Chapter Nine

Some days earlier, the same day Charley and his grandson had visited Rod and Kelly at their ranch, Holliday at his shooting range, plus nearby Fort Clark where they'd talked Sergeant Stone into joining the outfit, some of the local Mexican bandits who had been plaguing the south-Texas settlements along the border for what seemed like forever, decided to attack one of the isolated ranches on the outskirts of Laredo.

These machete-wielding *desperados* had crossed the customarily peaceful river with the intention of robbing the unsuspecting local ranchers and their families. They chose a small, isolated ranch house with a swirl of smoke rising from its chimney.

Elisabeth Hanna Rogers, the only Caucasian survivor of that bloody incident, it was thought, had been preparing breakfast for her husband, Newt, and their twelve-year-old son, Michael, when the three of them heard riders approaching outside their small ranch house, located east—by three-quarters of a mile—of the Rio Grande River.

Newt Rogers told his wife to stay inside while he and

the boy went out to check on just who it was had come a calling so early in the day. The two males took their hunting rifles with them so Mrs. Rogers would feel somewhat secure in their absence.

Terrified upon hearing rough Spanish-speaking voices arguing with her husband several moments later, Mrs. Rogers found herself frozen, unable to draw the curtain so she might look out. The woman could only listen as she sat trembling at the kitchen table. All she could hear were the harsh Mexican voices, plus the calming words of her husband, Newt, protesting the foreigners' presence on what he told them was private property and American soil.

The arguing outside went on for about three minutes before the voices finally paled off. The group, both men and horses, had moved away from the front porch.

Finally, Mrs. Rogers built up enough courage to go to the window and peek out. By then, she could only see the backsides of the heavily armed Mexican riders moving away down the entrance road. One thing caught her eye. It was a bright red neckerchief worn by one of the intruders.

Her husband and son walked along sullenly beside the Mexicans and their horses. There was another man also being nudged along by the small gang. He was the family's loyal ranch hand, a *mojado* who answered to the name of Humberto.

The Mexican trespassers, along with Newt Rogers and their son, had been out of sight for barely a minute before she heard the two gunshots. One, and then the other. After that, all she could make out were the distant sounds of Spanish-speaking voices yelling and horses hooves riding away.

Humberto came running up the road toward the house shouting something in Spanish. Elisabeth Rogers stepped out onto the porch to meet the frightened man. He stopped, eyes wide. He beckoned anxiously for her to follow.

Setting her fears aside, she ran after him through the gate and on down the dusty road, until she found herself sliding to a stop. Hidden halfway behind several spindly cactus plants, she could see her husband's body lying facedown in a pool of sandy blood. With a hand to her mouth in disbelief, she took another few hesitant steps forward, until her son's body came into view. Humberto was kneeling over the boy, genuflecting. The bandits had cut off both the boy's and the husband's heads. It was only then that Elisabeth Rogers knew it was all over—that they were both dead, and that her life had been changed forever.

Humberto dug two shallow graves and they buried Newt and Michael side by side, under a newly planted pepper tree near her vegetable garden. They prayed together in both English and Spanish for the two human souls.

After that, Elisabeth Rogers had the hired man hitch the two horses to the wagon, while she packed a few essentials, including her late husband's horse pistol, and both hunting rifles.

No words were spoken between the ranch hand and the widow, for Humberto could tell that an extreme change had taken place in the woman whom he had known as a nervous, yet considerate, lady—a transformation from the person she had been only hours earlier to a human being filled with a deep, seething vengeance inside. A blood lust for revenge, brought on entirely, he knew, by the cold-blooded, gruesome murders of her only loved ones.

* * *

"Name's Mitchell Pennell," said the large, scraggly bearded civilian with the frayed homespun clothing that smelled of more than one man.

He was talking to Sergeant Stone.

"I'll be traveling with you," Pennell continued. "Charley Sunday told me we we're going to be partners."

The two men were situated a few yards from the campfire near their bedrolls.

Sergeant Stone held out his muscular hand and the two of them shook.

"Tobias Stone," said the black man, forcing a smile. "Sergeant . . . United States Army."

Pennell held the lead rope to a Mexican burro.

"Roscoe found this here burro roaming wild and he give it to me."

The animal's rope harness was hitched to the front of a small, dilapidated, two-wheeled cart, stocked to just below the rim of its weather-beaten bed with ample Mexican Army–issue supplies, packed into gunnysacks.

"It was a good thing I found us this cart, too, and that you stumbled onto that Mexican food supply cache, Sergeant," said Pennell. "We can store our bedrolls in the cart, too, don't you think?"

"We've got us enough air-tights, hardtack, bacon, beans, corn, 'taters, an' tortillas to get us all the way to Mexico City if we was goin' that way," said Pennell. "I found a few more somethin'-or-others in that adobe, too." He smiled, showing uneven teeth. "Things them Indian women down here in Mexico like ta barter fer." He winked. He reached into one of the gunnysacks and withdrew a handful of shiny trinkets and beads, letting them sift through his fingers as if they were a solid gold treasure.

Sergeant Stone shook his head.

"I don't think we'll be needing them kind of trade goods, Mr. Pennell," he told him. "We gotta be keeping our time pretty tight. We only got a few days to do what it takes the United States Army a month to do. Matter of fact," he continued, "I don't think we need to be taking that scrubby chip wagon you found along with us, neither. Just a couple of good horses should do us fine, don't you think?" he added.

Pennell lowered his eyes, tugged at his chin.

"I suppose the Lord'll look on both you and me in a better light if we don't go off looking for women along the way." Pennell removed his hat to reveal a once shaved head with a new crop of short, growing stubble covering his scalp.

"I reckon I should be asking forgiveness from the Lord . . . and from you, too, Sergeant Stone . . . for my coveting like a sinner one more time. I thank you from deep down in my heart, sir. I can see now that you're a God-fearin' man."

Sergeant Stone nodded.

Underneath it all, he thought, *this Pennell fella seems to be an all right person himself. He seems to be a Believer, too. He ought to make a right fine trail mate on this little journey we're about to set out on . . . If I've got him pegged right.*

"I'll go see if anyone else wants the cart," said Pennell. "We'll use the burro to carry our supplies. Like you said . . . without any of the beads and trinkets."

He tossed the bag of now useless items into a pile of rubbish nearby.

The Sergeant nodded, watching the large man as he climbed aboard the sagging cart and took the burro's lead rope in hand. Then Mitchell Pennell slapped leather to the animal's rump. The burro struggled to turn the vehicle around, then Pennell was able to move the cart past Sergeant Stone and on toward the front of the adobe.

"Ask Rod and Kelly if they might have a use for it," said Charley to Pennell when he was told the cart was available. Just give those Mexican Army supplies the sergeant found to Roscoe. He'll put 'em to good use."

Pennell nodded.

"The sergeant and me sure don't need that old cart, we just thought you might be able to think of someone who could put it to better use."

"That's nice of you, Mitchell," said Charley.

"Thanks," said Pennell. "Thanks for getting me out of that hell hole."

"I put you in that hell hole, Mitchell," said Charley. "Who better to get you out?"

Pennell smiled, then he turned and moved away.

You bet your butt I put you away, thought Charley. *Even though you saved my life, you still had to do your time, and in the long run it wasn't up to me anyway.*

The year had been 1873 when Texas Ranger Sergeant Charles Abner Sunday had finally caught up to the outlaw, Mitchell Pennell. Charley had been following Pennell for seven days, with his prey heading west, then down, leading Charley into the badlands of the Texas Big Bend.

Pennell had robbed two banks in Del Rio, leaving a teller half-dead at the first bank and a bank guard wounded during the second assault.

Charley had been sent out after him.

It was late afternoon when Charley, still on Pennell's trail, found himself entering the tiny border town of Lajitas—just a stone's throw from the Rio Grande River.

The town's three establishments were an adobe trading post, an open-front, tent saloon, and a small, crumbling horse barn where travelers could get their mounts shod or a wagon repaired, if need be.

Charley spotted Pennell's horse tied off in front of the saloon—a tentlike structure with an open front. A quick glance inside showed him his quarry was not visible, so he nudged his horse over to the trading post where he dismounted.

Charley tied his mount to one of the yucca staves used to hold up the adobe building's porch roof. As he walked toward the open doorway, he passed three Mexican peons who were using the porch as a central location where the local ranchers, who were looking to hire day workers, could find them.

Charley nodded to the stoic brown faces, then went inside.

The interior of the building was dark and cool—it resembled Bill Röessler's general store back in Juanita more than what Charley remembered a trading post should look like.

There were three rows of boxed and canned goods in the center of the store, with glass countertops on either side of the room filled with bolts of fabric, knives, pistols, ammunition boxes, and trinkets of all kinds. Rifles were hung on the wall behind one of the counters, plus blankets, trappings, and harnesses were hanging from ten-penny nails and hooks everywhere, it seemed.

There was a small desk piled high with papers that had a sign reading POST OFFICE, LAJITAS, TEXAS, hanging over it.

There were no post office boxes visible, and no cash register. Just a bearded Caucasian man in rolled-up shirt-sleeves who was sitting on a high stool behind one of the glass counters looking through a pile of wanted posters while fanning himself with one of them.

"Constable?" said Charley.

The man looked up—his expression showed disinterest.

"I figured you must be the constable because of those posters you're looking through."

It was Charley speaking again.

"Maybe," said the man, getting to his feet. "Maybe I'm the constable, and maybe I'm not. Fact is, we don't have no official law dog here in Lajitas. Jake Cassidy's my name . . . and besides being asked to keep the peace around here when I'm able, I'm also the postmaster, the proprietor of this here establishment, and the blacksmith."

He nodded toward the door where Charley could see the barn across the way.

"Only thing I ain't," the man continued, "is a bartender. Abel Fernandez owns the saloon across the way, and he pours the whiskey. I don't imbibe so I never get over there much to see ol' Abel."

"That's too bad," said Charley, "since you're such close neighbors."

"What can I do you for?" said Jake Cassidy.

"Oh," said Charley, "you wouldn't have happened to see a man ride into your town about a half an hour ago, or so, would you?" said Charley.

"You the law?" said Cassidy.

Charley showed him his badge.

Jake Cassidy wasn't too happy to see Charley's circled star.

"People down here don't hanker much for Johnny Laws, mister," he said.

Charley swung around with his Walker Colt in his hand—it was pointed directly at Cassidy's midsection.

"Well you'd better start hankering for this Johnny Law,

amigo, because I mean business. I know he's here. His horse is tied right over there at the saloon."

"Then why don't you go over to the saloon and ask for him?" said Cassidy. "I surely can't help you do that."

"Nope," said Charley, "but you can run over there and ask that bartender to step outside for a few minutes."

"Sure enough," said Cassidy . . . "I can do that."

"Because if you don't, I'll put a bullet in your gut," warned Charley. "Now go," he urged the man, "and don't say a word about my being here."

He pressed the gun's barrel against Cassidy's stomach.

"Now move," Charley ordered, "and you better make your story sound convincing."

Cassidy nodded. He moved around the counter and slowly stepped through the door.

Charley followed, except he stopped just before going outside and stood watching from behind the door's frame.

From his position, Charley could see into the saloon. When Cassidy went inside the worn canvas structure, Charley was able to watch, and if the trading post owner was giving the bartender more information than he was supposed to, he'd do something about it later.

Charley knew he hadn't said any more than he was supposed to, when in less than thirty seconds, Cassidy came out of the saloon. He was followed by the barkeep, a dark-skinned *mestizo*—a mixed breed. Together they crossed over to the barn and disappeared inside.

Charley waited a moment before he stepped out of the trading post doors and began walking slowly across the dirt to the saloon.

Once he was closer, he could see the silhouette of Mitchell Pennell sitting at one of the few tables inside the establishment, located to the right of the makeshift bar, hidden somewhat back in the shadows.

As Charley was about to step into the shaded interior, Pennell's voice stopped him.

"Behind you, Ranger!" the outlaw yelled, followed by a flash of exploding gunpowder that came from under the table.

Charley fired back. His bullet caught Pennell in the shoulder, spinning him out of the chair.

"Not me, you sonofabitch!" yelled Pennell from the floor where he had fallen. "There's two guns right behind you."

In an instant Charley realized that Pennell had fired at someone in the street in back of him, and not at himself—a warning to him of his own personal danger.

Charley turned just in time to see Cassidy, beside the fallen bartender. The trading post owner was raising a shotgun, getting ready to aim the deadly weapon at him.

The Walker Colt spat two spinning wads of lead that caught Cassidy in both his chest and throat. The trading post proprietor went down spinning, splattering arterial blood all across the sunbaked street.

Charley came out of his reverie as Pennell was moving over to where Roscoe was still busy washing the breakfast dishes.

"Here ya go, Roscoe," said Pennell as he lifted the gunnysacks out of the cart, setting them at Roscoe's feet. "These supplies belong to you now. Charley's orders. But he wants Rod and Kelly to have the cart."

"I'll see that they get it as soon as I'm done here," said Roscoe. "And thanks," he added.

Pennell unhitched the burro, holding the animal's lead rope in his hand. He watched as Charley, still a few yards away, fastened the buckle on his saddlebag and turned to Fuerte, nearby.

"If you are ready, *mi amigo*," said Charley.

"Let us go now," said the Mexican.

Both of them stepped up into their saddles and spurred away from the camp.

Rod and Kelly had accepted the two-wheeled cart from Pennell; they began loading their bedrolls and supplies into it immediately. Henry Ellis would ride in the cart with his new puppy, while his horse would pull the two-wheeled vehicle.

Holliday and Feather were packed up and waiting for Roscoe to finish up his chores.

"Think we oughta help ol' Roscoe with them airtight tins Pennell just brung him?" said Holliday.

"Only if some of them tins is full a' whiskey," said Feather. "I been goin' on now fer around three days without somethin' to wash the dust out a' my gullet."

"Most likely we'll run across some little villages along the way that's got a *cantina*, Feather," said Holliday. "I hope you can last it out 'til then."

"I've waited before . . . reckon I'll just have ta do it again," said Feather.

Roscoe, now in position on the chuckwagon's spring seat, snapped the reins and had the mules take him over to where the two men were talking.

"If you fellers are done jawin' 'bout things an' such," he said, "I suppose we should be gettin' a move on."

CHAPTER TEN

The bandit known as Pedro Jose Bedoya was the first to spot the two-horse wagon with the American woman driving, as it trundled over a low shimmering rise on the dusty trail leading away from the river.

Bedoya turned to the four men riding with him, dedicated *bandidos* like himself. Bedoya, the leader of the pack, had given them orders, shortly after the raid on the Brownsville train, to ride hard for Laredo with the news that their well-planned attack had been stopped by some armed men traveling with the brand-new *gringo* army troops.

The five battle-weary bandits had spent two days and nights in the Mexican section of Laredo, spreading their account of the train attack, while drinking heavily and celebrating.

That morning, they had saddled up again for the long ride back to their base camp in the far desert, fifty or so miles to the west of the Texas town.

"It appears the American woman has lost her way," said Bedoya in Spanish, chuckling aloud and pointing. "Follow me, *hombres*. We will take her back to our camp as a memento of our stay in Laredo. I may wish to make her my bride. Ha." He laughed. His *compadres* cackled with him as they spurred away, galloping down a long, sandy slope toward the approaching wagon.

By the time Elisabeth Rogers was aware of the advancing horsemen, it was too late to turn her team and make a run for it. Instead, she reached below her feet and withdrew her dead husband's pistol, tucking it under her traveling skirt, then covering the substantial bulge it made with a crocheted lap blanket.

As the riders came closer, several of the men drew their weapons and began firing into the air, startling Elisabeth's horses. She struggled, reining them to a rumbling standstill.

The first thing she noted was the bright red neckerchief worn around the leader's neck. With her hand clasped firmly around the butt of her husband's revolver, Elisabeth pulled back the hammer and waited until the five Mexicans brought their mounts to a halt alongside her team.

"Aha," whooped the one who was smiling the widest—the one who wore the red neck scarf. She took him to be their leader. The grinning Mexican edged his apprehensive horse up next to the wagon seat. So close, in fact, she could smell the past few days oozing from his pores.

"What, may I ask, is a woman as beautiful as you doing here in this godforsaken land? And all alone?" Bedoya asked in broken English with both of his eyes twinkling. "There are many dangerous *bandidos* roaming these badlands, have you not heard?"

Elisabeth forced a smile as she slowly slid the hefty gun from beneath the folds of her skirt, still using the lap blanket to conceal the weapon.

"I'm all right," she told the Mexican. "I really am. You

and these men wouldn't happen to have been on the Texas side of the river yesterday morning, would you?" she asked calmly, still maintaining her smile.

"What business is that of yours, señora?" said Bedoya, changing his disposition to one of annoyance. "We go where we wish to go . . . Mexico, Estados Unidos. Anywhere we want . . . we go."

"I was just curious," Elisabeth continued, ignoring what the man had just told her. ". . . curious if you had been to a ranch near Red Rock, a ranch with three freshly planted pepper trees and a vegetable garden in the front yard?"

"As I have told you, señora," repeated Bedoya, "where we have been is not your business."

"The woman has a pistol," shouted one of the men in Spanish as he reached for his own gun.

Before he could clear leather, Elisabeth's pistol exploded from beneath the blanket; its spinning projectile propelled the man backward, knocking him from the saddle.

By the time Bedoya and the others had calmed their rearing horses and attempted to reach for their own guns, Elisabeth was holding them all at bay.

"Don't anyone move," she commanded, throwing back the smoking coverlet to reveal the large barrel of her dead husband's revolver.

"I'm as keen to kill all four of you the same as I did that one."

Pedro Jose Bedoya and his *amigos* raised their hands slowly. Bedoya made an attempt to speak. "But, señora—"

The Colt roared once again and Bedoya's horse crumpled beneath him, a gaping hole between its eyes.

"*I* do all the talking, mister," said Elisabeth Rogers. "You just do the listening. Now, all of you," she motioned with the gun's barrel, "drop your weapons."

The other remaining bandits followed her directions. Bedoya, pinned under his dead horse, struggled to pull himself free.

"You too, mister," she demanded with a squint to her eyes, "before you go trying to get yourself out from under that poor animal."

The others watched cautiously as their *jefe* labored to remove his sidearm from its holster. The sheath of concho-studded leather was caught beneath the man's pinned leg and his saddle.

"I do not say something like this usually to a woman," grunted Bedoya, "but you are already dead in this country . . . *puta*."

He feigned spitting.

"Don't you go getting any ideas about trying to frighten me," she told him. "Because this woman's put any fear she ever had *way* far behind her."

She raised the gun quickly, pointing it at Bedoya's head. "You killed my family, you rotten bastard. Now it is I who take my just retribution."

She pulled back the hammer one more time.

A large bead of perspiration bubbled to the surface on the bandit's forehead. He raised a hand. "No," he begged. "I did not kill your fam—"

The bullet's impact split the skull of the man directly behind him from forehead to spine, killing him instantly. The knife he had neatly removed from his neckband, ready to throw at Elisabeth, dropped to the ground as he toppled from his anxious horse.

The other two reined back, splattered with the man's blood, terrified they might be next.

"No, please, señora," said Bedoya, his hand over his heart. "Please believe me. We had nothing to do with any killings of *Americano* ranchers in Texas. We have been in

Laredo for the last two days. There are witnesses who saw us there."

Elisabeth thought for a moment, considering. Then she lowered the pistol's barrel slightly.

"All right," she said. "The rest of you just git. Move . . ." She raised her voice. "Now."

Once he'd pulled himself free, Bedoya swung into the dead man's saddle. Then he and the two remaining bandits wheeled their mounts around and spurred out as rapidly as they could in a westerly direction, leaving their dead companions—*and* Elisabeth Rogers—in the wake of their whirlwind departure.

Sergeant Tobias Stone, now dressed in worn trail clothing and a wool broad-brimmed hat, finished the Lord's Prayer under his breath as he rode alongside Mitchell Pennell. The burro, with their supplies dangling from two gunnysacks, followed along on a rope tied to the sergeant's saddle. They were deeper into Mexico, fourteen miles southwest of the adobe campsite where they had spent the previous night. It had been six hours since they had left the others behind and started out. No one in the camp had paid the two men any attention as they disappeared into the morning, except for Roscoe Baskin. Roscoe had waved to the two of them as they passed him by, and said, "Good luck."

"Been in the army long now, have you?" asked Pennell.

"Thirty-eight years," answered the sergeant, squinting ahead. "If you want ta count the time I spent in the war."

"You married?"

Another question from the sergeant's hefty trail mate.

"Fifteen and a half years," said Stone. "I got me a good

woman . . . and a big, strapping son. He's almost fourteen years old now, he is," added Stone with a smile.

"I ain't never been hitched up myself," said Pennell, shaking his head. "If I ever do marry up, it'll be with one a' them *pelado* Injun women from down here, I suspect. They seem to be the only female folk that'll have anything to do with the likes of me."

They rode along for a while, saying nothing to one another. Their horses' hooves appeared to crunch in harmony over the parched alkali of the northern Mexican desert. Every so often one would kick a rock, expanding a very soft sound into a jarring cacophony in the unremitting quietness that surrounded the two riders.

Finally, the sergeant broke the silence.

"She is more than a good woman, my wife," he told his new companion, picking up from where he had left off several moments earlier. "She is the *best.*" He turned in his saddle to face Pennell. "I'm just sorry I can't be with her more than I am," he added with a poignant twinge to his voice. "And my boy, too."

"Where are they now," asked Pennell, "your family?"

"Back at Fort Clark," answered Stone. "The fort where I'm stationed, most of the time . . . near Juanita. We make our home there."

"That's a long ways from here to there," said Pennell.

"Yeah," mumbled Stone, "a long, long way from here to there."

There was a trail of sorts, some may have called it a two-rut wagon route, but even that was debatable. It split off from the road leading away from the camp with the adobe building and headed northwest, where some cloud-covered mountaintops were visible in the far distance.

Two hours out of the camp, Charley Sunday and his traveling companion, Roca Fuerte, came across a deserted two-horse fence-wagon on that desolate byway. The wagon was lying on its back, turned turtle, with no sign of team nor driver.

Upon further investigation, both Charley and his friend determined the wagon to be American-made, and that it was definitely not an ancient relic left along the way by some earlier Mexican army expedition or a lone Mormon pioneer.

Charley dismounted. He slowly circled the wagon, his trained eyes searching for any evidence that might lead him to an explanation for the vehicle's presence in such a remote location.

After several minutes, he appeared to give up. He re-mounted, swinging into the saddle and tucking both toes into their respective stirrups. That was when Roca Fuerte saw the corner of the fabric.

"Señor Charley," he called out. "I think you may have missed something." He nodded toward the wagon's upside-down spring seat.

Charley's eyes followed Fuerte's gaze. The ex-Ranger saw it, too—a small piece of material that poked up from under the capsized ranch vehicle. He swung down once again and moved over to the wagon, closer this time.

Kneeling down, and using his gloved fingers, Charley wiggled the piece of knitted handiwork, pulling it out gradually so not to damage it. Finally, a small, hand-crocheted coverlet was revealed.

Charley held it up so Fuerte might see it better. "Looks like a lady's lap blanket to me," he said. "And it looks like it's got a close-range bullet hole in it, too. Dead center."

He wiggled the finger he'd stuck through the charred perforation to show the retired *federale*.

Fuerte shook his head slowly. "I hope that bullet wasn't meant for her. And what on earth would an American lady be doing down here all alone in Mexico, anyway?"

"Maybe she was out here doing the same thing we are," said Charley. "Looking for something . . . or someone. And, Roca," he added, "there are powder burns around this bullet hole. Either someone shot through it at real close range, or she was the one doing the shooting."

Sergeant Tobias Stone and Mitchell Pennell had been on the trail since before dawn. They had eaten their morning meal in the saddle, chewing on hardtack and jerky, then washing it down with warm water from their canteens. Like their horses, the supply burro had been fed a cup of oats before they had started out.

The night they had spent previously had been very chilly, windy at times, with gusts strong enough to spook the burro and the horses.

The sergeant had even gotten up in the cold, blowing darkness to stand with the livestock, whispering softly into the ears of the frightened animals, soothing their tensions with his soft voice and gentle hands.

Tobias Stone knew animals well, having been born on a large farm in Mississippi—once a great plantation before the Southern Rebellion had exploded. He had grown up sharecropping with his family and working part-time for the plantation's hostler—taking care of the estate's livestock. He had thought, back then, that being a hostler, the caretaker of the horses and livestock for a large plantation, was what he would grow up to be. But he was wrong. His parents died, without warning, in a cotton-gin mishap, shortly after Tobias turned sixteen. And on the same day they were killed, the land they had sharecropped for what seemed like a lifetime to the teenaged Tobias was turned over to another family. Plus, his part-time position with the hostler was taken from him, too. Only then had it become clear to the young Tobias Stone that he was really a nonentity as far as the plantation owner was concerned, and that he had only been accepted earlier because his parents had been meeting their established quota.

A day or two later, after he and his younger siblings had buried their mother and father, the five of them were given their freedom by the plantation's owner—who knew the war was going badly for the South—and they were allowed to go their separate ways, with Tobias ending up in Kentucky.

After several run-ins with some staunch segregationists—Confederate supporters who, in all likelihood, had never seen a free Negro—Tobias Stone went north and joined the United States Army. The main reason being that in the army, he could eat regularly and have a warm place to sleep.

Instead, he was ordered into battle. He fought in many bloody skirmishes during the war's final days, one time even avoiding capture only to find himself fighting in the muddy ditches once again.

Following the war's end at Appomattox, his company was moved west and split between the western fortifications where he would learn to fight and kill Indians.

Over the years Tobias Stone eventually ended up stationed at Fort Clark in west Texas, near the border with Mexico—and he was happy there with his own kind, the Seminole-Negroes.

At Fort Clark he also met the woman who was to become his wife. She worked as a washerwoman for the soldiers, keeping their union suits, socks, and uniform shirts clean with a weekly washing down at the nearby creek. She also beat the dust out of their greatcoats, pressing the uniforms until they looked like new. Her name was Ethel Rosa Johnson.

Sergeant Stone thought back to those days, so long ago, back to when he first laid eyes on his future wife. *She was so pretty*, he thought, *so sweet, so lovely*. And when he spoke to her that first time, she was so shy.

It had taken him over two months to convince her to stroll with him, another month before she would consent to go on a chaperoned picnic. And it would take an entire year until she finally accepted his proposal of marriage. Even then, it was six months again before the actual event would take place.

After their wedding, they had spent two wonderful years together, living in one of the married Negro enlisted men's private quarters at Fort Clark. A vermin-infested wooden hut, actually, just four walls with its windows open to the elements—plus the door was off the hinges.

But Tobias found the things he needed to correct those problems, and he was, in time, able to turn the quarters into a comfortable home for the two of them. A year later, their son had been born.

Rosa understood military life; she also had a great belief in the Almighty. She knew they would eventually be reunited in God's Glorious Kingdom, no matter what befell them.

"Whoooa-up," said Pennell in his usual gruff manner. He held up a hand so the sergeant would pause, too.

"What is it?" asked Sergeant Stone, coming out of his thoughts.

Speaking in a low voice, Pennell whispered hoarsely as some flying desert insect buzzed around his left ear. "I seen something move. Over there," he said, pointing toward a rocky configuration about fifty or so yards ahead.

"It was a man," he went on, "a Negro man . . . black like you. He ducked behind them rocks when he seen us coming."

Sergeant Stone slowly withdrew his sidearm. He checked the chambers. At the same time, Pennell slid his rifle from its rough-leather scabbard, licking his thumb then wetting the hammer, out of habit.

"Was he armed?" whispered the sergeant.

Pennell shook his head. "I didn't see no weapons, but he could have friends. You wanna ride on over, or do you want me to try and get around behind him first?"

"There'll be no need for that," said a raspy voice that came from directly behind them.

The two men turned abruptly to see the blued, twenty-eight-inch double-barrels of a Remington 10-gauge shotgun pointed directly at them.

Behind the gun was a Negro—black like Sergeant Stone, as Pennell had described—who wore the distinctive clothing of an Indian chieftain.

"You come with me," said Billy July. "You are my prisoners. And please, gentlemen, if you will, hand me your weapons."

Chapter Eleven

The origins of the Seminole-Negro came about in the eighteenth and nineteenth centuries when runaway slaves, along with free Negroes, turned south in desperation, toward the isolated swamps of Spanish Florida. They were seeking sanctuary from their white oppressors. They found welcomed refuge with a coalition of tribes known as the Seminoles—Indians who populated that remote region of tangled vegetation and sultry everglades.

Over the years, and through many intermarriages, the runaway Negroes became as the Seminoles themselves, taking on the culture of the Indians while still holding on to particular aspects of their ancient, African customs and adopted Protestant beliefs. They began to dress as the Indians and became excellent farmers, mainly because of their recent heritage as slaves. Many of them were from families who had worked in the fields for generations.

In the early 1800s, the United States decided they needed the Florida lands for themselves. They made war against the Seminoles, which by then included the Seminole-Negroes.

When the Spanish eventually turned Florida over to the

United States in 1819, the Seminole resistance began to dwindle, and when it became clear that runaway slaves were continuing to defect to the Florida Indians, the U.S. government decided that the Seminoles must be moved for good. They passed the Indian Removal Act in 1830. The tribes revolted. Several wars ensued, with the Seminole-Negroes fighting alongside their brothers of the Seminole Nation. After eight years of brutal fighting, and with many battles lost to overwhelming American odds, the remaining Seminole Indians and the Seminole-Negroes surrendered. They were eventually moved west to Indian Territory.

Later on, in the Territory in the late 1840s, after many disagreements with the neighboring Creeks and with no help at all from Washington to rectify these disagreements, the leaders of the tribes led the Seminoles, and the Seminole-Negroes, out of the United States and into Mexico. It was there, across the Rio Bravo, that they chose to settle.

Once they were south of the border, the Seminole-Negroes were given the name *Mascogo* by the Mexicans living in the area. For years to come they would continue to fight alongside the Seminole Nation, warding off attacks by hostile Comanche tribes, Lipan Apaches, and even a few bold slave traders.

Not only did their color, and the name *Mascogo,* distinguish them from the Seminoles, but their way of thinking would also separate the two groups.

In 1856, following a devastating smallpox epidemic, the Seminole Nation negotiated a treaty with the U.S. government. It guaranteed them their own reservation—so they slowly began to migrate north, leaving the *Mascogos* behind.

Following the War between the States, a series of Indian

raids were taking place along the border with Texas. The U.S. government, remembering the Seminole-Negroes and their aggressiveness in battle, reached an agreement with some who had remained in Mexico. They were promised their own reservation in Indian Territory if they would serve as U.S. Army scouts until the raids had been eliminated. Most of the *Mascogo* men joined up, bringing their families along with them. They would be assigned meager dwellings on unusable government land close to the army post at Fort Clark. And when their services as scouts were no longer needed, and the promises made to them all but forgotten, those who survived either migrated north to Indian Territory or drifted back south into Mexico, settling near the little town of Nacimiento in the state of Coahuila.

"What do you make of him?" asked Mitchell Pennell in a gruff whisper as he and Sergeant Stone rode along slowly, their hands tied in front of them so they could rein their own horses. The burro had now been tied to Mitch Pennell's saddle by its lead rope. They were reluctantly following Billy July, the black man with the shotgun who dressed himself as an Indian chief.

Stone shook his head. "I dunno," he answered quietly. "Fort Clark, where I'm stationed, has quite a few Seminole-Negro troops. But I never seen one dressed like that man is dressed. He looks to me like one of my own kind. But he ain't. I can plainly see that. Can't you?"

Pennell shrugged. "Injuns, black folks, they're all the same to me. Only thing making me follow this man is that dad-blamed scattergun he's carrying . . . plus these ropes around my wrists."

"You two don't have to be talking so secretive back there," Billy July called out, throwing a warm glance back at his prisoners. “Why don’t you ride on up here, closer, so we can all get to know one another better?”

When neither the sergeant nor Pennell responded, he turned again, stopping directly in front of them. He raised the shotgun. “Either nudge those horses on up here next to me,” he demanded, “or I’ll blow both those animals out from under you, and you can walk.”

Billy July waited as the two men caught up to him. When they were all together, he kicked his horse and continued on his way. The two Americans did the same.

“Now,” Billy July continued, “since I already know all about you two . . .”

“You . . . know all about *us*?” said Mitch Pennell.

“Of course I do,” answered Billy July with a slight smile on his lips. “I’ve been following you ever since you crossed into Coahuila with your friends. And when you all split up, I decided to follow you two and listen in on your conversations every time you found a reason to talk.”

“Mr. July,” said Pennell, “why don’t you tell us about you? About what’s a black man doing all the way down here in Mexico? And why are you wearing that Injun fumadiddle, instead a’ dressing like me and my friend here?”

Billy July chuckled. “When we get to where we’re going, I suppose you’ll find out the answer to that. Plus anything else you might be wondering, as a matter of fact.”

He laughed again, this time much heartier than before.

As the threesome continued on, the echoing peels of Billy July’s vigorous jubilation rang loud and clear across the desolate, desert landscape.

Don Roberto Acosta y Castro, and his estate foreman, Luis Hernandez, along with a number of the Don’s best fighting men, had reached the two-story adobe building.

The remains of the two campsites belonging to those who had been there most recently were still in evidence.

The Don had his men dismount, then the premises were searched thoroughly until they regrouped again at the front, around Don Roberto and Luis. Nothing unusual had been discovered except for the fact that Armendariz, and his unruly band, had camped there earlier. After they had moved on, evidence showed that a second group of horsemen had arrived. They also made their camp among the adobe ruins.

"What do you make of it?" Don Roberto asked Luis.

"Two parties . . . camped so close to each other, one after the other," said Luis, "can only mean that there are others, besides us, who are following the trail of Armendariz and his gang."

"Is it possible that this second group of riders could be *Rurales*?" asked the Don.

"I do not think so," said Luis. "But we must make sure that the men are aware of the possibility that they could be *Rurales*. We don't want to be getting into an altercation with the federal police."

Don Roberto nodded, agreeing with his foreman.

"Do you think maybe we should make our camp here for the rest of the day?" said Luis.

"I do not know why not," said Don Roberto. "These men we follow leave many tracks behind them. Those tracks will still be here in the morning if we do not follow them now. Tell the men we will camp here," the Don continued, "we might just find some other clues if we keep our eyes open."

Charley Sunday and Roca Fuerte sat cross-legged beneath a jagged overhang on the bank of the Rio Sabinas.

They were sharing some dried jerky and watching the afternoon sun shine down on the storm clouds that had been hovering for days on the western horizon.

After the discovery of the wagon, the two men had set out in several different directions looking for the woman they figured had been the wagon's driver. When none of the trails they had chosen panned out, Fuerte decided they should continue on toward the northwest. And if they happened to run across her tracks again, they would investigate.

"Any chance of finding a town of some size before nightfall?" asked Charley as he opened a tin of peaches with his penknife.

"You must be tired of sleeping with the scorpions," said Fuerte, chuckling. "Well, I am thinking that we might run across a small village in a day or two."

"But not by tonight," said Charley, plopping a couple of pieces of fruit into his mouth, then drinking some juice directly from the can.

"No," said Fuerte, "not tonight."

Charley handed the can of peaches to his friend, who immediately slipped more fruit slices into his mouth. Charley took off his jacket and rolled it into a ball. He placed it behind his head to be used as a pillow. He lay back, closing his eyes.

"We will rest here now, is that your plan, Señor Charley?" asked Fuerte, devouring the last several slices of peach before drinking the remainder of the juice.

"Yes, Roca," said Charley without opening his eyes. "I figure if we get a little shut-eye now, we can make twice the distance if we travel after dark. *And* we won't have to bake all day in the Mexican sun like we've been doing ever since we left our camp by that adobe house."

Charley winced before continuing. "I just wish we

could find us a place with a real nice featherbed every now and then. I got me this kink in my get-along that's really been bothering me."

"Ah, Señor Charley," said Fuerte, "you have had that old kink in your get-along ever since we rode together on opposite sides of the river. You are just getting soft in your old age, that is all."

"I suppose you're right, Roca, I suppose you're right," mumbled Charley as he pulled his hat down over his eyes. "Now get yourself some sleep. We'll be heading out again just as soon as the sun goes down."

Fuerte buried the empty peach can in the sand, using his boot. Then he settled back on his own rolled jacket next to Charley. Before he allowed himself to drift off, he, too, pulled his hat's brim down over his eyes.

Chapter Twelve

Having come across the long-standing Mexican settlement of Santiago de la Monclova earlier in the day, Rod, Kelly, and Henry Ellis had hidden themselves, their horses, and the two-wheeled cart behind some tall cactus outside the old municipality's adobe walls. They were waiting for the sun to set before entering the town. They were hoping to find someone who would sell them fresh meat for the puppy, oats for the horses, and maybe a warm meal for themselves.

Come nightfall, they left two of the horses hidden in some heavy overgrowth, then they took the boy's horse and the cart and walked on foot. The boy carried the puppy in his arms. They were all supposed to stay together and keep their eyes open for anything or anyone who looked suspicious.

By the time the three of them had made it through the maze of small adobe structures that made up the outer city, each one with its own particular sounds and smells, they found they were about to enter the center of the settlement. They could see there was a dance in progress a few blocks away in the main plaza.

Within moments, Rod found a small side street he assumed would lead them around the main square. He figured the route would most likely take them through several dark alleyways, so they could avoid the main section of the city where families liked to stroll.

It was when he, Kelly, and Henry Ellis—with the puppy still in his arms—were leading the boy's horse and cart through one of those poorly lit passageways that the boy saw the quick movement of a shadowy figure out of the corner of his eye. The form was dark and shaped like a human being. Whoever it was had obviously been observing the three of them before slinking around a sharp corner where they had disappeared completely.

"Did you two see that?" Henry Ellis whispered loudly to Rod and Kelly.

They both nodded. They had also seen the humanlike figure ahead of them.

All three knew something wasn't quite right when they could hear no footsteps fading into the distance. Whoever it had been had stopped close by and was waiting for them to follow—waiting for one of them to round the corner in pursuit.

"No," whispered Rod to the others. "No. We will not fall for some robber's trickery and be found the next day with our money gone and our throats slit."

As quietly as they could, Rod, Kelly, and Henry Ellis began to backtrack. They turned the horse and cart around quietly, then went in the opposite direction until they had completely circled the small block of adobe buildings. They were again on the same street they had been on before. Only now, they were walking down the dusty lane from the reverse direction, putting them behind the waiting thief.

Rod stopped abruptly, holding his breath. He could see

the dark figure—whoever it was—hunkered down in the shadows, waiting there in the darkness for them.

The mysterious figure wore a large floppy-brimmed hat and a cape of some kind. *Quite possibly,* thought Rod, *because this is Mexico, it might even be a* serape.

Slowly, silently, Rod motioned for Kelly and Henry Ellis to stay where they were.

"What do you think you're going to do?" whispered Kelly.

"I'm going to go and get that bastard," Rod answered.

"It's too dangerous, Rod, I can't let you do that," she whispered again.

"I can help," cut in Henry Ellis. "I can walk on ahead of you and maybe I can draw his attention away, so you—"

"No," said Kelly. "I don't want anything to happen to either one of you."

Rod put his hand on the boy's shoulder.

"I thank you for offering, Henry Ellis, but I have to do this alone."

He turned to his wife.

"Sorry, Kelly," he said, "but this is just the way it has to be."

Rod undid the leather flap on his army-issue holster. He drew his artillery-model, single-action, army Colt .45—the pistol he had been issued when he'd joined the Rough Riders. He'd had quite a few learning sessions with guns during his short training period, especially with revolvers—and he knew how to shoot.

He wasn't worried at all about his own safety when he began his lone advance down the street toward the crouching figure.

What Rod didn't know about was the other one—the partner in crime—until that cohort had walloped him good with a leather-covered piece of lead. The rap on the head knocked him senseless but not all the way unconscious. He fell to the ground.

He lay still on the sandy street, feeling the warmth of his own blood as it trickled down the side of his neck, then onto the ground beside his right ear, which had planted itself in the sand next to a hitching post. He felt the rough hands of his assailant as the robber rolled him over and then rummaged through his pockets for whatever it was the thief thought necessary to bludgeon him for.

He could also smell the anxiety oozing from the man's pores plus the odor of the mescal the man had recently consumed. The robber bent lower to check under Rod's boot tops, looking for anything he thought the outsider might have hidden there.

All the man found was Rod's money pouch, with the remainder of his last month's earnings inside.

Six dollars, Rod thought to himself, as he lay there in the sand. *This sonofabitch wants to kill me for six lousy dollars*. He heard the man swear to himself as he flung the empty money holder into the night. Then Rod heard the sound of a razor-sharp blade being drawn from a leather sheath. He blinked, trying to open his eyes. When he did, he saw the blur of the man's bulk hovering over him with a hand raised. In it, the attacker held a knife. The blade flashed its deadly glint, a reflection of the moon overhead.

Rod tried to move. He couldn't. All of his strength had been drained by the solid whack he had taken to the back of his head. He closed his eyes, awaiting his forthcoming demise. He knew for sure his life was moments from ending. But before he could think of the proper words to put into prayer . . .

"No, Manolito, no."

It was a woman's voice. "We cannot kill him now," the voice continued in its heavy Spanish accent. "*El jefe* would have us both hanged if you did. We are here for another purpose. I have subdued the woman and the boy. It is the boy we want . . . they are both tied up. We will wait until Colonel Armendariz has had a chance to see the boy . . . then he will probably order us to kill these other two."

Rod opened his eyes, keeping them in a tight squint. He peered between his half-open lids, hoping the two thieves would still take him for unconscious. The voice belonged to the person he had originally been pursuing, the one with the floppy hat and *serape* he had mistaken for a cape. And she was female.

Rod continued to watch the two as they argued in whispers above him. The man who'd almost killed him was still in shadow, but Rod could see the woman's face every now and then as a single ray of light cast from an oil lamp in a nearby window bounced across her brow. She was young, and she was beautiful . . . and she was the enemy.

Chapter Thirteen

Holliday and Feather Martin had been in the saddle for nearly two days and had yet to come across another human being. Roscoe, driving the chuckwagon, had kept up with his two companions as best he could.

The two men on horseback were now dismounting several yards from the open mouth of a large cavern. Roscoe reined the wagon up beside them. A few minutes earlier, Roscoe had recommended the threesome might use the cave for shelter if indeed the heavy black clouds overhead decided to open up and deposit their store of water onto the open desert below.

The wind had picked up a half hour earlier, causing the clouds to close in around them. And now, as they spurred their mounts and drove the wagon into the shelter of the cave's opening, the rain began to fall.

What had begun with light sprinkles minutes earlier turned into a heavy downpour by the time the three men had unsaddled their horses and unhitched the mule team quite a few yards inside the cave's mouth.

They built a little campfire with wood gathered along

the way during dryer weather, a habit Roscoe had acquired years ago when he could see that a storm was approaching.

They spread their bedrolls by the fire. A wide overhang above the cavern's mouth kept any dampness from reaching them, even when the wind was blowing. They had situated themselves deep enough inside the cavern to also shelter them from some of the sound of the storm's fury.

It wasn't too long before Roscoe had a pot of coffee boiling. He sat down beside Holliday with two cups, next to the wagon, handing one cup to the old trick-shooting expert. They sipped and talked as they reminisced about their journey.

"I don't believe this trail we're on will ever produce any fleeing bandits," said the quick-draw artist.

"I'm with you, Holliday," said Roscoe. "I'd bet all the money I ever earned in my lifetime that no human being has ever been where we are now. Look around," he added.

Holliday took a sweeping glance at the steep, curving rock walls that surrounded them. At one point he could see Feather digging at something farther on back in the cave.

"Hey, Feather," he called out, "come on back here . . . get yourself a cup a' steamin'-hot Arbuckle's. It'll warm you up—take the rattle out a' yer bones."

"I'll be there in a minute," Feather called back, his voice echoing. "Right now I think I mighta found something that could be of interest to all of us."

Roscoe reached over with the coffeepot and topped off Holliday's cup.

"Here ya go, Holliday," he said. "Don't let ol' Feather Martin's stubbornness keep you from relaxin'."

Holliday blew on the newly poured coffee in the tin cup, then he took a sip.

"I sure hope this rain lets up by mornin'," he said. "I'd hate for us to get stuck here for another day and be late for our rendezvous with Charley and the others at that Mexican fort."

An object, made of partially rusted metal, landed in the sand between the two men's feet.

"What's that?" said Roscoe.

After a closer look, it became clear that the thing was an old Spanish helmet—similar to those worn by the early Conquistadores.

Feather was walking away, but he called out again as he reached his position behind the two men.

"There's more back here that goes with that metal hat, fellers," his voice echoed. "I found some bones, too."

Sergeant Stone had figured all along that the Negro who dressed as an Indian must be taking them to a small encampment, or maybe an actual Indian village of some sort. Mitchell Pennell, on the other hand, had disagreed—before they had been forced to ride up closer to Billy July—arguing that they were being taken to some remote location. Pennell felt sure the strange man who had apprehended them was going to steal all of their earthly possessions before he shotgunned them both and strung up their naked bodies for the Mexican vultures to devour.

"I hear man-eating predators can strip a dead man's carcass down to a bare skeleton before the devil's shadow lengthens by a quarter of an inch," Pennell whispered to the sergeant. But his words turned out to be contrary to fact because to their surprise Billy July led them through a high-walled narrow entrance formed by layered sandstone, then on into a sheltered passageway. Two silhouetted sentries were posted on either side, high above them, both with large-caliber rifles held at the ready across their chests.

"Where in the Sam Hill is he taking us?" whispered Pennell.

Stone hushed the man with a flick of his eyes; he could see where they were being led.

The slender corridor through which the three were riding opened up into a box canyon—a verdant oasis—a sanctuary with a pleasing cluster of desert vegetation growing from lush, fertile soil. Presumably all this was being fed by an underground stream.

The submerged watercourse briefly popped to the surface near the trunks of several cottonwood trees to form a comforting blue pool.

A group of dark-skinned women and children could be seen wading at the water's edge. Some of the women were doing laundry farther down. They laughed and carried on, beating the wet clothing against a series of flat rocks, unaware of Billy July and his two captives as they arrived.

The prisoners were led past the pool to a spindly, waist-high tree stump near a small hut built from rocks and palm fronds. They were instructed to dismount and tie off their horses and the burro. After they had done that, Billy July indicated they should follow him once again.

He escorted the two strangers over to the meager shelter, pointing out that they should stay outside while he entered the structure. He disappeared through a narrow flap of sewn animal skins, serving as a door.

When it appeared as if they were alone for a moment, Pennell leaned over to Stone. He asked softly, "What do you think this place might be?"

The sergeant shrugged. "Looks to me like an outpost of some sort," he answered in a hoarse whisper. His eyes whipped back and forth, checking to see if they were being watched. "They look to be black, African people like me," he continued. "Except for the way they're dressed. They gotta be Seminole-Negroes."

Most of the camp's inhabitants who were visible wore various Indian attire, mixed together with other worn and tattered pieces of cast-off clothing they had procured somewhere or another.

"They sure do look different," said Pennell, scratching his ear with one of his bound hands. "Kinda like In-dins. Kinda like you," he concluded.

There was movement within the hut. Stone motioned for Pennell to hush. The animal-hide flap was pushed aside and Billy July ducked out through the tiny opening. He was followed by a smaller Negro man who was also dressed in elaborate Indian regalia. They stopped in front of Sergeant Stone and Mitch Pennell, scrutinizing, looking the two Americans up and down.

"This is our leader, John Thomas Bodie," said Billy July. "He would like to ask you both a few questions."

Sergeant Stone nodded. "We'll do our best to oblige, sir," he answered.

The smaller man stepped in closer; he looked the sergeant directly in the eye. "Why does a black man ride with a white man?" he wanted to know.

The sergeant shrugged.

"He's my partner," was his sincere answer. "The two of us have been scouting a trail together."

Tobias Stone, being an honest man, could never lie.

"Why do you scout a trail in Mexico?" the chief asked. "Are you not both from the United States?"

Stone nodded again.

"We are here to do a job," he said. "There are others with us who do the same. And, yes," he went on, "we do come from across the border. We come from Texas, and we are—"

There was an elated shriek from inside the hut, and the flap was pushed aside with passion. Elisabeth Rogers, looking quite weary, very dirty, and completely worn out, stepped out into the sunlight.

"Texas?" she said. "Did I hear someone say they were from Texas?"

The storm that had sent Roscoe, Holliday, and Feather into the shelter of the cave had moved on, eventually settling over the desert floor some fourteen and a half miles northwest of the cavern, directly above what was usually a dry and dusty Mexican village but for the rain.

On this day it was neither dry nor dusty. Every particle of dust on the main street had been turned into a soggy, watery muck.

It was into this pitiable rural hamlet that Charley Sunday and his companion, Roca Fuerte, found themselves riding after a grueling two days in the Mexican wilderness.

The hard rain had been coming down steady for several hours. Charley and Fuerte, buttoned up securely in their meager jackets, then covered even more by oilskin slickers, hunkered low under their dripping hats, which they had both pulled down over their ears to keep the harsh wind from blowing them away. They were finding the welcome they had thought they might get from the citizenry of the first town they were encountering to be not all that friendly. Dark, fearful eyes peered out suspiciously from dreary windows and gloomy door frames, as the two ex-lawmen—one American, one Mexican—sloshed across the muddy village square.

More than a few Mexican army wagons, plus several

canvas-covered military ambulances, had been unhitched and left out in the storm along the side of the street.

More than likely, thought Charley, *the pulling-livestock is being kept in some covered corral or barn nearby, out of the weather . . . out of sight.*

Both men knew this was a sign that there were federal troops somewhere close by. But right then, no human activity could be observed by either one of them.

The two dismounted in front of a sagging *cantina*, located among an irregular row of adobe storefronts lining the plaza. They faced a large Catholic church across the way. The two men tied off their horses before stepping under the *cantina*'s leaking porch roof to gather their thoughts.

The downpour continued to pound everything around them. It was very cold. Both men could see their breath as it steamed in the icy air.

"It just might be they have that featherbed you've been hoping for somewhere in this village, Señor Charley," said Fuerte with a twinkle.

Charley grimaced. He looked up as more lightning flashed overhead. "If they do, Roca," he answered through the deafening rumble of thunder that followed, "I suspect it's as foul smelling as this saloon we're standing in front of."

Fuerte chuckled. "Is a bad smell going to bother you too much if I take you on inside this *cantina* and buy you a shot of whiskey . . . and get us out of this storm for a few minutes?"

"Of course not, Roca," said Charley. "Nothing smells so bad that I'd turn down a friendly drink."

Fuerte clasped his friend by the shoulder, urging him toward the door. A harsh blast of wind helped the two along, pushing them toward the entrance.

Four blanketed Mexicans were huddled beside a small table in one corner of the cold and damp room. They were playing a game of dice, bouncing the ivories off the lower wall nearby. Their backs were to the solid double-doors that shielded the bat-wings inside. One of the door handles turned, and the rain-swept wind ushered in the two storm-drenched figures. Charley Sunday and Roca Fuerte stopped just inside, reaching for the door behind them.

Three drunken federal soldiers laughed their way past the two men, moving out into the storm, headed back to where they were quartered.

Once the soldiers' voices were drowned out by the clatter of the rain on the building's tin roof, the two men closed the door. They shook off, shedding an abundance of rainwater onto the once sleek, but now cracked, black-and-white-tiled floor.

There were empty tin cans, glass pitchers, and numerous pots and pans spread out on the floor around the room. They had been put there as receptacles to catch the rainwater that dripped from various leaks in the ceiling above.

Charley removed his hat and slapped it against his knee, knocking off even more water. "Whoooeee," he exclaimed, once again shaking his entire body like a dog after a cold swim. "C'mon, Roca," he said, "let's get us that belly warmer before it gets any colder."

"Or wetter," added Fuerte, whacking some of the accumulated dampness from his own saturated headgear.

The two men moved to the small bar, an antiquated piece of furniture, more than likely a personal possession of whoever owned the little *cantina*.

An old European clock had been affixed to the wall above the back-bar; its Roman numerals told the two newcomers it was three thirteen in the afternoon.

Fuerte rapped on the counter, glancing around for any sign of a bartender. Charley checked the cracked and dirty mirror's reflection, keeping his eyes on the four Mexicans behind them beside the table in the corner. They were still throwing the dice and talking among themselves in Spanish, showing no interest at all in the new arrivals.

A sleepy face raised itself from behind the bar counter, startling both men. A month-old *Ciadad Acuña* newspaper fell away from the man's face and onto the bar top beside Charley's arm. The bartender flashed a lopsided golden smile for a welcome.

"*Buenas tardes*," he said, a greeting to them both.

"*Dos* whiskeys," said Fuerte. He looked the man square in the eye. He did that with all men he met for the first time.

The bartender nodded. "*Dos* whisk-eeys," he repeated, trying to mimic Fuerte's gruff manor. He got a cold stare in return. He turned away and began preparing the drinks.

"Kinda wet outside," said Charley to the bartender. "You get these gully washers down here all the time?"

The bartender looked over with a shrug. "*No comprendo*," he said. He finished pouring the two drinks.

"They get rain like this in winter," said Fuerte to Charley. "The Sierra Madre Oriental mountains west of here are mostly the cause of it, though not as much as the Sierra Madre Occidental range further west. It has even been known to snow there if it gets cold enough."

Something caught the Ranger's eye. The newspaper the bartender had dropped on the bar top had been folded back, and there was a blurry photograph of a man on horseback on the third page.

Charley leaned in closer. He squinted. "Hey, Roca," he

whispered, "look over here. I don't have my magnifiers with me. Can you make out a name under this photograph?"

Fuerte leaned in. He took a glance over Charley's shoulder.

"It is Colonel Armendariz, for sure," he said. "The man we are looking for—"

The ex-Ranger's firm hand fell atop Fuerte's wrist, stopping him cold.

Fuerte turned to Charley and saw that his look was now focused across the bar to the mirror behind the bartender.

In the reflection, he could see that the four Mexicans who had been playing dice were now all silent, having let their blankets fall to the floor. Every single one of them wore leather bandoliers across their chests. Heavy pistols hung at their sides.

Charley spoke softly to Fuerte. "You can duck, or you can draw, Roca. I'm betting there's gonna be some killing around here real soon. And I intend to make sure it isn't me . . . or you . . . that're going to be the ones that die."

Knowing that there would at least be one out of the four who would have some idea of what he was about to say, Charley, his back to the four, cleared his throat. What he was about to say came slow and easy. He gradually turned until he could make direct eye contact with one of the men in the mirror.

"A Colt revolver is a piece of unique, cold steel, *mi amigos* . . . it doesn't differentiate between a man's size or the color of his skin."

He bent down slowly and withdrew the Walker Colt from his boot.

"This gun has killed both brown men and white . . . plus more Indians than I'd care to count."

He made a slow, pronounced pivot, turning around altogether, facing the foursome directly.

"Now you *hombres* have just two choices," he went on, "thin and none. If you as much as blink, I've made up my mind to put out your lights. So you have just one minute to get things right with your Maker because, whether or not you like it, this is your judgment day, *amigos*. And that means it's *all* over. So go ahead anytime and start counting your blessings. And, by-damnit, that's a damn fact," he added.

The bartender made a flick of his eyes below the bar. Fuerte figured he probably kept a weapon there, so he wagged a finger in his direction.

The man stepped back, realizing he probably shouldn't get involved.

The air in the small room was becoming very close. No one spoke. The two former lawmen continued to stare down the four Mexicans. The rain's constant drumming on the *cantina*'s rooftop was the only sound to be heard.

Charley did not blink. Neither did Fuerte. Nor did the Mexicans, for that matter. Everyone involved knew that the first one who made a move would be the first to die.

Fuerte wished he could ease his hand just a little closer to his own weapon.

The bartender slid just a little farther away.

It was a standoff. All it would take was for one man to make the slightest mistake.

Seconds ticked away on the ancient wall clock above the back-bar. As the moments passed, the ticking became almost deafening.

The door was suddenly flung open by someone entering from the outside. Lightning flashed. At the same moment, thunder roared along with six pistols. Both Charley and Roca Fuerte had fired their weapons in the direction of the Mexicans, knocking down two of them and setting up a smoke screen. Four Mexican bullets whizzed by the ex-lawmen's heads, slamming into the mirror behind them. The bartender ducked as shards of reflective glass exploded all around him. Charley and Fuerte dropped to their knees and took careful aim before disposing of the other two.

The fifth man, the unexpected one—the one who had entered the door sparking the anticipated gun battle—turned around as quickly as he had come in and ran back outside into the rain-drenched street. He found his horse, mounted, and galloped away into the blinding sheets of rain that totally obscured his mud-spattered getaway.

Roca Fuerte and Charley Sunday stopped their pursuit as they reached the porch; neither fired their weapon after the departing rider.

Fuerte yelled over the roar of the storm's onslaught: "Are we just going to let him ride off like that, Señor Charley?"

"Nope," said Charley. Then he turned. "By the way those men inside acted when they heard you say Armendariz's name, they must have been part of his gang, wouldn't you think?" The ex-Ranger slid his weapon back into his boot. "We'll just go ahead and follow that one. Take our time. More than likely, he'll lead us right to Betty Jean and Kent."

Chapter Fourteen

"What's that?" asked Henry Ellis under an overcast sky as he pointed off across a deep, high-desert valley to a point just above the foothills of a large flat-topped *mesa*.

Kelly and Rod, with Henry Ellis riding in the cart holding the puppy in his arms, were being led by their captors. They had stopped for some rest beside a configuration of boulders that overlooked a peaceful, but dry, creek bed. The thought of rippling blue water flowing a few hundred feet below the faint trail they had been following for the past hour and a half made Kelly hope for some rain.

While the Mexican man and woman stayed in their saddles, speaking Spanish, and smoking hand-rolled cigarettes, Kelly tried to figure out just where they might be going by listening carefully for familiar Spanish words.

They had stopped when Henry Ellis had asked about several wooden structures poking up through the arid vegetation in the distance. The Mexican woman, who had been riding behind Kelly, looked up at the sound of Kelly's voice. She could see the American boy was still pointing. She followed her captive's finger with her eyes, finally spotting the questionable objects across the valley's wide span.

"Oh." She shrugged. "That is the Black-Seminole burial grounds. Our present government, which we despise, has given them permission to live in our country."

"The Black-Seminoles bury their dead above ground because they have lived in swampland. They are *not* our enemies," said the man. "Having been granted special permission to be here by the government does not make them bad people." He turned to Rod. "We leave the Seminole-Negroes alone because one day we may need them ourselves—"

"Or *they* may need *us*," interrupted the woman.

The man collected the reins of his horse. "We had better be going," he told them all, "if we plan on getting to our camp before nightfall."

Sergeant Stone, Mitchell Pennell, Billy July, John Thomas Bodie, and Elisabeth Rogers sat together in the hidden canyon campsite around a small, crackling campfire, in front of the hut beside the pool. They had just finished their evening meal. Several Indian women were removing the simple utensils they had employed, taking them to the nearby pool where they prepared them for washing by rubbing the dishes with sand before rinsing them in the cold water.

While the flames from the fire threw their shimmering patterns on the thoughtful faces, they were all served a warm, tangy drink by another Black-Seminole woman.

The sun had only just set. The canyon had been in deep shadow since midafternoon, right after Billy July and his prisoners had arrived. An uncomfortable chill was on the evening's air. "Another storm must have set in some distance away," John Thomas told them. The gracious Black-Seminole leader also offered the newcomers an animal-skin shelter to sleep under, just in case the hideout canyon experienced some showers of its own before dawn.

The talk going on now was not only about the weather. It also concerned Elisabeth Rogers's dilemma: the fact that her husband and son's murderers were still out there—on the loose—running free.

The four men had listened intently to the Rogers woman's story while they ate, with each one of them conjuring up a way in which they might help her find those who had committed the intolerable crimes.

Billy July was the first to offer a sensible solution to the problem by releasing his claim to Sergeant Stone and Mitch Pennell. He granted the two men their freedom by allowing them to continue on their way in the morning, if they chose to do so. There was a condition: they must keep a steady lookout for the bandits Elisabeth Rogers had described. They were to either report back to the two leaders at the Seminole-Negro camp as to the whereabouts of the killers, or they could take matters into their own hands by slaying the assassins themselves.

"I have another idea," said Elisabeth Rogers, directing her suggestion to the leader of the small band of Black-Seminoles. "I know I owe my life to both you, Mr. Bodie, Mr. July, and your people. It was Mr. July who found me after my wagon overturned and my horses had run off. I thought I was going to die out there in that horrible desert . . . until you showed up." She smiled. "It was you who brought me here, Mr. July," she went on. "It was you who treated my injuries and fed me. And I am forever grateful to you for that, believe me. But now . . . now I must leave."

John Thomas Bodie and Billy July exchanged puzzled

glances. "I must continue in my pursuit of justice," she went on. "Vengeance, some may call it, but until I know that those who took my family away from me have paid for their crime . . . Until I know, without a doubt in my mind, that the men who murdered my husband and son have paid the ultimate price . . . *with their lives* . . . I cannot . . . I will not . . . rest."

"You must not go alone into the desert again, Mrs. Rogers," said John Thomas Bodie. "We would be sending you to your own death for sure if we were to allow that."

Elisabeth reached over. Smiling softly, she stroked the older man's arm. She shook her head. "I don't plan on going anywhere alone from here, Mr. Bodie. I mean to travel with these two Texas gentlemen." She indicated Pennell and Stone, sitting on either side of her. "I am sure they will not mind if I"—she drew in a deep breath and expelled it—"if I ride along with them."

Partly because of the overcast sky, night fell rapidly on the muddy ground Charley and Fuerte rode across on their galloping horses. Within a ten-minute span, the surrounding desert was under complete darkness. The rain had let up less than an hour earlier, and the storm clouds overhead were beginning to disperse. This eventually allowed a soft, eerie glow from the moon overhead to illuminate the usually arid region.

Charley Sunday, and his Mexican companion, Roca Fuerte, found that they had to walk their tired mounts along the barren lip of a deep gully. At the bottom of the steep slope, the channel was churning with four feet of swift-flowing storm runoff.

The two men were following a set of well-defined hoofprints, left by the horse belonging to the man who had fled the *cantina*. They knew they were close to their prey—so close, in fact, the rainwater on the saturated ground hadn't had time to entirely settle into the crescent indentations made by the animal's iron shoes.

"Do you th-think we will catch up to this man soon," said Fuerte, shivering in the night's chill.

"Don't you go worrying yourself, Roca," answered a just as chilled Charley Sunday. He removed his slicker, tying it on top of his bedroll behind his saddle. "I'll wager we'll have him in our sights within the hour."

"I s-sure hope so," said Fuerte. "Because I'm beginning to th-think my toes will fall off by midnight if we don't."

"Hell, Roca," chuckled Charley, "your toes aren't going anywhere. Not as long as you keep your boots on."

The men rode along a little farther, a quarter of a mile or so. By then, a large slice of moon had been exposed completely by the scattering clouds, and the two could see better than they had expected.

Suddenly Charley reined up.

Fuerte did the same.

The ex-Ranger cocked an ear and squinted off into the murkiness ahead.

"We found him, Roca," Charley whispered. "He's right up there about fifty yards in front of us. Just waiting to put our lights out."

Fuerte whispered back, "He thinks he is going to ambush us, does he?"

"Not if Samuel Colt has anything to say about it," said Charley, acknowledging the large revolver in his boot top.

He dismounted as quietly as he could, hoping a loud squeak of the saddle leather would go unnoticed by the waiting bandit-assassin.

Fuerte also dismounted. Just as he planted his feet firmly on the ground, gunshots, with bright muzzle flashes, erupted from the darkness to their left. Both men grabbed their rifles, sliding them out of the scabbards.

They dove for cover over the side of the ravine, sliding down the shale and into the freezing water that was flowing briskly along the narrow channel.

"G-geezes-G-god-a-mighty," yelped Charley as he hit the icy surface.

Fuerte mumbled the equivalent in Spanish. He immediately began to scramble out.

Charley pulled him back by his gun belt into the rushing current. "No, Roca," Charley ordered. "We need to stay right here. Those shots came from over yonder." He pointed to the rim of the ravine where they had just been. "Not up that way."

He indicated the direction where he had said the killer would be. "I'm afraid our friend has friends of his own."

"D-damn, Señor Charley," said Fuerte. "I'm about to f-freeze my toes off."

Both men held their balance as the murky water swirled around them.

"We gotta draw them in," said Charley. "Stay as low in the water as we can, at least until they show themselves . . . make them think they killed us both so they feel safe enough to come down here looking."

"I d-don't know if I c-can hang on that long, Señor Charley," said Fuerte. His lips looked to Charley as if they were beginning to turn blue. "C-cold never d-did me any good anyway." He shivered.

"We aren't going to be waiting long, Roca," Charley whispered. He nodded toward the brink of the rift. "Here they come now."

The two ex-lawmen ducked lower into the water.

Shadowy figures began to appear at the top of the slope—silhouetted *sombreros* worn by several men with rifles. They moved slowly—carefully—edging their way over the lip, then using their boot heels to dig into the saturated shale to keep them from slipping or falling down the precipitous incline.

In the brackish water below, Charley Sunday and Roca Fuerte waited. Only their rifles and eyes showed above the surface of the churning water.

Charley's look shifted to Fuerte beside him. He spoke only with infinitesimal movements of his eyes, indicating to his partner that they must wait until the approaching men were even closer before they would make their move.

Bits of gravel and wet clots of sand slid into the water around the two former lawmen. The menacing forms loomed larger and larger as the bandits drew closer. They moved slowly, carefully picking out a safe trail to the water's edge.

When they were no more than seven feet away, Charley nudged Fuerte, and together they rose from the rushing flood, slamming cartridge after cartridge into the breeches of their rifles while yellow flame and spiraling lead crashed into the midsections of the startled attackers.

The bandits, four in all, were caught completely by surprise. They never had the chance to fire one shot in return. Instead, their lifeless bodies tumbled past Charley and Fuerte into the foaming channel, only to be carried away by the floodwater's sucking undercurrent.

Charley's gloved finger pressed against Fuerte's lips, preventing him from letting out a whoop of relief. Roca looked quickly to Charley who shook his head. The ex-Ranger motioned in a direction farther up from where the four men had come.

Another figure in a large *sombrero* was stopped in his tracks at the top of the incline. It was apparent to the former Ranger that the man at the top of the ravine couldn't see what had happened to his friends.

"*Hombres?*" the man called out. "*Ustedes están bien?*"

There was a moment.

"*Now!*" shouted Charley. Both men fired their rifles simultaneously, kicking up four-foot rooster tails just below the reluctant bandit's outline. The man scrambled to the ridge behind him, unharmed.

More ricochets and mud spirals followed, taking huge bites out of the rain-soaked earth.

A quick reflection of the moon off one of the man's large-rowel spurs flashed as he disappeared over the rim of the deep ravine.

Charley scrambled out of the water and began climbing up the incline after the man. Even though he was slipping and sliding, in less than a minute he was still able to make it to the high point where he'd last seen the man.

Once there, he was joined by Fuerte. The two of them stopped, breathing hard, wiping mud from their hands and rifles, listening as hoofbeats faded away into the night.

"Our horses," said Fuerte, looking around frantically for their mounts.

Charley let a hand fall on his friend's shoulder. "They have to be around here somewhere, Roca," he said. He put two fingers between his teeth, then whistled.

"Th-that is n-not right," said Fuerte, shivering even harder now. "My s-saddlebags contained all of my d-dry clothing . . . plus, our sleeping blankets were tied to our s-saddles. W-what are we g-going to do now?" he added.

"Well," said Charley Sunday, "I suggest you look right over there, Roca."

Fuerte followed Charley's gaze until his eyes fell on both horses.

Dice had heard Charley's whistle and was now leading

the way for Fuerte's horse over to where the two men were standing.

Charley took Dice's reins in his hand.

Fuerte did the same with his horse.

"I always train my riding horses to answer to my whistle," Charley told his friend. "You should do the same, Roca. Otherwise you might just find yourself stumbling around in the dark one night while you go half-crazy looking for him."

There was a flutter of bats overhead as a cloud of the tiny creatures flew past the campfire, then departed through the cave's opening in what appeared to be a single motion.

Holliday, Feather, and Roscoe stopped digging for a moment to take note of their findings. Farther back in the cave they had discovered what remained of the body of the Spanish soldier who had belonged to the helmet. He was now only bones—with an Indian spear sticking out of the ground where his heart once pumped blood. The man's partially intact skeleton was stretched out on its back beside his armor. The dead soldier's rotting clothing was draped over his rib cage, torso, arms, and legs. The knee-high leather boots he had been wearing when he died looked almost as if they could still be worn. But when Holliday attempted to remove one of the decaying leather leggings, it crumbled into dust from the pressure of his grip.

Alongside the skeleton, and next to the hole in the cave floor the three men had been digging, was a padlocked iron box.

"Don't ya think it's about time we opened that thing up and looked ta see what's inside?" said Holliday.

"He's right, you know," said Feather. "Maybe there's enough gold in there ta make us all rich. And if there is, or isn't, we should stop diggin' either way."

Roscoe said, "Whether there's gold inside that box, or nothin' at all, we still gotta leave it here until we can bring Charley and the others back and show 'em what we found."

"Why's that?" Feather wanted to know.

"Because Charley told me that since we're guests in another country, there are certain things we shouldn't do without checking it out with the Mexican government first."

"What kinda things?" Feather wanted to know.

"Stealin', fer one," Roscoe said. "And that's the same as thinkin' somethin' is ours when we know damn well it ain't."

"Well," said Holliday, "none of what we found belongs to the Mexican government, that's fer sure. Maybe the Spanish government . . . ?"

"Maybe we oughta open her up now, just so we know what we're talkin' about," said Feather.

"I don't know why not," said Roscoe. "Go ahead. Just remember . . . whatever it is, we have ta leave it here."

"You two back off a bit," said Holliday as he drew one of his nickel-plated revolvers, aiming it at the large, ornate padlock.

The men backed away just as Holliday fired. Bits and pieces of the rusted padlock were spun away by the glancing bullet, leaving the iron box free to be opened.

The men scrambled back to the box, all of them grabbing the lid and flinging it back.

The first thing revealed was a sheet of thick copper with the Spanish Crest engraved on its face.

All three men let out sighs of disappointment.

That was until Roscoe reached in and removed the copper sheet.

There it was—glistening with the reflection of the campfire's flames: pounds of silver and gold coins, sparkling jewelry, and silver goblets—enough treasure to make rich men of the trio, even when split three ways.

"Close 'er up," said Roscoe. "Close 'er up tight an' start makin' a damn good map a' how we get back ta this cave."

All Holliday and Feather could do was show disgust at their friend's decision.

"Go on now," said Roscoe. "Put 'er back in the hole and throw some dirt on it. We gotta meet Charley and the others at that old Mexican fort pretty soon. Remember?"

Chapter Fifteen

Colonel Alfonso Natividad Armendariz y Rodriguez—the man who had become infamous throughout northern Mexico as the spineless brother of a celebrated bandit hero, had been born in the year 1848 to sharecropper parents in the Mexican state of Durango. According to legend, he turned mercenary when he was in his teens. He was supporting himself through those dubious means in the neighboring state of Chihuahua when the Revolt of 1877 occurred allowing Porfirio Díaz to become president of Mexico once again. Armendariz was twenty-nine years old at the time. It was then he made the decision to join his brother, and he became a ranking leader in the brother's gang of mercenaries.

Still a coward at heart, Armendariz left his brother's bandit gang soon after he'd participated in his first altercation with government troops.

He took a small group of uneducated peasant bandits with him when he deserted. He formed those followers into his own gang and began offering his services to anyone for the right price. Armendariz's climb to a position of power wasn't necessarily something he had accomplished himself. But he had an animalistic charisma, he was clever, and he appeared to be full of life when observed by outsiders, which had helped his celebrity grow. Though he lacked interest in politics, he had become a leader of men through his desire to make money any way he could.

Rod, Kelly, and Henry Ellis had been prisoners in Armendariz's high-desert camp for three hours before they ever saw the notorious *bandido*. When they finally did see him, they hadn't a clue it was Armendariz at all.

The image of the gang leader Rod had kept in his mind for the past few years had come from a blurry newspaper photograph he'd seen in a San Antonio café some years earlier. It had been a posed, news-camera photograph of a Mexican man on horseback, wearing a large *sombrero* with two brass and lead-filled bandoliers slung across his chest. The rest, Rod's mind had created over the years: the handsome, mustachioed face, the twinkle in the man's eyes, the smile, even the wink the horseman was giving the newspaper readers from his triumphant position in the saddle as he twirled a slender *cigarillo* in his long fingers.

Now, the man Rod was looking at across the busy compound, the man with the thickset body who hobbled along on makeshift crutches, the one Manolito had pointed out to them as his beloved leader, Colonel Alfonso Armendariz, wasn't matching up at all with Rod's mental image of the bandit leader. This Armendariz—the real Armendariz—was shorter, well under the six feet or more Rod had imagined him to be. He was stocky, maybe even fat, and his hair looked very much like that of the Seminole-Negroes who lived in that area: thick and matted. He also had a small black mustache, not the full, droopy style worn by most of the other men.

But it was his eyes Rod would later come to remember him by the most. Colonel Alfonso Natividad Armendariz y Rodriguez's piercing dark eyes made the young Indian shiver all over—just the thought of those eyes made him feel totally inept.

Later on, after the prisoners had been fed and night had fallen over the bandit camp, Henry Ellis had managed to talk one of the guards into bringing him some scraps for the puppy, while at the same time watching exactly where the man had gone to find the leftover bits.

As the boy watched the puppy gobble up its meal, he turned to Rod and Kelly who were sitting to his left on some large boulders they were using as a place to rest.

The trio was being kept in a triangular, fenced-in area. A small cove in onc of the many rock formations offered the perfect place for an improvised cell. Wire cattle fencing was stretched across the open front of the recess, creating a third wall, with barbed wire laced between the squares of the first barrier's links.

While Rod and Kelly talked among themselves, Henry Ellis wandered off to check out the periphery of their little niche.

He stepped off the footage of the fence, plus the security of the enclosure next to the rocks and boulders at each end of the wire barrier. When he got in close to study the thickness of the fencing, he looked up for a split second and found himself face to face, through the wire, with Colonel Armendariz himself.

The surprise of the extreme closeness made him step back a few paces.

"What are you planning to do, *boy*?" said Armendariz. "Are you planning to escape from me once again?"

"Oh, no, mister . . . Gosh no . . . I mean, Colonel . . . Armendariz," said Henry Ellis. "I was only getting familiar with this space where my friends and I are being kept prisoner."

"Well," said the Colonel, "please get any ideas of running away out of your mind for now. It has taken me too long to capture you in the first place. I would not be pleased if you caused me even more trouble by escaping again."

"No . . . no, sir," said the boy. "I would never do that to you a second time."

Armendariz started to turn away.

"Colonel, sir?" said Henry Ellis.

"What is it, boy?" answered Armendariz. "Can you not see that I am a very busy man?"

"Uh, Colonel," said Henry Ellis. "I was just wondering how you got hurt."

"Oh, these," said Armendariz, indicating his crutches. "I will tell you if you promise me you will tell no one else."

"I promise you, Colonel . . . You have my word."

Armendariz leaned in very close to Henry Ellis before he spoke. So close, in fact, that the boy could smell the odor of the cigars he'd been smoking, as well as the sickening stench of tequila fermenting in his stomach.

"I fell off my horse," he whispered.

He began to laugh.

Then Henry Ellis started to laugh.

Finally Armendariz's chortle grew louder and louder, coming from his belly, until his eyes began to tear up.

He raised a finger to his lips.

"Shhhhh," he said.

Then he turned and hobbled away.

Henry Ellis moved back to where Rod and Kelly were sitting.

"You made a new friend?" said Rod.

"I'm going to need you two to take care of Buster Number Two for me," said Henry Ellis. "I've found a way out . . . except the space is only big enough for a person my size."

Rod and Kelly leaned forward—they appeared to understand.

Henry Ellis went on, "I'll steal a horse and try to get to that Mexican fort where we're all supposed to meet. Then I'll bring my grampa and the others back to help get you both out of here."

"That sounds pretty dangerous," said Kelly.

"Who else can go?" said Henry Ellis. "The space I'm going to try to escape through is not even big enough for you, Miss Kelly."

"Let him go," said Rod to his wife. "I know he can do it."

The boy handed Rod the dog's makeshift leash.

Kelly picked up the animal and fastened an end of the rawhide strip around its neck.

"If the guards come again, we will tell them you are sleeping."

Rod took off his coat and wrapped it around some rocks, then he shaped it until it resembled a human form. He set it down behind one of the boulders so only one part of it could be seen.

"I want to thank you two for being so good to me," said Henry Ellis.

The three of them hugged.

The boy made his way along the fence line until he disappeared behind the rock formation on the right where the fencing followed its contour. Squeezing his body a few more feet between the rocks and the fence, he dropped to his knees, then down to his belly. Once there, he slithered under the wire like a snake. Whenever it could, the barbed wire took a bite out of his shirt and trousers.

Once outside the confines of the makeshift jail, Henry Ellis slipped on through the bandit camp until he came to the picket line of horses.

He knelt down in the shadows as a guard made his rounds.

It wasn't long before the boy had one of the animals untied and was leading it away from the camp. When he thought he had gone far enough, he swung up onto the horse's back, then nudged the animal on down a sandy dune that led him even farther away from the Armendariz camp.

Chapter Sixteen

1961

"Why didn't Henry Ellis take the puppy with him when he escaped from the bandit camp?" said Noel.

"He was afraid the pup might bark and give him away, stupid," said her brother, Caleb.

Their great-grandfather cut into their conversation.

"First of all, Caleb," said Hank, "your sister's not stupid. Her question about why the boy didn't take the puppy with him was perfectly all right for Noel to ask. I even wondered about that for a long, long time myself."

"But I'll still bet he didn't want the pup barking and giving him away before he had gone far enough from the bandit camp," said Caleb.

"He also didn't need to take the puppy with him when he knew he had a lot of hard riding ahead," said Hank. "Plus, he knew the pup would be safe with Rod and Kelly . . . and he also knew that if the dog wasn't there behind the fencing making his puppy sounds, the bandits might get suspicious and take a closer look . . . and find out that Henry Ellis was missing."

"Meeting the bandit chief must have been very scary for

Henry Ellis," said Evie. "If just looking at him bothered Rod, a grown-up, imagine what being face to face with him did to Henry Ellis."

"Oh, Henry Ellis wasn't scared of Armendariz," said Hank. "The bandit leader might have looked mean, but the boy could see when he was up close and talking to him that the bandit was all bluff and no bite."

"I'm just glad he got away," said Noel. "I sure hope he found his grampa Charley, though."

"You just sit tight, li'l darlin'," said Hank. "Go get yourself another dessert. I'll be getting back to Henry Ellis in a minute or so."

Chapter Seventeen

1900

Don Roberto led his small band of *vaqueros* across the open desert toward some sketchy cloud formations that were forming on the western horizon. They were following the tracks of two horses. This particular trail had been a gamble for the Don, as the larger faction they'd been trailing had broken up into clusters of twos and threes heading out in different westerly directions.

A rider appeared in the distance, coming out of a towering pile of boulders. As the rider got closer, he was recognized as Luis Hernandez, the Don's foreman. As he reached the column of riders, Luis reined up sharp in front of Don Roberto.

"I follow the two sets of horses' hoofprints, plus those of a burro, as you asked me to do, Don Roberto," said Luis. "Then I find hoofprints of a third horse joining the others."

"Maybe it was one of their friends meeting them," said Don Roberto.

"No," said Luis, "I don't think so. This new horse, he has no shoes."

"That could make him an Indian," the Don said to Luis. "The only Indians in this part of the country are the Black-Seminoles. Our government has advised the citizens of Mexico to stay away from the Seminole-Negroes. It is probably better that we go back and choose another trail to follow. No matter who we follow, they are bound to lead us to Armendariz and my guests that he has abducted."

The Don motioned for his men to do an about-face, then he and Luis rode to the other end of the column, where the Don instructed the riders to follow him.

Charley Sunday saw the Mexican fort for the first time as he and Roca Fuerte crested a low rise just fourteen miles from the trail they had been riding for the last day and a half. At Fuerte's suggestion, the two men had slowed their pace, and now they rode on toward the crumbling citadel at a more comfortable stride.

The fort had been constructed from the dirt on which it now stood. Adobe bricks not only made up the walls of the ancient stronghold, but adobe had also been used in the construction of other structures inside the fortification, as well as the several barracks buildings.

The old fort's adobe bricks had been rounded and chiseled by the weather through its many years of exposure to the harsh elements found in northern Mexico's unforgiving environment.

"From what I can make out," said Charley as they neared the broken-down edifice, "we're more than likely the first members of the outfit to get here."

Fuerte's eyes scanned the adobe walls, still a couple of hundred feet in front of them.

"I do not see any signs of life, Señor Charley," he said.

"None except for those wild burros over to the right of the main gate."

"I'm not sure just how wild they are, Roca," said Charley. "They could belong to someone who is already inside."

"No," Fuerte argued. "They look wild to me."

The two men kept riding toward the ancient stronghold. Nothing except for the two burros moved.

As they approached the decaying wooden gate, Charley noticed that it was propped open halfway, then held in place by a dilapidated military wagon.

Charley nudged Dice to continue on, and they entered through the half-open portal.

Once inside the walls, they could see that they were alone, indeed, as each and every adobe building that faced the small parade ground had been left with doors wide open and stores scattered. Weapons, canteens, and several decaying bodies of Mexican army soldiers as well as their horses were lying here and there around the parade ground.

"I knew this fort was abandoned," said Fuerte, "just not abandoned that short of a time ago."

"It looks like a detachment of the federal army decided to use this place again recently," said Charley. "But I wonder who it was they were using it to protect themselves from? I don't see any arrows . . . that eliminates an Indian attack. Plus there's no blood visible from bullet wounds on any of them."

"Maybe we should check out the commanding officer's quarters," said Fuerte. "There may be something there that might be able to tell us more."

The two men roamed the crumbling fortress for a time and found nothing, except more woundless bodies.

"It could be they were poisoned," said Fuerte when the two men met in front of the main building once again.

"But not necessarily poisoned here at the fort. The original name for the land this garrison is built on was Dead Water Flats. That was because all the water the original builders discovered in the area turned out to be contaminated. When it was operating, the Mexican army used to bring fresh, barreled water to this fort by the wagonload.

"All I can figure is that these particular soldiers decided to use this fort again after its long abandonment, but somehow they weren't told in advance that the local water could kill them . . . and that is why they are all dead."

"The water killed them?" said Charley.

"Man and animal have the need to drink every day, Señor Charley," said Fuerte. "Every man and beast you see here took no longer to die than a half hour to forty-five minutes. The officers must have come across one of those tainted water holes just before they got here and let every man and animal have their fill. By the time they had started to settle inside these walls, the poison took effect."

"There are two ways to prove what you say, Roca, my friend. One is to find some of that deadly water, and the other is to examine the fort's infirmary."

They found the fort's infirmary near the storeroom. The small, one-room building contained even more dead.

"It is apparent to me," said Fuerte, "that there was almost no time at all for the medical officer to treat these soldiers before he also died."

Charley's eyes drifted across the room to where a body draped in a white coat lay with his face on the top of a desk. Underneath his chest was an open journal, in his hand, a writing pen.

Charley walked over to the body, lifted it up, and pulled the journal from under him. The pages were blank.

"You're right, Roca," said Charley. "It looks to me like their medical officer consumed some of that poisoned water, like you said. Killed him dead, just like the others . . . before he could make out his report on the situation. And that's a fact. Come on, Roca," Charley added, "we need to clear out some space for everyone to sleep when they get here."

Mitchell Pennell and Sergeant Tobias Stone were the next to arrive at the abandoned fort, along with Elisabeth Rogers, who now rode the burro.

The threesome were met less than fifty yards from the main gate by Roca Fuerte, who had ridden out to greet them.

They exchanged a few words, then Fuerte led them toward, then through, the main gate. He explained to them the presence of the Mexican soldiers' bodies, while at the same time warning them to drink only from their own personal canteens.

When the newcomers were all the way inside the compound, they were greeted by Charley, who stood guard above them on the front wall.

"Pennell . . . Sergeant Stone," he called down to them. "Welcome." He turned to Fuerte. "Roca, come up here and relieve me so I can show our new arrivals where we set up our camp."

Fuerte called out, "Yes, sir, Señor Charley. I will be there as soon as I can get these men a drink of safe water."

Fuerte grabbed his canteen from his saddle and handed it to Pennell. The ex-convict took a healthy swig before passing the canteen to Elisabeth, then to Sergeant Stone.

"How'd you know the groundwater around here wasn't safe to drink?" questioned Charley as he climbed down from the wall to join the others. He passed Fuerte who was on his way up.

The sergeant answered, “They taught all of us Fort Clark soldiers to recognize bad water. It sure don’t look like the Mexican army has the same kinda training, does it?”

“They’re all dead,” Charley told him.

“We gonna bury ’em?” asked the sergeant.

“I figured we’ll all pitch in tomorrow morning and dig one very big grave . . . use it for all of ’em, including the horses.”

“That’s gonna be one hell of a hole,” said the sergeant. “It’ll be nice to have more men.”

“I’ll tell you what,” said Charley, “we’ll not only wait until the others get here, we won’t start digging until they do. I just hope the smell doesn’t bother anyone tonight at suppertime . . . or while we’re sleeping.”

Elisabeth, standing some distance away, caught Charley’s eye.

“Who’s the woman?” he asked the sergeant. “We came across a wagon on the trail,” he continued, “could it have belonged to her?”

“More than likely,” said Pennell. “We met her when we were captured by the Black-Seminoles and taken to their camp.”

“Seminole-Negroes?” questioned Charley.

“There’s a bunch of ’em livin’ down here in Mexico, Charley,” said the sergeant. “Pennell and me were caught off guard, and one of ’em got the drop on us. He took us prisoner and made us follow him to his camp. That’s where we met up with Mrs. Rogers . . . they had rescued her after her wagon rolled over and her team got away.”

“Did I hear someone mention my name?” said Elisabeth, who had gotten to her feet and was now moving closer.

"That you did, ma'am," said Charley, holding out his hand to her.

The two of them shook.

"I'm Elisabeth Rogers," said Elisabeth.

"Charley Sunday," said Charley, tipping his hat.

A little over an hour later, Elisabeth finished telling her story to Charley. She had filled him in on the circumstances that had brought her to Mexico, beginning with the morning her husband and son had been murdered by the gang of roving Mexican bandits. And her meeting up with more bandits upon entering Mexico, and having to kill two of them—plus overturning her wagon while trying to get away. She also told them about the short time she had spent with the Black-Seminoles, until the Sergeant and Mitch Pennell were brought into the camp as prisoners of Billy July.

"Are you any good with a gun?" asked Charley when Elisabeth was done speaking.

"Like I told you, I've had to kill a couple of men just to get this far," she answered.

"That's good to know," said Charley. "You see," he went on, "we're down here looking to find my daughter and her husband. They were abducted in Brownsville nearly a week ago by a gang of Mexican bandits. Our intent is to find the people who abducted them and free my family, then take them back to the United States. That may include having to use our guns to persuade the abductors . . . when we find them."

Fuerte called out from his position on the wall, "Someone is coming, Señor Charley. It looks like three men, plus the chuckwagon."

"We'll be right up and join you," said Charley. "That should be Roscoe, Holliday, and Feather."

Night had begun to fall when Elisabeth was telling her story. Now it had gotten much darker, which made it difficult for Roca Fuerte to identify the two riders and the wagon's driver from that distance.

Fuerte was joined by Charley, the sergeant, and Pennell on the wall. Charley had brought along a lantern. They all strained their eyes to see, until Charley was able to recognize the three men for sure as their friends.

He swung the lantern back and forth, then yelled out, "Roscoe, Feather, Holliday! Over here; it's Charley. Come through the front gate . . . I'll meet you just inside."

Charley climbed down the steps, followed by the others.

Once the threesome had made it through the entrance gates, Charley held up the lantern and led them over to where the others had already set up a temporary camp.

After some anxious handshaking all around, Charley turned to Roscoe.

"I'm so glad you still got some vittles packed away in that wagon," he said. "Break 'em out. We'll help you any way we can. I don't know about the others, but I'm starving."

"I'll help with the cooking," said Elisabeth. "If no one minds."

Roscoe threw her a hard glare, which couldn't be seen by the others.

"Who's she?" Roscoe whispered to Charley.

"Doesn't matter," said Charley, "she's one of us now. And try to be nice, Roscoe," he added as he moved away.

"Why, I'd be more than pleased to have you assist me, ma'am," said Roscoe. "And your name is . . . ?"

"Elisabeth Rogers," said Elisabeth.

"Like I said, she's part of our outfit," Charley called back to him over his shoulder. "She joined up with Sergeant Stone and Mitch Pennell out on the trail. She's got no other place to go."

Roscoe untied, then slung, a gunnysack down from the wagon's bed. He began going through it.

"Can ya peel a potata, ma'am?" he asked her.

"I can peel as many potatoes as you've got," she replied.

"We just can't use very much water, that's all," said Charley, explaining the dead bodies all around. "The only good water we have around here is what's left in our canteens."

"Hey," Roscoe said, "maybe I'll just bake them 'taters in my Dutch Oven, 'stead a' boilin' 'em." He yelled out, "Why don't you get me a cook fire goin', Feather . . . Grab the rest a' the boys and see if you can rustle up any firewood."

Holliday moved in beside Charley.

"It was a rough couple a' days out there, Mr. Sunday," said Holliday. "We had rain, wind, sun, and a lot a' different kinds a' weather."

"I'm sure you did, Holliday," said Charley. "And so did we, if that matters anything to you. Now get out there with the others and find Roscoe some firewood."

After supper, everyone sat around the fire relaxing and enjoying the cool evening. Charley moved in beside Fuerte and Roscoe with three cups of steaming coffee. He set them down on a flat rock and began to pack his pipe bowl with tobacco from his pouch.

"These makings just don't seem to taste right ever since

Fuerte and me found ourselves neck deep in a ditch with the high water rising."

He found a match and struck it on a nearby rock, bringing flame to the pipe's bowl. His continuous sucking and puffing kept the glowing, red-hot tobacco burning strong.

"I always keep some extra matches in my saddlebags, wrapped in oilskin. That's why I still got some that'll fire up. Took me half of one night to clean the mud out of my Walker Colt, dry it, oil it, then reload. Cleaning ourselves up wasn't that easy, either, was it, Roca?"

"We finally came across a little creek where the water was clear enough to use for bathing," said Fuerte.

"And the rest is history . . . just look at us now?" said Charley. "I'm going to get up on that wall again and keep an eye out for Rod, Kelly, and Henry Ellis. The rest of you can either sleep out here in the yard . . . or inside the officers' quarters. Me and Roca cleaned it all up for you inside."

Chapter Eighteen

Charley Sunday woke up a little before dawn to the echo of hooves on hard rock. A single horse was approaching. Charley was still on the wall where he'd fallen asleep several hours earlier. He raised his head and peered down the barrel of his rifle. In the setting moonlight, on the road leading up to the front gate of the adobe fort, was a lone rider. He was astride a spirited Mexican horse, riding bareback, headed toward the stronghold's entrance gate.

The sky was growing lighter with the beginning of the new day, finally allowing Charley to recognize the rider as his grandson, Henry Ellis.

A wide grin spread across the old rancher's face. He stood up, then he moved down the adobe steps two at a time.

"It's Henry Ellis," he called out to the others who were still sleeping on the ground and inside the officers' quarters. "It's my grandson."

The boy rode in through the gate, and as soon as he saw his grandfather, he slipped off the horse's back and ran to Charley, arms out.

"Grampa Charley," he called out, then the two were hugging, patting one another on the back.

"I was so worried, Grampa," said the boy. "I was afraid I wasn't going to find you."

"Well, you found me, all right," said Charley. "Now we're all together again."

Henry Ellis's eyes dropped to the ground.

"We're all together, except for Rod and Kelly," he said.

"What's happened to them, son?" said Charley.

"The three of us were captured by members of the Armendariz gang," the boy said. "I was able to escape . . . But Rod and Kelly weren't that lucky."

"Did you see your mother and father?" asked Charley. "Did you see Betty Jean?"

The boy shook his head.

"No, Grampa. I was looking for them the whole time I was there . . . Rod and Kelly, too. But we never saw them . . . or anything that might have led us to believe they were even there."

Having heard Charley talking outside, Roscoe, Feather, Fuerte, and Elisabeth came out of the officers' quarters and moved over to join Charley and Henry Ellis.

"I'll bet you're mighty hungry, son," said Roscoe. "I'll have breakfast goin' just as soon as Feather and some of the other gentlemen around here build me a fire."

He moved away and Feather followed right behind.

"Would you know how to get back to that bandit camp if you had to, Henry Ellis?" asked Charley.

"Sure," answered the boy. "Easy as pie."

"Then that's where we're going, just as soon as we've all had something to eat."

"What about the bodies?" Pennell yelled over to Charley.

"No time for digging now," said Charley. "We'll just

have to leave them where they are for the time being. Someone'll be along for 'em, I reckon."

With Henry Ellis and his grandfather in the lead, the outfit, minus Rod and Kelly, once again found themselves riding in formation—a single column. Only now, they were following the boy's directions that they hoped would lead them to the Armendariz camp.

At times they rode at a trot, at others in a slow gallop. They rode over stone bridges, past seemingly deserted villages, down sandy trails, and through trickling ravines. They trudged across open land and through several deep canyons. They waded through even more ravines and streams, and would intermittently stop to rest. They would eat only when their horses began to show weariness and hunger. Otherwise, the small group continued on, forcing themselves to the limit. Roscoe, driving the chuckwagon, always seemed to be last, playing a game of "catch up" every inch of the way.

By late afternoon, after Henry Ellis had told Charley he thought they were pretty close to the Armendariz camp, the outfit gathered around some large boulders, in the shade of several spindly trees, for an afternoon break.

When they had rested and watered the horses, Charley had them back in their saddles and on the trail once again.

Don Roberto and his men entered the same small village Charley and Roca Fuerte had ridden into during the raging storm a day or so before.

The streets were still quite muddy, and several store

owners, whose establishments were nothing more than covered stalls, were still shoveling, sweeping, and cleaning up their inventory before opening for business.

The Don spotted a Mexican army officer and some of his soldiers hitching several teams of horses to the army wagons that were standing out on the street. Don Roberto gave his men an order to stay where they were, while he and his foreman, Luis, rode over to where the officer was standing.

"Did you happen to see two strangers ride through this town in the last day or so?" asked the Don in his native language.

The officer pointed to the *cantina* across the plaza.

"Two men, one a *gringo*, one a Mexican, who no one had seen before, killed four *bandidos* over in that *cantina* two days ago, during the storm," the officer replied in Spanish.

"Would anyone mind if my friend and I looked inside the *cantina*?" said Don Roberto. "We might be able to tell you who those strangers were if we can see the location where this shooting took place."

"Go ahead," said the officer. "The local police have already removed the bodies."

"For that I am grateful," said the Don. "But I would still like to see where the killings took place."

He moved off toward the *cantina* with Luis following.

The double doors, closed during the storm, were now wide open as Don Roberto and his foreman, Luis Hernandez, strode through the swinging bat-wings.

Once inside, they had to wait a few seconds until their eyes became accustomed to the darkness within. When the Don was eventually able to see what was around him, he spotted the bartender leaning against the counter, polishing some glasses. Don Roberto moved over to the bar with Luis beside him.

Speaking in Spanish, he said, "Are you the owner of this establishment?"

The bartender looked up at the taller man.

"Yes . . ." He paused. "Well . . . I am the brother-in-law of the owner," he answered. "But I am in charge."

"Were you a witness to the shooting that took place in here recently?"

The bartender opened up, retelling his version of what he had seen. He was sure the dead men were members of the Armendariz gang, but he had a little trouble describing who the two men were that had done the killing.

"All I can really tell you about those two men who shot the bandits is that one was a white-haired Mexican . . . and the other one, an old *gringo*."

"Well," said Don Roberto, turning to Luis, "a *gringo*, he says. I am beginning to wonder just how many *gringos* are in our country searching for Armendariz and his men."

"Maybe this *gringo* is a relative of those who were abducted," said Luis.

"That is a possibility," said the Don. "And if this old *gringo* is possibly related to the Pritchard family, then how is the white-haired Mexican involved?"

The bartender raised his hand to get the Don's attention.

"Señor," he began. "I think I have seen the white-haired Mexican before . . . it was a long, long time ago, many years, but I think I recognized him from when the *Rurales* were protecting this town from the *bandidos*."

"Fuerte," said Don Roberto.

"No," said the bartender. "That is not the name the old *gringo* called him. He called him Roca."

* * *

After the outfit decided to take a break for the evening meal, Charley and Fuerte went on ahead to continue searching for Armendariz's camp. When the two men were close enough to smell food cooking, and to hear Spanish-speaking voices, they dismounted and tied off their horses.

"Come this way, Señor Charley," whispered Fuerte.

Charley nodded, then he quickly followed his Mexican friend until they were both forced to crawl along on their bellies until the camp came into view.

The two men stopped—they both lay flat in the wild grass and peered into the camp. The first thing they took notice of was the makeshift jail—plus the fencing that made up the enclosure where the remaining two prisoners were still being kept. Both prisoners were now tied, back to back. Another precaution since the boy had been found missing.

"There's Rod and Kelly right over there," whispered Charley. "Now where do you suppose they're keeping Betty Jean and Kent?"

Fuerte shrugged, then he motioned for Charley to duck down even lower as a rider approached the camp from behind them.

The rider was recognized by the guards before he was allowed to enter. Soon he was trotting over to a group of bandits who sat in the shade of a tent's overhanging flap, playing a card game.

When the rider approached, Armendariz stood up to greet him.

The two traded words in Spanish, then Armendariz sat down again, picking up his cards to resume playing his hand.

"What'd they say?" whispered Charley.

Roca Fuerte turned to him and spoke softly.

"Armendariz thanked the man for delivering the two

Americanos to the *hacienda* of the person who paid for their abduction. Then the man asked the colonel just when they were going to move the other two Americans. He was told the boy had escaped. Just having to say the word 'escaped' appeared to make the bandit leader uncomfortable.

"After a moment, Armendariz went on to say that the Indian and his woman were still prisoners and would go along with the rest of them when they all moved out later that afternoon."

Before Fuerte could go on any further, he was interrupted by the barrel of a rifle poking at his temple. He turned slightly to see that Charley also had the barrel of a rifle pressed against the side of his head.

Two surly bandit guards had found the observers in the tall grass outside the bandit campsite. They urged the two infiltrators to stand, using their rifle barrels to prod them.

As they started to get to their feet, Charley jumped up fast, kneeing the man nearest him in the groin, then he brought his Walker Colt down hard on the man's head. Blood spurted as the guard went down.

At the same time, Fuerte had come up with a knife in his hand, gutting the other bandit with a single swipe. Fuerte caught the man before he fell, gently letting his body crumple to the ground.

Charley grabbed one of the rifles. "C'mon, Roca," he whispered, "we need to get back to the others."

Fuerte nodded and picked up the other man's rifle.

They found their horses, mounted, then moved silently away from the bandit encampment.

When Charley figured they had gone far enough that they wouldn't be heard, he spurred out faster. He was immediately followed by Fuerte.

* * *

The rest of the outfit was situated just far enough away that they did not hear the scuffle, plus it had been handled very quietly. When Charley and Fuerte appeared, coming from the outland beyond, Roscoe was the first to get to them.

"What'd you find out?" he asked. "Are they there?"

"We saw Rod and Kelly . . . and we learned that they have already sent my daughter and her husband on to the *hacienda* of the person who hired Armendariz and his gang to abduct them."

Feather moved in beside his friends.

"Ain't we gonna break out Kelly and Rod anyway?" he asked.

"No . . . I don't think so, not just yet," said Charley. "I figure we'll let them go with the bandits, then we'll sneak them away when we have the chance. Right now they've got those two tied up tighter'n I've ever seen before. There's no way we can break them away from that gang right now without causing some kind of a ruckus."

"Sounds like those bandits are pretty upset that I got away," said Henry Ellis, who had only just joined the small group.

"Rod and Kelly were tied up tighter'n two calves in a forty-man roping contest, son," said Charley. "We'll figure out a way to rescue them on the trail. Now, I need two men to replace me and Fuerte to watch that camp. You don't have to get in as close as we did; I just need you there to let us know when they start to pack it up."

The bandit gang began preparing for their departure about an hour later. Holliday and Feather, who had volunteered to take over observation duties for Charley and Fuerte, both rushed over and mounted their horses, moving away quietly—on their way to report that the gang was about to break camp.

Charley found his grandson near a clump of bushes where he sat on a log with a forlorn look on his face. As the older man knelt down beside the boy, he could see that Henry Ellis had been crying.

The boy jumped slightly when Charley put an arm around his shoulder.

"It's all right, son," said Charley, rubbing Henry Ellis's neck. "Everything's going to turn out all right."

Henry Ellis looked up into his grandfather's eyes. A single tear continued to run down his cheek.

"I'm sorry that I let those bandits capture my mother and father," said Henry Ellis. "I shouldn't have run out on 'em. I've caused you so much trouble, Grampa," said Henry Ellis.

"You know better than I do that you had nothing to do with any of that," said Charley. "Don't you be feeling sorry for yourself for no reason. Coming like you did, to get me, was probably the smartest thing you ever did."

"Sorry, Grampa," said the boy. "I know you're right."

Charley nodded. Then he winked at the boy.

Henry Ellis went on, "It's a shame that you and Señor Fuerte weren't able to see my mother and father. Now we only have the word of one of those bandits saying that they were taken to another man's *hacienda*. Do you really think we should believe what you heard that bandit say?"

"Don't you forget that your mother is also my daughter, young man," said Charley. "And I believe they were taken to this man's . . . *hacienda*. The same *hacienda* we will have under surveillance as soon as Armendariz leads us to it."

Henry Ellis's eyes dropped to the ground—he was slightly embarrassed for having questioned his grandfather's integrity.

"I saw the pup," said Charley as he tousled the boy's hair. "He was with Rod and Kelly. Did you ever find any time to train that young dog?"

"Well," said the boy, "he comes when I call him, he rolls over, and when he needs to go, he whines so I know to take him away from the camp and out into the open."

"I love you, Henry Ellis," said Charley after a moment. "I hope you know that."

"I love you, too, Grampa," echoed the boy.

"I love the way you're growing up into a man," Charley went on. "Not just the physical changes . . . but in other ways, too. Your attitude, for one," said Charley. "I've also seen how you can be calm and coolheaded in situations that would have had several grown men I know stumped. And you're learning to ride well . . . 'bout as good as most cowboys I've known."

There was a long pause as both man and boy did some serious pondering.

"Grampa?" said Henry Ellis, looking up.

"What is it, son?" answered Charley.

"Do you really think we'll ever find them?"

"What makes you say that? . . . Are you thinking about giving up?"

"No sir, Grampa. It was my mother and father who were abducted. A man never gives up when it's his family that's involved."

By nightfall they had reached some higher country. Sergeant Stone and Mitch Pennell had been appointed temporary scouts for the outfit. They came riding back to inform the others that Armendariz and his men had just set up another camp for the night.

"How far away from us are they now?" Charley asked.

"No more than a mile or so farther on than their last camp," said the sergeant.

"Then we're far enough behind them to have a very small campfire this evening. Feather," he called out, "I'm putting you in charge of firewood again. The rest of you, give Feather a hand. And don't worry about getting your hands dirty."

It was late in the afternoon when Charley and Fuerte decided to make a wide sweep around the Armendariz camp. They were off to check out what lay ahead.

What they found was a vast green valley with a very large adobe *hacienda* set dead center between open farmland and limitless, unfenced grazing land.

A quarter of a mile from the *hacienda*'s high walls and double-gated entrance was a small village. Fuerte said this was where the *hacienda* workers lived out their lives while working for the landowner, and they had done the same for the owners who had come before him.

The *rancho*, with its surrounding acres of growing crops plus the additional acres of grassy land for cattle, when combined, looked to Charley like a single verdant basket, surrounded on all sides by purple, high-desert mountains. The grassy sections were being used to feed a grazing herd of well over a hundred thousand cattle. Charley thought it was the prettiest piece of acreage he had ever seen.

The two onetime lawmen watched from their vantage on top of a steep hill as two Mexican riders, coming from the direction of Armendariz's camp, galloped through the herd, scattering the cattle as they made their way to the *hacienda*'s wooden gates.

Because it was getting quite dark by then, Charley and Fuerte turned their horses around and headed back to their own campsite, using the same roundabout way they had come.

As the two Mexican riders approached the *hacienda*'s fortified walls, they were recognized by the armed guards and given permission to pass through the heavy gates.

Once inside, they were joined by four mounted guards who led the two men across the courtyard and over to the main house.

As the visitors dismounted, one of the men let his *sombrero* slide to the side of his head, revealing his face.

"Don Sebastian did not tell us it would be you, Colonel Armendariz," said one of the mounted sentries, Andrés, who was the captain of the guard. He bowed from the saddle. "I am sure he will be delighted to see you."

"I am dressed in the clothing of one of my men to protect my identity, in case someone saw us on our way here," said Armendariz. "I prefer that no one knows that I am paying the Don this visit."

"*Sí*, Señor Colonel," said the captain of the guard as he dismounted. "If you will follow me, I will take you to Don Sebastian."

The two men dismounted, then they followed Andrés up several stone steps, across a large sandstone patio, and on to a set of outsized copper-plated front doors, which were positioned between two stone stairways that led to a balcony above.

Andrés swung one of the heavy doors open and the new arrivals followed him.

Once they were inside, Andrés told the two men to stop, as the huge copper door of the main house—*la casa grande*—was closed behind them by one of the guards who had remained outside.

They took in the magnitude of the enormous room in front of them. Most outstanding were the identical eighteen-foot hand-carved stone fireplaces that opposed one another across the tiled floor from each side of the room. The width of the room stretched over forty feet across, from chimney to chimney, and the room's length looked to be at least seventy feet long, from entryway to the rear wall, behind the staircase.

The high ceiling had been painted similar to the Vatican's Sistine Chapel in Rome—but instead of heavenly figures lounging against soothing backgrounds, these painted replications were from hell itself, done in reds, yellows, and orange swirls, depicting Man's darker side.

The entire area was furnished with heavy dark oak, hand-carved chairs and tables scattered here and there. Great tapestries, depicting Mexico's troubled history, covered every wall from top to bottom—and celebrated jewelry and costly keepsakes were kept under glass, in polished cases, located throughout the extended space.

As the men stood staring, a voice called out, echoing through the enormous room.

"Colonel Armendariz," said the voice, "your arrival here this early is quite unexpected."

The colonel, and the man who was with him, searched the room with their eyes. No other person was visible.

"I am here to see Don Sebastian Ortega de la Vega," said the colonel in return. "I have already delivered to him the Americans I was engaged to bring to him . . . and now I would like to be paid for that task."

"In time you will get your money, Colonel Armendariz," said the hidden voice. "I received from you both the mother and the father earlier today. But I am afraid I didn't make myself clear enough . . . I am really more interested in the boy . . . their son. Are you planning on bringing him to me any time soon?" he added.

"The boy has escaped, Don Sebastian," said the bandit leader . . . "*But*," he said quite loudly, "my men are searching for him as we speak. He cannot have gone that far."

Armendariz could tell by the following silence that Don Sebastian was not that pleased with him at the moment.

"I told you I wanted all three delivered to me, Colonel," the Don's voice went on. "Our agreement was for the entire family . . . and you have not delivered them to me as you guaranteed you would."

"But, Don Sebastian," said Armendariz, "I swear to you on my mother's grave that I will have the boy for you by tomorrow."

"Again you make promises that you do not know you can keep," said the voice. "Now, you and your companion get back on your horses and leave my *hacienda* . . . and do not come back until you have brought the boy with you. Only then will you be paid the price we agreed on."

Charley Sunday and Roca Fuerte rode into the outfit's camp, dismounted, and tied off.

Henry Ellis ran up to them babbling about something.

"Slow down, son . . . slow down," said Charley. "You'll have to talk slower if you want us to be able to understand what you're saying."

"Sorry, Grampa," said the boy. "All I wanted to know was if you saw my mother and father."

The two ex-lawmen exchanged looks. They turned to the boy with expressions of complete fatigue.

"Just like before, Henry Ellis," said Charley. "I'm sorry, but we never did see them. We do know several men from Armendariz's camp went there to visit with whoever owns that *hacienda*. We saw them ourselves, just before the sun went down."

"Why don't you three come on over here and get yourself some supper," said Roscoe, cutting in.

Later on in the evening, they all sat around the dwindling campfire and discussed the many ways they might use to get the captives out of the *hacienda*.

No decision had been reached by the time the boy decided to throw in his own two cents' worth.

"Why don't we break Kelly and Rod out of Armendariz's jail first . . . before we try to find my mother and father. Both Kelly and Rod are good with guns, and we just might need them if you're planning on breaking into that *hacienda*, Grampa," said Henry Ellis. "You said the outer walls themselves were over twelve feet high."

Charley nodded. Then he addressed the entire outfit.

"All right," he said. "My grandson's come up with a pretty good idea. We'll go ahead and break Rod and Kelly out of Armendariz's camp before daybreak. Then we'll hit the *hacienda* at full strength."

"May I interrupt, Señor Charley?" said Fuerte. "Not even counting the number of sentries guarding the main house, there are at least a hundred and fifty more militiamen who he must keep in those barracks we saw behind the *hacienda*. Plus there are those who work in the fields for the owner. That doesn't include the *vaqueros* who watch over the cattle. As it is now, we are very undermanned. If you plan to attack them head-on—"

"Henry Ellis is right," said Charley, interrupting his friend Fuerte. "Our first objective will be to get Rod and Kelly out of Armendariz's camp. And we must use stealth," he added. "We must send someone into that camp who can find Rod and Kelly. Untie them and lead them back here. Someone who looks so insignificant, no one in that camp would ever suspect he is one of us."

Feather Martin, appearing to be dressed in Mexican clothing—he'd punched any creases from the crown of his hat and flattened the brim, then thrown an old blanket over his shoulders—strolled boldly through Armendariz's camp. He nodded to the bandits he passed, then he sat down on a rock near a gathering of men who were relaxing around a campfire.

"Here," said one of the men to another bandit, handing two bowls of beans to him. "Take these to the prisoners . . . they are probably very hungry by now."

The man with the bowls moved away.

Within moments, the diminutive cowboy, with his oversize headgear, slithered away from the others and followed the man with the bowls of beans.

Feather stayed in the shadows and watched as the man with the bowls entered a tent that had been set up as a temporary jail cell. It was guarded on each end. The man emerged several moments later without the bowls.

That must be where they're bein' kept, thought Feather, then he slipped around to the side of the tent and slid himself under the canvas siding.

Feather looked around. For some reason he felt cramped.

He eventually realized that was because he was beneath a small, folding, camp table. He could see Rod's and Kelly's feet as they sat together on a cot across from him. He could see they were tied securely and could only assume they'd been gagged.

Carefully, he shoved his head out from under the table and made a noise with his tongue and teeth.

"Ssssst," he said.

Rod and Kelly both looked over. They couldn't talk because they both had large pieces of cloth stuffed into their mouths to silence them, just like Feather had figured.

As soon as the little cowhand saw their wide eyes of recognition, he slid out from under the table and started untying them both—starting with the pieces of cloth that were gagging them.

Kelly was the first to have the piece of cloth removed.

"Feather," she whispered, "how did you get here?"

Feather shushed her with a finger to his lips, then he pulled out Rod's gag. Immediately he began to work at the ropes that had been securing the two.

"You just keep quiet and I'll have you out a' here quicker'n you'll ever know," whispered the tiny cowboy. "Hold still," he told Kelly.

He had them both untied within minutes. They stood up and shook the kinks out.

Feather got to his feet beside them.

"Here," he said to Rod, "this is for you."

He handed Rod a Colt .45, single-action.

"Charley told me ta give it to ya," he went on quietly. "He figgered you might need it."

"You got us to this point, Feather, now how do we get out of the camp?" asked Kelly.

"Same way as I come in, I 'spect," said the little cowpoke. "Just follow me."

He dropped to his knees and slithered under the table. After a quick peek to make sure no one had come up on that side of the tent, he slid on under the siding. Rod and Kelly followed.

As they made their way to the edge of the camp, two of the bandit guards stepped out of the darkness.

"Identify yourselves," shouted one of the *sombrero*-wearing men as the three Americans were nearly to the horses.

Blam! Blam! . . . barked Rod's Colt—the two men were taken out in short order.

The trio untied and mounted three horses, then they spurred away as quick as they were able.

Within a short span of time, Rod, Kelly, and Feather had arrived back at their own camp.

Henry Ellis ran to greet them.

"Douse that fire," Charley told Roscoe. "The rest of you, and that includes Feather, Rod, Kelly, and my grandson, take the horses behind those rocks . . . get everything out of sight. Someone besides us had to have heard those gunshots."

Everyone did what Charley asked them to—and when the six members of the bandit gang who'd been ordered to follow the escapees rode by in a cloud of dust, Charley's insides felt much better. So did the rest of the outfit.

They waited in hiding until the six bandits came back up the trail, having realized that those they were chasing had somehow gotten away.

Charley and the others were able to hear the men talking among themselves in Spanish as the group passed by again. They were now riding slower, on their way back to the Armendariz campsite.

"What were they saying, Roca?" Charley asked Fuerte after the bandits had passed.

Roca answered, "Many things of interest to us, Señor Charley. Most of which we already know. But there was something that was said that we have no knowledge of."

"And what might that be?" asked Charley.

"Just the name of the man we are seeking . . . the man who paid Armendariz to abduct your daughter and her husband. He is the owner of the large *hacienda*, and the vast farm and grazing lands in the green valley. He is a very wealthy rancher by the name of Don Sebastian Ortega de la Vega."

"I don't think I recognize that name," said Charley. "Have you heard of this Don Sebastian before?"

"*Sí*, Señor Charley, I have," said Fuerte. "Don Sebastian Ortega de la Vega is one of the most powerful illegitimate businessmen in all of Mexico . . . though he hasn't made a public appearance in many years, and he does not socialize with any of the other wealthy families in this state. He does all his business through attorneys in Matamoros and Mexico City. And his vast cattle herd keeps growing, in spite of having no records of sales. Other than that, no one knows much about this man, except that he guards his *hacienda* as if it were a Spanish castle."

They ate in the dark that night, sitting around what used to be the campfire, the pit now filled with charred pieces of wood. After every morsel had been wiped from his plate, Charley took out his pipe, filled the bowl, then lit the tobacco with a Blue Diamond match.

"The faster we move, the less they'll be expecting us," he told the others.

"Do you still have a plan, Charley?" asked Kelly.

"No more of a plan than any one of you folks might have," he answered, "but it may work."

He turned to Sergeant Stone.

"This should be so simple we won't be needing your tools, Sergeant," said Charley. "I suggest you bury them right here where we are, just for now, in case we're run off, or something worse. The rest of you will only be needed as backup for Henry Ellis and me."

"That's your plan?" said Kelly. "Just you and Henry Ellis are going to climb that twelve-foot wall all by yourselves and take on that man's own personal army? I knew you were crazy, Charley Sunday, but not that crazy."

"He is crazy, Señora Kelly," said Fuerte, "but this time, I think, he is crazy like a fox."

"I get it," said Rod. "Since our little outfit is so overwhelmed by the number of men this Don Sebastian has behind him, we are safer if we use as few of us as possible to breech the *hacienda* wall."

"And that's going to be Henry Ellis and me," said Charley, for the second time. "The rest of you will be waiting for us when we come out with Betty— . . . with Henry Ellis's mother and father."

"When is all this going to take place," Pennell wanted to know.

"We'll leave here just as soon as I lay out your positions for you, then I'll tell you what to expect from the guards inside the *hacienda*'s gates. First of all, I'll be needing a very long rope, and something to tie at one end that can be used as a grappling hook . . . plus my grandson."

Chapter Nineteen

Charley and Henry Ellis hid their horses—plus the two extra ones they had brought along with them for the boy's parents—between the tall stalks of a cornfield, which had been planted several yards away from the *hacienda* wall. They stacked brush, weeds, and cornstalks around the animals, hoping they wouldn't be seen by anyone who might happen to come near.

Both man and boy then set out through the corn rows, making their way toward the *hacienda* wall about a tenth of a mile away.

Charley carried a long, coiled rope over his shoulder; the boy carried Charley's Winchester rifle.

When they had traveled several hundred feet and could see the moon's glint off a wall guard's rifle barrel in front of them, Charley held the boy back so he could speak to him.

"This is as far as you go, Henry Ellis," he whispered. "You stay here, and use my rifle if that guard up there sees what I'm up to and tries to take me out."

Henry Ellis levered a shell into the rifle as quietly as he

could, all the while keeping an eye on the position of the wall guard.

"All right," said Charley, "when you see I've done my job . . . come a running. I'll toss the rope down to you and you can climb up."

The boy nodded, and his grandfather moved forward toward the wall.

As Charley arrived at the base of the wall and was preparing to throw the rope that was attached to the makeshift grappling hook, he heard the sound of bubbling water somewhere nearby. He turned to his right and could see that some of the adobe bricks at the wall's base had never been set by the builders. Instead, a knee-high arch had been constructed in their place so a small creek could flow out of the *hacienda* grounds unheeded.

He sized up the small opening with his eyes. He smiled softly, then he recoiled the rope, turned around, and disappeared between the rows of corn.

He found his grandson where he'd left him. He told the boy about the hole in the wall that had been left open for the creek to run through.

"I want to go," said the boy.

"Henry Ellis," said Charley, "I don't think I want to let you do that. It's too dangerous."

"But I can do it, Grampa, I know I can."

"You saw the diagram of the *hacienda* Roca drew in the dirt back at our camp, didn't you?"

Henry Ellis nodded.

"There wasn't much detail," said the boy, "but at least what I did see should give me an idea of where I am, once I get inside the walls. Now, can I go, Grampa? Please?"

"You're beginning to change my mind, son . . . besides, it is your mother and father."

"Thanks, Grampa," said Henry Ellis. He gave Charley a big hug, followed by a quick wink.

"It's a pretty small opening, son, but I'm sure you'll fit," said Charley.

"This'll change your whole plan, won't it, Grampa?" said the boy. "Now I'll be the only one who sneaks into the *hacienda* and rescues my parents."

"With you going under the wall," said Charley, "rather than me going over, it won't give them much of a target to shoot at. Just think about that, son. You can do it." He added, "I have faith in you. They won't even know their security has been breached."

"Thanks, Grampa," said the boy.

"You realize we don't know where your folks are being held," said Charley, "so it'll be all up to you to find them on your own. Do you understand any Spanish?" he asked.

"*Un poquito*," said the boy. "I've been studying the language since I was in the third grade."

"Well, you might have to do a little translating in your head if you hear any of those people inside that *hacienda* talking with one another. Do you think you can handle that?"

"*Sí, mi abuelito*," said Henry Ellis. "That means grandfather. Oh," he said, "you don't want me to go into the *hacienda* unarmed, do you?"

"Here," said Charley, reaching into his vest pocket. "I almost forgot."

He handed the boy a small, over and under, two-shot, 32-caliber derringer.

"Put this in your pocket . . . and use it only if you have to," he said. "And remember, I'll be right here if you need me. You haven't forgotten that coyote call I taught you when you were a little boy, have you?" he asked.

The boy shook his head.

"No sir, Grampa," he answered. "I can still do it."

"If you feel you're between a rock and a hard place, just make that coyote howl," said Charley. "When I hear it, I'll be over that wall faster'n a cat with its whiskers on fire. I'll find you wherever you are, and I'll give you a hand. Do you understand all I've told you, Henry Ellis?"

The boy nodded.

Charley took his grandson by the shoulders and gave him a squeeze, along with a tender look.

Henry Ellis stood on his tiptoes and kissed his grandfather on the cheek.

The boy turned, and with a good pat on the butt from Charley, he started out toward the wall.

Once Henry Ellis had squeezed himself through the small arch at the base of the wall, he stood up, putting his back against the inside of the whitewashed adobe barrier, staying in the shadows cast by the moon overhead.

He hadn't been able to accomplish that small maneuver without getting some of his clothes wet. So now, as he stood there trying to figure out what his next move would be, he also felt the chill of the night, brought on by a light breeze whipping at his damp clothing.

Before his teeth had the time to start chattering, the boy made a visual inspection of every building that was standing within his view of the courtyard. Only a few of the windows were lighted. He knew there must be occupants inside.

I wonder which one of those rooms they're using to hold my parents? he thought to himself. He decided that he'd have to look into every one of the windows, all around the main house, to determine where they were being held.

He changed the level of his observation. Now looking in either direction, he studied the position of every guard he could see between himself and the *casa grande*—he counted seven. He made a mental note of their positions before starting off toward the main building.

He used the walls, then the side of another adobe structure, to keep himself from being seen. Suddenly, he stopped in his tracks. Four uniformed guards had just stepped out of the building beside him. They appeared to be headed for the barracks building across the courtyard.

The boy hugged the wall and watched as the four guards entered their sleeping quarters, calling it a day.

For the first time, Henry Ellis was aware of the loud voices and singing emanating from inside the building beside him.

A quick peek through a curtained window showed the structure to be the guards' recreation room—a place for the members of Don Sebastian's militia to drink together and share their stories of previous deeds.

He realized at that moment he would eventually find himself between the *hacienda* and this guards' recreation building when he would be leading his mother and father to their freedom. There seemed to be no other way out. Plus he must also figure out another safe route to get them to the wall after they passed the guards' building, since the courtyard was very wide at that particular point.

He waited for another few moments, until he was sure no other guards would be leaving the building, then he quickly ran the few steps across an open area until he saw some more guards coming. He quickly found refuge behind some bushes alongside the *casa grande*, and he crouched down behind them.

* * *

Charley was waiting patiently between the corn rows when a strange noise made his ears perk. He reached for the Walker Colt in his boot, and as he resumed his stance he heard Rod's voice.

"Henry Ellis," came the young Indian's whispered call a second time.

"Over here," Charley whispered back. "And it's me, Charley."

There was some rustling between the corn stalks, then Rod was beside him. Both of them were just as surprised as the other to find themselves where they weren't supposed to be.

"I thought Henry Ellis would be standing guard, not you, Charley," whispered Rod, who was armed with an army-issue Colt.

"And you're supposed to be with the others waiting as backup for when we bring my daughter and her husband out of the *hacienda*," whispered Charley in return.

"They knew we were there, Charley," said Rod. "I don't know how they knew it, but Armendariz's men got the drop on all of us before we knew what was happening. I somehow managed to escape during all the commotion."

"Captured?" said Charley. "They captured the whole outfit?"

"There's just you, me, and Henry Ellis left," said the young Indian. He glanced around. "Where is Henry Ellis, anyway?" he asked.

Charley made a motion with his hand, indicating the *hacienda* wall behind them.

"He's in there," he told Rod. "I was about to go over the wall as planned, then I saw a small hole in the adobes used as a passageway for a creek that runs through the grounds. Henry Ellis asked me to let him go. There was no way I could have fit through that hole anyway."

"So you allowed Henry Ellis to go instead," said Rod. "There's nothing wrong with that, Charley."

"Well," said Charley, "I know that boy pretty well, and believe me, I know he's up to it."

Henry Ellis sat with his back against the *hacienda* building's wall; he was still hidden securely behind the thick bushes. The boy knew he had to leave this little hide-away soon so he could continue with the search for his parents.

Before he had the chance to move, Henry Ellis heard several men's voices speaking in Spanish. They were coming from an open window above his head.

"Armendariz has captured the band of Americans who have been following him since they left Brownsville," said one of the voices in Spanish.

"What about the old Texas Ranger, Charles Sunday?" asked the second voice, also speaking in Spanish. "And the boy . . . have they caught the boy yet?"

"Those two are still missing," said the first voice. "I have my men out looking for them right now."

"Whatever it takes," said the second voice, "you will find them, and bring them both to me."

"As you wish, Don Sebastian. I will have them all in my custody before the sun rises tomorrow morning."

"In the meantime"—it was Don Sebastian's voice again—"I will go and check on the two prisoners. I will be very angry if something bad should happen to them."

Charley and Rod stood next to the outside wall, near the arched opening made for the creek—the tiny opening used by Henry Ellis earlier to gain access to the courtyard.

Charley was swinging the long rope again, and when it felt right, he released the grappling hook end and the rope uncoiled as it reached the top of the wall, disappearing over the apex.

"Good," said Rod. "Now, just pray that it has grabbed on to something."

Charley pulled on the rope until it was taut—the improvised grappling hook had done its job perfectly.

Charley handed his end of the rope to Rod.

"Good luck," he said.

"This time, pray for me, Charley Sunday," said Rod. "And pray for Henry Ellis, too."

"Of course I will," said Charley.

Rod shinnied up the rope to the top of the wall, using his feet to brace himself. Then he took a quick look around the *hacienda* grounds, in case there were any guards present. When he was sure no one had seen him, he slid over the top of the wall and dropped the twelve feet down the other side to the ground.

Charley waited a moment or two, just in case something might have gone wrong with Rod's unconventional entrance into the *hacienda*'s premises, then he turned away and began coiling the rope.

"Hold it right there, Señor Sunday," came a heavily accented voice from behind. "And hand over your gun . . . at once!"

Chapter Twenty

1961

"Oh my," said Noel as she slid over closer to her Grampa Hank. "Just when everything's going right, something always comes along to spoil it."

"Why did they build the *hacienda* on top of a creek bed, Grampa Hank?" asked Caleb.

"So they'd have something to drink when they were thirsty," said Josh, who had stretched out on the grass and was looking up at the stars while he spoke.

Hank said, "Did you know that here in America, even today, both farmers and ranchers like to have their houses near a creek or a stream, so they won't have to go too far for water? Well, it was the same down in old Mexico back then. The *hacienda* owners would build their homes near a creek or stream for the same reason; they had to have water close by. Don Sebastian's choice to build the little exit arch in his wall for the stream proved to be his undoing. His plans for the *hacienda* walls had been based on the fact that the normal size of a Mexican man was just too large to fit through that little arch—and much too small for a soldier in full fighting gear. He never expected that a boy, the size of Henry Ellis, would be able to use the arch to gain entrance into his private sanctuary."

"So, what happened, Grampa Hank?" said Noel. "What happened next?"

Chapter Twenty-one

1900

Henry Ellis had made it as far as the corner of the *casa grande*. He decided he'd stay there, behind the bushes that surrounded the main house, until he could check every window and door he came to.

Most of the rooms were unoccupied, others contained a guard or two, as he stopped momentarily beneath each casement, checking to see if his parents might be inside.

He had nearly circled the entire building, with no luck, when he heard his mother's voice coming from a small window on the far end of the *hacienda*'s lower floor.

After the boy had stopped to figure out from which window her voice was coming, he moved cautiously to that opening and stood up on his tiptoes. He got his ear as close to the shutters as possible. Once he was set firmly in place, he held his breath and listened as best as he could.

It was a man's voice with a heavy Spanish accent that was now speaking. And since Henry Ellis could also hear his mother's voice every so often, he was sure he'd stumbled across a conversation between his mother and her captor.

"I beg of you, tell me, where have you taken my husband?" Betty Jean asked the man.

"For the time being, your husband's whereabouts are not your concern, señora," answered Don Sebastian, the man to whom the other voice belonged.

"He is my husband and I want to be with him," said Betty Jean's voice. "He has become a very sick man. He needs me."

"I will have your husband brought back to you only when you can tell me where your son is," said the Don. "Until then, I must keep the two of you separated."

Henry Ellis felt sick to his stomach when he realized this man also wanted him in custody.

He let himself down to the ground where he would wait until his mother was alone in the room.

Charley had been taken to a place where the rest of the outfit was being held—in a break in a small wooded area, close to the *hacienda*'s outside wall. Here Don Sebastian's guards—along with some of Armendariz's men—could watch over them with no possibility of escape.

"Señor Charley," shouted Fuerte when he first saw the guards bringing the ex-Ranger into the area. They stopped to untie him.

"Roca, *mi amigo*," Charley answered back. Then he threw his arms around his friend.

"My friend," said Fuerte, "I thought you might be dead. Please accept my apology. I do not know how they found out we were here. Is it possible there is a traitor among us?"

"I don't think so," said Charley. "I can vouch for every single one in my outfit. I handpicked them all."

Some of the others were drifting over to where Charley

and Fuerte were standing—Roscoe was the first to reach them.

"Looks like they got you, too, C.A.," said Roscoe. "Where's the kid?"

Charley shushed him with a harsh look.

Roscoe nodded slightly to let Charley know that he understood he should keep quiet about the boy.

"And Rod?" said Kelly, whispering. She moved in beside them.

Now there were even more gathering around. Charley kept his voice low as he filled them all in.

"Both Henry Ellis and Rod are inside the *hacienda*'s walls," said Charley. "Hopefully, we'll figure out how to get away from these guards before Henry Ellis and Rod need our help getting Betty Jean and Kent out of that place."

Kelly looked up at Charley. "You say that Rod is inside the *hacienda* walls with Henry Ellis?"

"That's right, Kelly. They're both inside," said Charley. "But not together. All we can do right now is to pray that those two will eventually meet up. Pennell, Sergeant Stone," he called out.

Charley's loud whisper brought the two men to his side. When they gave him their full attention he went on.

"You two men edge your way around to the east side of this enclosure. Holliday, Roscoe, you two work your way over to the west. I'll take the north . . . and Roca, you take the south. When I see that all of you are in position to take out the guards nearest you, I'll holler."

"We can do that, Boss," said Feather.

"It'll be no problem," added the sergeant.

"The sooner we get this done," said Charley, "the sooner we can get back to the *hacienda* so we can be there for Rod and my grandson."

* * *

Henry Ellis was still waiting outside the window to the room where his mother was being held. The man who had been talking to Betty Jean had just left the room, closing the door behind him. *Those two sure talked for a long time*, the boy thought to himself before jumping up and grabbing the bottom of the window frame. He pulled himself up until he could see his mother inside.

"Mother," he whispered.

Betty Jean jumped at the surprise of hearing her son's voice.

"Over here, Mother," he said again.

This time she turned and saw Henry Ellis's face centered in the casement.

"Oh, my dear God," she said out loud. Then she whispered, "Thank God you're alive, Henry Ellis."

She moved over and helped him as he climbed through the open window the rest of the way.

After he joined his mother inside, the two of them hugged for the longest of time—then she leaned in and showered the boy with kisses from forehead to chin.

"My boy," she said, "my son . . . oh my. It's so good to see you, Henry Ellis."

"Where's Father?" the boy wanted to know.

"I wish I knew myself," she said. "He was feeling under the weather this morning, so they sent several men over here to get him. I must assume they took him somewhere for treatment."

"Is there a hospital here on the *hacienda* grounds?" asked the boy.

"There certainly should be, by the size of this place," she said. "It's like a small city."

"That's where he must be, then," said Henry Ellis.

"Where else would they take a man who was complaining of feeling ill?"

"If it helps," said Betty Jean, "they must have turned to the left when they went out the front door. I could see them through the window when they crossed the yard. Then they disappeared behind some of those other buildings."

"First," said Henry Ellis, "I want to get you out of here and to a safer place before I go looking for Father. Follow me . . . I think I saw just the right place when I was finding my way over here." Henry Ellis added, "You'll just have to promise me one thing, Mother . . . that you'll stay there until I get back with Father."

His mother nodded.

"I promise you, Henry Ellis," she said. "I promise you with all my heart."

Rod had found his way as far as the guard's recreation building. Once he was there, however, he felt trapped because the door leading to the inside was now open, and every so often a guard or two would either enter or exit the building, making it impossible for him to go on any farther.

Once, when he decided to go around to the other side of the building, he spotted the two gate guards—with rifles ready—surveying the inside courtyard instead of the surrounding acreage outside the walls.

Something's gone wrong, he thought to himself, then there was an opening, a space in time between the guards' coming to and leaving the building.

He took a chance and ran toward the *casa grande*, diving under the bushes. He found himself approximately where Henry Ellis had hidden when he first got to the main house.

* * *

Henry Ellis led his mother down a long hallway that opened up into the *hacienda*'s great room. Both he, and Betty Jean, were overwhelmed by the room's size, but finding a way out was their main dilemma at that moment.

"Stay close to me, Mother," said Henry Ellis. "Those two doors over there are the front entrance, I'm sure. We need a door that will lead to the outside, where our presence will not be so obvious."

"What about that one?" said Betty Jean, pointing across the vast room to a single door located beside one of the opposing fireplaces.

"It'll do for a start," said Henry Ellis.

With his arm around his mother's shoulder, the boy led her across the tile floor to the other side.

After a moment of fidgeting with the door's handle, the boy opened the portal and ushered his mother through the door and out into the fresh air of the courtyard.

Henry Ellis scanned the open space in front of them, his eyes finally stopping on the creek that flowed through the property.

"C'mon, Mother," he said. "Follow me."

Holding her hand, he made a dash for a small building constructed of rocks that appeared to straddle the running watercourse. In no time at all, mother and son slipped through a small arched opening in the structure's wall and disappeared inside.

From his position in the bushes, Rod had seen the two make their dash for the creek house—the place within the *hacienda*'s walls where food items were kept that needed the natural refrigeration offered inside.

Though the interior was exposed to little or no light, and it was quite a few degrees cooler than it was outside,

Henry Ellis figured that at last he'd found a place to hide that was somewhat safer than anywhere else he'd thought of before.

"You stay here, Mother," said Henry Ellis. "I'm going to find out just where they're keeping Father."

"Please, Henry Ellis," said Betty Jean, "please don't leave me here alone."

"I have to go, Mother," said the boy. "I promised Grampa I'd get you both out of this place . . . together."

"You should do what your mother wants you to do, Henry Ellis."

There was the sound of a splash.

Both of them turned to see Rod—with his gun in hand—as he entered through the same door they had used.

"It's all right, Mother," said Henry Ellis. "This is Rod Lightfoot . . . he's a friend of Grampa's and mine."

Betty Jean began to breathe easier.

Charley, Fuerte, and the rest of the outfit were herded into a tighter circle. Extra guards had been added to oversee the group.

About then, a fancy carriage drove up containing Colonel Armendariz and Don Sebastian.

The driver stopped the carriage in front of the captives. Both men stood up, getting the prisoners' attention.

"I am Don Sebastian Ortega de la Vega," the Don began. "And I am sure that you know my friend here, Colonel Armendariz? We are here to ask for your surrender.

"We know that the boy and one of the other Americans are inside the walls of my *hacienda* . . . and as long as we know that, there is no chance of their escaping."

"You have my daughter and her husband in there, too," shouted Charley from his position in the crowd.

"If you will come closer and identify yourself, señor," said the Don, "perhaps I can tell you more of my plans for all of you."

Charley stepped forward.

"Ah, Señor Sunday," said Don Sebastian. "I assumed that was you. I know you are the leader of this band of Texians . . . with the exception of Señor Fuerte over there . . . and I'm ready to make you an offer."

"An offer?" said Charley. "What kind of an offer?"

"I will release every one of these prisoners into your custody . . . that will include the boy and whoever it is with him inside those walls . . . in return for a ransom of fifty thousand American dollars."

"That's one hell of a lot of greenbacks," said Charley. "What makes you think I have access to that kind of money?"

"I have read that you are a rich Texas rancher . . . Plus, I know all about your cattle drive last year, and I have been advised of how much money you must have collected by now from certain American corporations for your endorsement of their products."

Charley broke into a laugh.

"Now ain't that something," he said. "You're assuming I'm a millionaire because of that?"

"You are correct, señor," said the Don. "Most likely you are a millionaire several times over."

"Well, I'm not," said Charley. "Not even my friend who backed me on that cattle auction, and the drive afterward, has that kind of dough."

"Fifty thousand dollars is the price I am asking, señor," said Don Sebastian, "for the release of the four people I have in my custody."

Roscoe, Holliday, and Feather were grouped together nearby, whispering among themselves while the two men talked. Finally, Roscoe broke away from the little gathering and turned to Charley.

"C.A.?" said Roscoe, then he whispered, "Holliday, Feather, and me can get you all the ransom money you need."

"Quit being silly, Roscoe," said Charley. "This is serious business we're talking about here."

"I mean it, Charley," Roscoe said again. "If the Don will excuse us for a minute . . ."

Don Sebastian nodded. Charley turned and joined Roscoe, Holliday, and Feather. They all leaned in for a whispered discussion. Finally . . .

"And you're sure of that," said Charley.

Roscoe answered, "Cross my heart an' hope ta die, it's the God's truth."

"And I'll swear to it on a stack a' Bibles," said Holliday.

Feather didn't seem to be as eager as the others, but he eventually agreed.

"It's true, Boss. We're all tellin' you the truth."

Charley slowly turned back to the Don.

"Give me two days and I'll have your ransom for you."

Don Sebastian's mouth grew into a large smile.

"Only the four of you will go," said the Don. "I will return to you your weapons and send some of my guards with you."

"No guards, Don Sebastian," said Charley. "Release the four of us, and we'll have your ransom back here in two days, just as I've said I would."

The Don pondered for a moment, then he turned to his captain of the guard.

"Andrés," he said, "give these four men their weapons . . . and bring them their horses."

Andrés shouted out some orders in Spanish, and they were followed out immediately. Rifles and pistols were returned to Charley, Roscoe, Holliday, and Feather. At the same time, two other guards brought them their horses.

All four of them mounted. Charley turned to those remaining members of the outfit.

"You'll be safe here," he told them. "We will only be gone two days at the most."

He turned back to the Don.

"And, Don Sebastian," he added, "we'll be needing the burro . . . plus that two-wheel cart Colonel Armendariz inherited when he took the Indian, his wife, and my grandson into custody."

He turned to the colonel.

"Do you think you can get along without it?"

The Don pointed across the yard to where the burro belonging to the sergeant and Mitch Pennell was tied beside the cart.

"Captain," said the Don, "would you please hitch the burro to the cart and bring them over here?"

Again, the captain called out an order in Spanish. Within moments, the rope attached to the burro and cart were handed over to Feather.

"Thank you, Don Sebastian," said Charley. "As I said, we will be back with the ransom in two days."

"If not in two days," said the Don, "these others will become my permanent prisoners."

"Two days it is," said Charley, so the other members of the outfit could hear him. Roscoe borrowed Henry Ellis's horse, then he, Charley, Holliday, and Feather reined around and headed for the open country as the sun began to rise.

Chapter Twenty-two

They had been away from the *hacienda* for less than three hours. The horses had just started climbing a steep embankment, where the road was leading them, when a man's Spanish-accented voice called out in broken English from somewhere close by.

"*Alto!* . . . Stop where you are, *amigos*," the voice said. "Stop, and throw down your weapons."

Roscoe and Feather made moves indicating they were about to follow the man's order, but Charley motioned for them not to be so hasty.

Charley's right hand slowly dropped down to retrieve his Walker Colt, which was sticking out of his boot top.

"Who are you?" he yelled. "And what do you want from us?"

He was met by silence.

Charley indicated to the others to go ahead and draw their weapons.

In moments, Charley and his friends could hear horses' hooves on shale, then eight Mexican bandits rode down from their hiding place behind a rocky formation to the left of them.

The Mexican leading this band of cutthroats was none other than Pedro Jose Bedoya, the same bandit who'd led Elisabeth's welcoming committee several days earlier. Charley recognized the man from the detailed description Elisabeth had given him, right down to the red neckerchief he wore.

All of them had their weapons drawn. In order to make it even, Charley motioned for his friends to raise their guns as well.

The two factions eventually met in the road's center—a flat area that could accommodate all the horses. As they faced off, Bedoya spurred out a little until he was facing Charley. Their horses' noses were almost touching.

Bedoya waved his pistol.

"I think . . . that I have ordered you to throw down your weapons," said the bandit leader.

Charley waved his Walker Colt, imitating the Mexican.

"I think," Charley began, "that throwing down our weapons might just get us killed. No, sir," he continued. "Since we already have our guns aimed at you and your men, throwing down our weapons won't happen any time soon, as far as I'm concerned. Now, what do you want from us?" Charley asked.

"We were most interested in what is in the little cart being pulled by the burro," said Bedoya. "Maybe you people are gold prospectors? No? Or maybe you are delivering a payroll to one of the mines?"

"We are prospectors, señor," said Charley, "but our cart has yet to be filled. You have come across us before we have had the chance to do any mining. Sorry," he added.

"Then you should not mind if we look into that cart," said Bedoya.

"Be my guest," answered Charley.

Bedoya motioned for one of his men to check it out.

"Bernardo," he said.

The man called Bernardo rode over and dismounted. He raised the lid on the cart and revealed it to be empty.

"Not even supplies for your stay in my country?" asked the bandit leader.

"All the supplies we need we carry on our horses . . . in our saddlebags."

"For some reason, señor, I do not believe you," said Bedoya. "But you have shown us that you have no gold, so we are all lucky that no bullets have been fired."

"Now, that's a fact," said Charley. "Why don't you and your men go back to where you came from, and me and my men will continue on our way . . . no bullets exchanged by either of us. Is that agreeable to you, señor?"

"*Sí* . . . I agree," answered Bedoya.

With all guns still cocked and aimed, both parties began reining their horses back, until there was a good separation between the two parties. Finally, Bedoya turned his animal around and signaled for his men to follow. The bandits scrambled back up the incline, then disappeared into the sparse vegetation behind some closer rock formations.

Since they were approaching from a different direction than they had come the first time, it took Roscoe, Holliday, and Feather a little longer to recognize the familiar landmarks they had hoped would help them locate the way to the cave.

They arrived at the cavern's entrance at dusk, just as the sun was going down—and just in time to set up a little campsite inside in almost the same spot the three of them had camped on their initial visit.

The threesome was able to show Charley the findings by torchlight—the Spanish soldier's body, his helmet, and after some digging, the iron box containing the gold and the other treasures it held within.

Charley couldn't help showing wonderment at the sparkling collection.

"So, what were you boys going to do with all of this if Don Sebastian hadn't asked us for a ransom?" he wanted to know.

"Well," answered Feather, "I recollect we was plannin' on comin' back fer it all after we got home ta Texas. We figured there was no use tellin' anyone about it if we wasn't close enough ta lay claim to, or protect, the stuff from the kind of men who are willin' ta kill fer things like gold treasure boxes."

"Well, at least you know now that it isn't only poor bandits who are willing to kill for treasure like this," said Charley. "Wealthy bandits will murder for it, too."

"At first, one of us was goin' ta stay with it until the others got back," said Holliday. "But the more we thought on it, the more we realized that it might be months, let alone years, before we could all get together ta haul it all out."

"Roscoe," said Charley, "it isn't like you not to tell me about something like this."

"Sorry, C.A.," said Roscoe, "but somethin' this big just had ta be kept secret . . ."

"I know, I understand," said Charley.

"I woulda told you once we were back across the border," Roscoe added. "Honest I would. But it wasn't gonna do nobody any good if we could never come back here . . . the three of us, I mean."

"Well," said Charley, "we best go ahead and bring the cart over so we can start loading 'er up."

"Yes, Boss," said Feather.

Feather, Holliday, and Roscoe ran to retrieve the burro

and cart—they led the animal over to where Charley was still standing beside the open iron box.

"All right," said Charley, "let's fill 'er up."

All four of them began shoveling the gold—coins, chalices, and jewelry—with their bare hands, from the iron box into the cart.

When they were finished doing that little chore, they backed away to admire their handiwork.

"What about him?" asked Holliday, pointing to the dead Spaniard.

Charley took another look at the mummified body and the armor, which half covered the crumbling bones.

"We'll leave him here," he told them. "We may be a lot of things, but we ain't grave robbers. And that's a fact."

He started walking over to where their horses were tied off. The others followed, with Feather leading the burro and cart.

"We can either head back now," said Charley, "or we can grab a few hours of shut-eye and leave later on toward morning. What'll it be, boys?"

They chose the two hours of rest.

A short time later, when they were all sitting around the campfire chewing on jerky and drinking coffee, Holliday had a question for Charley.

"The load we got in that cart sure looks like it'd trade out fer a lot more'n fifty thousand American dollars, Charley."

"Probably would," said the ex-Ranger. "But I'd rather we take more with us than not enough. We want to make Don Sebastian happy, don't we?"

"Yes, Boss," said Feather.

"You always seem ta know what yer' doin', C.A.," said Roscoe, "that's fer sure."

"Maybe we oughta cover it up with somethin'," said Feather. "If we happen ta pass someone on the trail back to the *hacienda*, and they see what we got, it could be all over fer all of us. Especially if those bandits happen ta show up again."

"If we meet up with anyone on the trail that's got the grit to try and take it from us, I welcome them to try," said Charley, pulling his Walker Colt out of his boot and spinning the cylinder. He cocked, then reset, the hammer before snapping the gate closed. "If every one of us just keeps their eyes open," he continued, "there ain't going to be no one trying to take this gold from us."

"Hey, C.A.?" said Roscoe, "if it does turn out that the gold is worth more than the amount the Don is askin' fer in ransom, do you think he'll let us keep the change?"

After they all had a good laugh, Charley said, "Go to sleep, Roscoe. Wake us all up in four hours, will you?"

Charley woke up in two hours. The campfire's flames were much lower, the still-glowing embers cast a much weaker light throughout the cavern. The others were snoring soundly beside him.

He could also hear the murmuring of Spanish-speaking voices.

He opened his eyes very slowly. Through crossed lashes he saw the bobbing of many *sombreros* in the flickering reflection of the fire—it was the gang of Mexican bandits they had encountered on the road earlier. They were also silhouetted by the glow of the moon outside the cavern. And it appeared their number had grown in size.

Charley counted twelve this time.

Charley knew that one move, one tiny word to the others, could get them all killed. Even so, his right hand slowly crept down to the butt of his Walker Colt that was protruding from the top of his boot. He slowly drew the large revolver, then he brought it up to his chest, where his bedroll was covering him up to the neck.

That number of men, so close by, confused him. *They must have followed us from where we parted back up the trail*, he thought. He felt lucky, though. In spite of the fact the bandits had found the cavern, his thought continued: *What if these men were* federales, *instead, hoping to capture someone doing something illegal? Or they could have been another band of Mexicans, Armendariz's gang, perhaps, who happened to stumble upon the cave by seeing the fire's light coming from inside, and were now exploring.*

Feather, sleeping comfortably on Charley's left side, passed some gas, then he turned onto his back where he immediately began to snore again.

Every single bandit nearby stood completely still, waiting for the smallish man to awaken. When he didn't, when he just kept right on snoring, the Mexicans let out a communal sigh of relief.

Roscoe, sleeping to Charley's right, appeared to have been disturbed by the noises Feather was making. But in no time, he was breathing in his customary way, as if nothing had happened.

"Bernardo," Bedoya called out in a whisper.

Within moments, Bedoya was joined by the one answering to the name Bernardo.

"*Sí, jefe,*" said Bernardo. "What is it you wish?"

"If the Lord is with us," said Bedoya, "we will not have

to wake these *Americanos.* We will search in their saddle-bags for money and other things of value, and when we are finished, we will be on our way."

"Are you not afraid of these *gringos*?" said Bernardo. "There could be more of them, you know."

"I am not afraid, Bernardo," said Bedoya. "But I recently came across an American—a woman—on the trail, who was very cunning. She presented herself as one thing but became another. And before I realized it, I had lost my favorite horse and two of my best men because of that woman. I do not wish for the same kind of confrontation with these *Americanos* . . . so we must do what we have to do, as quickly as we can, and be back on our journey again, before they know what has happened."

"*Sí*," said Bernardo. "I will tell the men."

It's a damn shame, thought Charley as he continued to lay low in his bedroll, watching the gang members as they rummaged through everyone's saddlebags. *Just a shame that I can't warn the others without having every single one of these cutthroats turn on us, followed by a hail of Mexican bullets.*"

So he had to watch—just lay there and watch—while they eventually spotted the burro and the two-wheeled cart.

When it was discovered there was gold inside, word of the finding was spread through excited whispers to avoid waking the Americans.

The bandits spent another few minutes searching the rest of the cave, with one of them crossing himself rapidly when he came across the body of the ancient Spaniard lying beside Feather's recently reopened excavation.

The gang members finally gave up. They left the cave, mounted their horses outside, and awaited the command from Bedoya to ride away from the cavern.

Charley continued to watch silently while one of the

bandidos rode his horse back into the cavern, then over to the burro. He untied the rope, then led the animal, the cart, and the gold it was carrying out of the cave. He joined the others.

Bedoya and the men rode away, disappearing into the mist of the creeping dawn.

Charley didn't wait for the others to wake up naturally; he grabbed his canteen and walked up and down the row of bedrolls, splashing water onto everyone's face.

Within moments, all three of them were awake and sputtering like fish out of water.

"Aw, geez," said Holliday.

"Cut it out, will ya, Boss?" shrieked Feather.

"Leave me alone, damnit, I'm tryin' ta sleep," shouted Roscoe.

"Get your lazy rear ends up, you slackers," yelled Charley. "The gold is gone. Those bandits stole it right out from under our noses."

Charley explained it all to the others over jerky and coffee, telling them that there was absolutely no way to have let them know what was going on without arousing the suspicions of the intruders.

"Well, what're we waitin' around here fer, if ya know which way they went?" said Feather.

"Oh, they'll be back," said Charley. All we have to do is stay right here where we are and get ready for a fight . . . then we just wait for them to come back."

"Fer heaven's sake, Mr. Sunday," said Holliday, "they got our gold. Why on earth would they want to come back here again?"

"Because after you yahoos killed off them wine bottles we found last night, and either dozed off or passed out, I took it upon myself to lighten that load of gold a mite, then I filled it back up with something to take up the empty space. After that, I put a single layer of gold on top of it all so it'd look like the whole cart was still filled with treasure."

"So, what makes ya think those bandits'll even look in the cart again before they get to wherever they're goin'?" said Feather.

"Because there's not one man alive I know of who wouldn't have the greedy urge to run his fingers through a chest full of Spanish gold treasure if he got the chance. These guys aren't any different than the rest of us . . . and that's a fact."

Out on the trail, Bedoya was doing just that. He had halted his column of men and ridden back to where the burro and cart were located at the tail end.

He dismounted, then he dropped to his knees, throwing back the oilskin cover. Next, he was digging his hands into the treasure trove.

A look of complete disgust crossed the bandit leader's face.

He slowly pulled his hands and arms out of the cart to reveal that they were covered in slushy, green, watery, horse manure—the substance Charley had used to replace the gold he had removed from the cart.

Don Roberto and his *vaqueros* rode over the summit of a slight hill and were confronted by the abandoned Mexican army fort in the near distance. The Don raised his hand to stop his troops, while Luis Hernandez was sent on ahead to scout.

They waited about fifteen or twenty minutes after the ranch foreman had entered the gates of the fort. The Don was about to give the order for the rest of them to proceed with caution, when Luis appeared, riding out of the gate, then turning and galloping back toward the group. He carried something in his right hand.

As he slowed his horse and reined up in front of Don Roberto and the others, he held up the object he'd been carrying. It was a hand-scribbled sign that read

XXX

POISON WATER

DO NOT DRINK

It was signed, Charles Abner Sunday.

"When I first entered the fort," said Luis in Spanish, "I ignored this warning sign in my haste to search every inch inside . . ." He doubled over in pain, yet he continued. "It was only when I was leaving . . . that I took the time to read this warning. I do not understand English that good, but I know the word poison. By then, it was too late . . ." He doubled over again, with even more pain. "I had already taken several swallows from a ladle in a bucket I had come across in there. So, I knew that . . . by then, I was . . . a dead man."

With that, he fell forward, tumbling from his saddle.

The Don caught the sign before it, too, fell.

"No one drink any water in or near this fort," he ordered. He dismounted and knelt beside Luis. Two other men were already at the man's side. They both gave the Don somber looks.

"He is dead," said one of the men.

Everyone present removed their hats, then crossed themselves.

"Bury him," said the Don. "Save his clothing and his Saint Christopher for his wife and family."

The two men picked up the body and moved it to the side of the road. Four others joined them with small shovels and began digging a grave, while another began to unclasp the chain around his neck.

The Don stood there quietly, contemplating the signature on the sign.

"Charles Abner Sunday," he mumbled to himself. "From where do I recognize that name?"

One of his older *vaqueros* nudged his horse closer to the Don.

"What is it, Ernesto?" said Don Roberto.

The one called Ernesto dismounted, facing his employer. He removed his hat, revealing a full head of white hair.

"I have meet this man, Charles Abner Sunday . . . it was a long time ago," said Ernesto. "When I was employed at a cattle ranch across the river. At that time, this Charles Abner Sunday was a Texas Ranger. A man known to everyone for his bravery and courage."

"Of course," said Don Roberto with a sigh of relief. "He is the father of the woman who was abducted . . . the wife of Kent Pritchard, who was coming to visit me. I remember her husband telling me about Señor Sunday when he was here in Mexico a few years ago. Do you think this Charles Abner Sunday is here in Mexico, Ernesto? Do you think it is Charles Sunday who we have been following?"

"Don Roberto," said Ernesto, "I not only think he is here . . . I think he has brought people with him to assist him in his search for his daughter."

"And I think we should not waste any more time standing around talking," said the Don. "This Charles Abner Sunday might just need our assistance."

"What did I tell you?" said Charley. "They came back."

He was standing behind a large boulder near the front of the cave and was speaking gently into Roscoe's ear.

The two of them were positioned to the right, inside the cavern's mouth. Holliday and Feather had split up—with Holliday on his belly behind a low, half-buried boulder in the cave's center, and Feather, perched on a protected ledge high above, about halfway up the left wall of the cave's interior.

All of them were armed with both pistol and rifle to choose from during the expected exchange of gunfire. Presently, they all held their Winchesters at the ready.

Charley's warning had made them aware of just how close the altercation was to happening.

Feather slid a few more cartridges into his rifle. With a swift single jerk on the lever, he sent the first projectile into its position in front of the rifle's firing pin. Then he set the weapon aside and drew his Texas Ranger–issue Walker Colt, checking the six loads inside the chambers. He spun the cylinder, then closed the gate.

Holliday did the same with his saddle gun, then he rolled onto his back, tucking the rifle under his left arm while he drew his right-hand pistol, opened the gate, rolled the cylinder, and checked the chambers. After that, he reversed the rifle to his right arm, then checked his left-hand six-shooter. A quick roll back onto his belly, and he was ready for bear.

Like Charley, both Roscoe and Feather were using their Texas Ranger–issue revolvers—Walker Colts. Although the large revolvers only fired six hand-packed conical bullets before they had to be reloaded again, Charley, Roscoe, and Feather had always been known to hit their mark with every pull of the trigger. They were such expert pistol shots, that most often, reloading during a fight was never needed.

Bedoya appeared, leading his men as close to the cavern's giant entrance as he could.

He had just given them the dismount order, when all hell broke loose, coming from the cave's opening. Flaming bullets rained down on the bandit gang, with every single, spinning piece of hot lead burrowing into human flesh. Several *bandidos* got off some return fire, but no one they were aiming at was hit.

When the fusillade subsided, Bedoya twirled his *sombrero* in the air—a signal to all his remaining followers to retreat until they could find adequate cover.

That was when Charley called for the second curtain of fire to be launched. The four Americans blasted away with their Winchesters, catching even more bandits in the same angles of cross fire as they had in the first volley.

By then, Bedoya and some of the remaining gang members were scurrying from one place to another in complete confusion. Eventually they were able to shoot back from the surrounding area where they had found some natural defenses to shield themselves.

Most of the Mexicans took pride in their marksmanship, but before they could find a target, swirling lead shapes drilled into their skulls and torsos.

By then Charley and his men had narrowed the number of bandits down to Bedoya and two others. The one called Bernardo was still in charge of the burro and the two-wheeled cart.

Feather took his chance and fired—his bullet caught the man directly between the eyes. Bernardo dropped immediately to the ground, leaving the dangling rope hanging loose from one of the burro's harness rings.

Holliday's rifle had run out of ammunition, so he'd switched to his matching six-guns. As one of the final gang members stood up and started running toward a loose horse, the old Wild West showman stepped out into the open and fired one gun after the other, until the running man was cut down in his tracks.

Now there was only one of the bandits left—Bedoya—and he wanted no more.

He held up a rifle with a piece of white material tied to the barrel. After several waves of the makeshift surrender flag, Bedoya stood up so his adversaries could see that he was unarmed and giving up.

Charley stepped out from behind the boulder he had been using as cover. He motioned with his gun for Bedoya to come forward.

The Mexican gang leader did. Following Charley's orders, he dropped his weapons and kicked them out of the way. He continued walking toward Charley with a face filled with confusion.

"You have killed all of my *compadres*," he said softly as he moved toward the cave's entrance. "And I could have prevented it myself. Why?"

He dropped to his knees and looked up to the sky.

"Why," he continued, "why did I not give the order to kill every one of these *gringos* last night when they were sleeping?"

"That wouldn't have saved you, *amigo*," said Charley. "Because one of us was awake . . . me," he said. "And I had this old Walker Colt aimed directly at your *huevos* . . . just in case you did give your men that order."

* * *

Charley, Roscoe, Feather, and Holliday rode through the *hacienda* gates with Bedoya behind them on his horse. His neck was in a noose with the other end tied to Charley's saddle horn. His hands were bound tightly behind him.

Another rope had been looped around Bedoya's belt several times and was helping him lead the burro and the two-wheeled cart it pulled.

There was an obvious strain on the wheels of the tiny cart, indicating to all that it carried a very heavy load.

Don Sebastian had received word from one of his outriders that the four Texans were returning. He had time to prepare himself and was now standing in his carriage with Armendariz at his side, inside the gates. Andrés, his captain of the guard, had also moved the members of the outfit that Charley had left behind inside the gates.

"Welcome back, Señor Sunday," said the Don. "I see that in addition to whatever ransom money you have brought for me, you also bring me someone I have not seen in many years."

He indicated Bedoya at the end of the rope.

The Don turned to Andrés, his captain of the guard.

"Untie Señor Bedoya and bring him to me at once," he said.

Andrés and several of the guard began moving toward Bedoya.

Charley immediately drew the Walker Colt from his boot top.

When he did, there was the sound of many rifles being cocked at the same moment.

"No, Mr. Sunday," said Don Sebastian. "You will please hand over your pistol to Andrés, my captain of the guard. And the others . . . they will also please give their weapons back to Andrés."

Charley nodded to Roscoe, Holliday, and Feather.

"Do what the man says, gentlemen," he said.

Andrés and three guards stepped forward. The Texans turned over their revolvers and rifles.

"Thank you, Mr. Sunday," said Don Sebastian, nodding to Charley, then leaning closer to face him. "I expected you much sooner."

"Sooner?" Roscoe whispered to Charley. "I thought he gave us two days."

"He did," said Charley.

The ex–Texas Ranger turned a very sober face to Don Sebastian.

"You gave us two days to bring the ransom . . . and we're here to deliver it even sooner than that."

"I gave you one day," said Don Sebastian with a look just as restrained as Charley's.

The members of the outfit began arguing back and forth until Charley stopped them all with a raised hand.

His eyes were still glued to the Don.

"You told us two days, Don Sebastian," said Charley. "And that's a fact. There's your ransom, in the cart . . ."

He pointed to the two-wheeled cart nearby.

". . . Not a boy's ransom," he went on, "but a king's ransom. There is your blood money, Don Sebastian . . . in gold, not American dollars. It's all worth the same . . . even more."

The Don motioned for Andrés to check out the contents of the cart.

The captain walked over to the cart and threw back its wool *poncho* cover. He lifted the lid to reveal the entire Spanish treasure—the glittering gold threw off brilliant reflections in every direction.

Eyes lit up all around.

"Bring me a coin," said the Don.

Andrés picked up one of the gold coins, took it over to his employer, and handed it to him.

Don Sebastian gave the coin the usual test by biting on its edge. The expression on his face showed he believed the coinage to be authentic.

"Are you satisfied, Don Sebastian?" said Charley, dismounting, then moving over to the two-wheeled cart with its golden shimmer.

"Very satisfied," said Don Sebastian. "But now that you have missed the deadline, it can only be a wonderful gift I must always be grateful to you for bringing to me."

"C'mon, Don Sebastian. Quit pulling my leg," said Charley.

The Don drew in a large breath of air and expelled it.

"I am not, as you say, pulling your legs, Señor Sunday. I am dead serious about what I am telling you. This gold now belongs to me . . . as do the boy and the Indian who are still in hiding on my property, along with the boy's mother and father. You may call it a penalty for your being a day late with the ransom."

"So, you now know it's Rod Lightfoot who is missing from the group," said Charley.

"With thanks to my friend, Colonel Armendariz, who reminded me that the Indian was not with his wife as he always is. Now, since you and your friends are visitors to my country, I would like to let you all go back to the United States unharmed.

"I will return your weapons to you after my men have escorted you back to the border. All you have to do in return is to promise me that you will stay on your side of the river from now on. Simple, no?" he added.

"Simple, yes," said Charley. "But not as simple as you think it'll be."

Fuerte stepped in beside Charley. He looked up at Don Sebastian, who was still standing in the carriage.

"Señor Sunday and his friends will go, Don Sebastian."

Charley nudged him hard, then he spoke under his breath.

"No one's going to send me and my outfit running back home to Texas with our tails between our legs, Roca. Oh no . . . I won't have that."

Fuerte raised his eyebrows to Charley, trying to make a point as he whispered to his friend.

"There are still no odds in our favor at this time, *mi amigo*. If we stay here and argue with the Don, Señor Charley, it will prove nothing. We have no weapons. We are outnumbered. We must do what he tells us to do."

Charley started to open his mouth to say something.

Fuerte cut him off.

"You must trust me, Señor Charley. You are in my country now . . . I know how things work here in Mexico."

"But I—" said Charley, and then in a whisper to Fuerte, "whatever you say, Roca. Under the circumstances I find that I must go along with whatever you say."

Charley looked back to the Don.

"All right," he said. "I will promise you, Don Sebastian. When your men escort us to the border, I assure you we will not return . . . you have my word on that."

Don Sebastian turned to Armendariz.

"If you agree, Colonel, we will soon be rid of these thorns in our side."

"I agree," said Armendariz.

"All right," said the Don, "send some of your men to get their horses."

He turned back to Charley.

"Some of my guards, along with the colonel and his men, will accompany you to the border. Like I said before, once you are there, your weapons will be returned to you."

* * *

Betty Jean and Rod continued to wait inside the creek house. Like Henry Ellis, they had not slept in two days.

Henry Ellis had slipped out into the courtyard earlier. He had spotted yet another building he thought could be the *hacienda*'s dispensary. He took a roundabout way of getting there because of the presence of more guards than usual in the area.

Once he reached the side of the building he hoped was the hospital, Henry Ellis stood on a rock so he could peer into a window.

By doing so, he found that it was indeed the hospital he had been searching for. There were only a few patients on the cots inside, and the boy figured they must either be *hacienda* workers or other guards who had been injured, or come down sick. His eyes searched the large room for signs of doctors and nurses, but he only saw one person in a white coat—it was being worn by a man sitting at a desk in a small office annex at the front of the building.

Henry Ellis took a better look, squeezing his eyelids together to improve his focus. By doing this, he was able to see that there was another man sitting across the desk from the man wearing the white coat. The second man wore a brown suit—an American-tailored suit. And when the boy was finally able to get a better look at the second man's face, he was relieved to find that the man in the suit was his father.

Now, to get you out of here, Father, Henry Ellis thought to himself. He found a side entrance that would take him inside. Once there, he began to make his way carefully toward the front of the building.

A few members of Armendariz's gang, along with six guards belonging to Don Sebastian, were chosen to get the

Texans their horses. When they returned, the outfit was ordered to mount up.

Dice, along with the other three men's horses, was now tied off to a hitching post. Charley swung onto Dice's back. Roscoe headed toward the chuckwagon, while Feather and Holliday were mounting up.

Charley waited in his saddle while the rest of the outfit searched for their mounts.

"Señor Fuerte," Don Sebastian called out to Roca, "you will not be going with them . . . you will remain as my guest at the *hacienda*. Please come over here."

Fuerte led his horse over to the carriage where he was met by two guards—one was pointing a rifle at him.

"Señor Fuerte," said the Don, "since you are a citizen of Mexico, I will make it my business to see that you are delivered to the proper authorities."

"I am in no position to argue, Don Sebastian," said Fuerte. "I will go wherever you wish for me to go."

The two guards turned Fuerte around, making him face the Don. They continued to hold his arms down at his sides.

Don Sebastian pulled a pistol from his sash, aiming it at Fuerte.

"Many years ago," said the Don, "when I was a much younger man . . . and you were leading the *Rurales* in this part of the country, you arrested me and some of my *compadres* for a robbery we did not commit. I am still grateful to this day that the judge at my trial understood that my friends and I had nothing to do with that robbery, and set us free. But still, on the day of my release, I made a vow . . . to find and kill the man who set me up to be arrested for a crime I did not commit."

With that, he turned slightly and pulled the trigger.

Don Sebastian's bullet caught Bedoya in the solar plexus, knocking the unsuspecting bandit leader back a few feet until he was stopped by the rear end of a guard's horse. And with a look of genuine surprise showing on his countenance, he slowly fell forward, facedown in the dirt.

An unexpected sigh of relief escaped from Elisabeth's lips.

Henry Ellis was walking down an aisle between the dispensary's beds toward the office annex at the front of the building when he heard the shot. It was only one shot, so he knew immediately that a battle hadn't started. He just kept on walking.

On occasion, he would have to slow down and quietly tiptoe when passing a bed that contained a sleeping patient. When he had gotten a little closer, he would speed up again, keeping his eyes on his objective—the office annex and the two men inside—still some distance down the aisle in front of him.

When he was about fifteen feet away, he dropped down to his hands and knees and crawled the remaining distance.

He had to be as quiet as he could to avoid making any sounds that might echo in the high-ceilinged room.

When he reached the door to the office annex he could hear a heavily accented voice, plus his father's voice, in deep conversation.

"As I told you before," said Kent, Henry Ellis's father, "I feel much better now. I would like very much to go back to be with my wife . . . I am more than certain she is very worried about me by now."

"Relax, Señor Pritchard," said the man. "You are in the right place for someone with your illness."

"I've told you many times that I feel just fine now," said Kent. "It was only this morning when I felt somewhat under the weather. Please send me back to my wife, sir. I beg of you with all I have in me."

"Sick or not sick," said the man, "the Don wants you here . . . and it is here you will stay. Even if I must order that you be restrained and sedated . . . by force, if that is necessary."

"You're not going to do anything to hurt my father, mister."

It was Henry Ellis with the derringer in his hand pointed at the man in the white coat.

His father had a very surprised look on his face.

"Henry Ellis," he said. "How did you get here? We thought you were—"

"I'm alive, Father," said the boy. "Look at me. Take my hand if you want, feel me, but I'm very much alive. Now," he said to his father, "I need a room with a lock and no windows for this other gentleman."

Rod ducked back farther into the shadows of the creek house interior, taking Betty Jean with him. He had heard Spanish-speaking voices and they seemed to be getting closer.

"Has anyone checked the building over the creek?" said one of the voices in Spanish.

"We searched that structure thoroughly, my captain," said the voice again in Spanish.

"And you found nothing?"

"*Si*, my captain . . . we found nothing."

"We must still search the building once again," said Andrés in Spanish. "We must go back inside and—"

He stopped speaking as another guard on horseback rode up and reined to a stop.

"Captain," said the rider, "your presence is required at the dispensary immediately. And bring the men you have with you. They may be needed."

Both Betty Jean and Rod breathed easier as the guards' footsteps faded into the distance.

"That was a close one," said Betty Jean.

Rod nodded.

Suddenly there was the sound of splashing water. Rod and Betty Jean turned just as Henry Ellis and his father entered the creek house from the rear of the structure.

"Oh, my God . . ." said Betty Jean, "it's you, Kent . . . you're safe."

The two fell into each other's arms and held one another very close for a time.

"I'm glad to see that you found him," said Rod.

He patted Henry Ellis on the back.

"Thank you, son," said Kent.

"You were wonderful, Henry Ellis," added his mother.

"I did it, Rod," said the boy. "I saved my mother *and* my father . . . plus, I didn't have to shoot anybody."

He showed Rod the derringer Charley had given him.

"Put that away, Henry Ellis," said Rod. "Hide it on yourself where they will never think of looking if they capture you again."

"Yes, sir, Rod," said the boy.

He turned away from them and tucked the tiny gun somewhere beneath the folds of his clothing. He turned back around, smiling.

In seconds the smile turned to one of complete surprise. Standing behind Rod and his parents were Andrés, the captain of the guard, and five of his *hacienda* sentries. Their weapons were pointed at the group.

"Hand over the gun," the captain said to Rod. "Or drop it. Either way, it doesn't matter to me. You are all under arrest."

* * *

An hour later, a well-guarded assemblage, which included every member of the outfit, was lingering in the *hacienda* courtyard where they had been ordered to wait.

After several moments, Andrés marched over to the Don's carriage. Don Sebastian leaned down so the man could whisper in his ear. When the captain had finished speaking, Don Sebastian sent him back to where he had come from.

"I am afraid your plans have changed slightly, Señor Sunday," said the Don. "I have been told that your Indian comrade . . . including the boy and his parents . . . those who have been evading my guards, have been arrested. They are being brought here as we speak."

Charley and the rest of the outfit were united with Henry Ellis, Betty Jean, Kent, and Rod, who could only try to smile as Kelly ran to him.

After consoling Henry Ellis, his daughter, and clapping her husband on the back, Charley moved to the front of the group, where he stood calmly and waited as the carriage containing Don Sebastian was brought around in front of him and stopped. Colonel Armendariz, now astride his horse, was right beside the Don's coach.

Don Sebastian stood up in the carriage. He spoke for all to hear. He was very polite.

"My American friends," he began. "It is unfortunate that we have all had to meet under such dreadful circumstances. My initial intention was to have Mr. and Mrs. Pritchard and their son delivered to me by Colonel Armendariz. But when the colonel's men allowed the boy to get away from them, my entire plan had to be changed. And when the boy brought you, Mr. Sunday, and the rest of these interesting people into my country, for no other reason than to rescue the boy's parents, I had to change my plan once again.

"But now that I have the boy, I no longer need the parents . . . plus I no longer need the Indian . . . or you, Mr. Sunday, or the rest of your friends.

"So, now your plan is to kill us all, I reckon," said Charley. "Is that correct?"

"Oh, no, no, no," said Don Sebastian. "On the contrary. Since I have what I need, and because I'm such a fine fellow, I am still going to have my men escort the remainder of you back to the border where your weapons will be returned to you . . . again . . . if only you make to me one very large guarantee."

"And that would be?" asked Charley.

"The promise is the same as I asked of you before . . . that you and your friends agree to stay out of my country and never cross the Río Bravo del Norte into Mexico, ever again."

"Well, sir," said Charley, "I don't rightly know if I could keep a promise like that."

"You will if you ever want to see your grandson again," said the Don.

Kelly, nearby, tugged on Charley's sleeve.

"In that case," said Charley, without blinking an eye, "I'll make you that promise . . . and speaking for the others, I'll promise for them, too."

The boy's parents began to protest.

"Betty Jean, Kent," said Charley, "I'm doing the dickering with this gentleman. You two just hush for now."

"I knew you would see it my way, Señor Sunday," said the Don, "once you knew what the consequences could be."

"So my daughter and her husband can go back with us?" asked Charley. "Is that true?"

"It is only the boy that I want," said Don Sebastian. "It

is only the boy I have always wanted. You may have his parents."

"And my friend, Señor Fuerte?" said Charley.

"I have been told that Señor Fuerte killed several of Colonel Armendariz's best gunmen. You will need to ask the colonel about Roca Fuerte."

Armendariz leaned forward in his saddle.

"I will agree to let Señor Fuerte go with the rest of them . . . *if* Señor Fuerte guarantees me that he will stay on the other side of the Río Bravo like the others."

Charley whistled to get his friend's attention, then he motioned for Roca to join them. Fuerte pulled away from the guards that were still restraining him just as soon as Don Sebastian nodded for them to let him go. Fuerte walked back across the open area and eventually found his place beside Charley.

"Thank you, my friend," Fuerte whispered when he was finally standing at Charley's side.

One of the guards brought Fuerte his horse, and he mounted.

"Well, sir," Charley said to Don Sebastian, "you have my grandson . . . and I have everyone else. That ain't such a bad deal.

"Isn't it about time the colonel's men and your guards escorted us back to Texas?"

Both parents, plus several members of the outfit, threw him puzzled looks.

Charley ignored them. He threw a look to Henry Ellis, who had been standing beside the Don in the carriage. Charley winked at the boy before turning back to the Don.

"Might I have a minute with my grandson?" he asked.

"I can see no harm in that," answered Don Sebastian.

Charley dismounted, then he moved in beside the coach. When he was facing Henry Ellis, the boy knelt down to Charley's eye level.

Henry Ellis wouldn't take his eyes off Charley. Finally the old rancher reached over and pulled the boy to him. As the two appeared to be embracing, Charley whispered into the boy's ear.

"No matter what I've told the Don," he said softly, "we will come back for you."

Tears began to form around the edges of Henry Ellis's eyes.

"I know you will, Grampa," he said.

"Just have faith," added Charley.

They pulled away from one another, with the boy giving his grandfather a slight nod.

Betty Jean, Kent, and the others looked on as Charley returned to his horse and remounted. Charley had to wipe away a tear of his own, but before anyone saw him do that, he whirled Dice around and called back to the rest of the outfit.

"C'mon," he yelled. "Everyone mount up who isn't already . . . we're going back to Texas."

Roscoe, behind the lines of the chuckwagon mules, watched Charley, waiting for his command for them all to move out.

The dismounted members of the outfit found their horses—along with Rod. The parents climbed aboard the chuckwagon beside Roscoe while Sergeant Stone gathered up the extra horses.

Henry Ellis called out.

"Miss Kelly, Grampa . . ."

They both turned around.

He was pointing to the saddlebags on Kelly's horse.

"Take care of my puppy . . . Take care of Buster Number Two."

Charley and Kelly nodded. She reached into her saddlebag and removed the pup, holding it up so the boy could see it.

"Thank you, Miss Kelly . . . I mean, Mrs. Lightfoot," said Henry Ellis.

"I'll take real good care of him for you, Henry Ellis," said Kelly.

Feather, who was nearby, nudged his horse in next to her. He reached over to pet the puppy. He used their closeness to relay a message to Kelly.

"Henry Ellis's grandpa ain't gonna let anything happen to his grandson, believe me," he whispered.

"I know that," said Kelly. "Please let his mother know if you get the chance."

Andrés raised his hand, then gave the signal for everyone to move out.

The heavy gates were opened for them, and everyone urged their horses through the wide opening.

Henry Ellis brushed the hands of Don Sebastian away from his shoulders, took a step forward, then stood silently in the carriage, watching them all depart.

Five members of the group turned their heads for a final look back at Henry Ellis—they were Charley, Betty Jean, Kent, Rod, and Kelly, who was still holding the puppy in her arms.

Henry Ellis smiled at the sight.

The gate was eventually closed behind the riders.

Don Sebastian turned to the boy.

"All right, Chico," he said, "you are now in my safekeeping. I expect you to cooperate by doing everything I ask of you."

"Yes, sir," said the boy. "I promise. You will have no further problems with me from now on."

Chapter Twenty-three

By the first night, Charley and his outfit—minus Henry Ellis—were camped among several large rock formations at the bottom of the foothills where they ate more jerky, canned beans, and coffee for their evening meal.

Don Sebastian's guards, plus Colonel Armendariz and his men, were camped circling them to prevent escape. The *hacienda* guards and the colonel's men were cooking some *cabrito* they had taken from a local farmer's goatherd.

Charley's group could smell the goat meat as it cooked over the open fires, but they made do with their jerky because there wasn't one of them who would stoop to asking for a handout.

After soaking it in his bowl of beans, Charley took a bite of jerky, wiggling the piece of dried beef back and forth, hoping to break off a chunk he could chew instead of breaking a tooth. When he finally accomplished that task, Roscoe turned to him just as he took a bite.

"It ain't as easy when ya don't got yer own choppers," he said. He attempted to chomp down on his own jerky. Nothing happened, so he dipped the dried beef into his bowl of beans as he'd seen Charley do, then tried again.

The dried meat appeared to have softened up some, so he bit into the jerky one more time and pulled even harder, until both his uppers and lowers popped free of his mouth.

Feather caught both pieces of the dental work in his hands before they hit the ground. He quickly tossed them back to Roscoe.

"Here ya go, pardner," said Feather. "I'm afraid yer' gonna have ta soak that jerky a whole lot longer than you just did before you try to sink yer pearly whites inta it again."

Roscoe picked up the coffeepot and poured a stream of hot coffee over his dentures—then he popped them back into his mouth. At the same time he poured more coffee into his cup. After a moment or so, he picked up the piece of jerky he had been trying to eat and put it in the cup to soak for a few more minutes.

"Now, don't any of you grab my cup by mistake thinkin' it's yours," said Roscoe. "Or you'll be makin' one heck of a mistake."

"Just as long as it ain't the same cup you keep yer fangs in overnight," said Feather.

"That's an entirely different cup, you old cowpoker," said Roscoe.

Feather moved over and shoved his chin into Roscoe's chest, looking up at him.

"Be careful of who you're callin' a cowpoker, Mr. Smarty Pants," he said.

"Cowpoke," said Roscoe. "I meant cowpoke."

"Quiet down, you two," said Charley, who was resting on his bedroll nearby. He nodded, indicating the guards and Armendariz's men. "Our guardian angels might think that you're disturbing their peace. They're apt to come over here and shut the both of you up."

About then, Fuerte moved in alongside Charley and sat on the end of the bedroll beside him.

"Did you find out anything, Roca?"

"It was a very good idea, Señor Charley, for you to suggest that I place my bedroll over there near the other camp. I was able to gather much more information than I believed I would."

"Well, go ahead," said Charley, "spit it out."

Fuerte leaned in closer to his friend.

"It is not a lie," he said. "Their orders are to take us to the border, then give us our weapons back . . . just like Don Sebastian said they would."

"No more changing the course in midstream?" asked Charley.

"That is correct," answered Fuerte. "For once, it appears that the Don was telling the truth."

The following day they were forced to travel over thirty miles in the broiling sun. During that ride, Kelly gave her hat to Betty Jean, who had been complaining about the heat even though she had been wearing a borrowed Mexican scarf to cover her head since they had left the *hacienda*.

Charley knew it would happen. After a while, Kelly became overheated. Andrés, the captain of the guard, had several of his men construct a makeshift travois stretcher for the woman to lay on while traveling. It had a shade made from twigs and a piece of cloth to keep the sun off her face. Charley hitched it to his own horse, while Rod rode alongside with his canteen and several wet neck scarves, to keep her hydrated. Elisabeth walked along beside Rod with her own canteen and a wet cloth, to keep her face moisturized.

The Mexicans shared their noon meal with the Americans, allowing Roscoe to consume pulled goat meat, soft beans, and a warm tortilla instead of the jerky he was becoming so fond of. They had stopped by a small stream where they could fill their canteens and have a drink of cold water along with the Mexican rations.

By nightfall, Kelly was beginning to come around. She was sitting up and sharing both food and drink with her friends when the sun finally dropped below the horizon.

Later on, in her bedroll beside Rod in his, Kelly dropped into a deep sleep, which, with her, always brought on vivid dreams.

In this particular reverie, Kelly found herself walking barefooted through white hot sand dunes. In her heart she knew she was seeking someone in particular within the dream. As moments passed, she dreamed she saw the silhouette of a well-dressed man with derby and cane standing in the shimmer of a mirage between two distant dunes. Something inside urged her on—plodding, trudging toward the vision of the man, yet never getting any closer. Finally she stopped. She drew in a long breath but could only watch as the man's figure waved what seemed to be a final farewell. Then he turned around and began walking away. But instead of trudging through the sometimes knee-deep sand, the man appeared to float above the dunes. After he had gone only a few yards, his outline appeared to shrivel up and he disappeared into thin air right before her eyes. She blinked.

When her eyes felt like they were opened again, she was no longer walking among the sand dunes. Instead, she was riding in a horse-drawn trolley car, moving down a big city's Main Street. She was alone in the trolley car, with only the driver in front of her. He sat in the seat behind the two sliding windows through which the lines passed, on their way to the horses' bits.

Other trolleys, carriages, gentlemen on horseback, and the occasional automobile surrounded her. They were traveling in both directions up and down the tree-lined roadway.

Suddenly, one of the carriages moved up from behind and started to pass the trolley. As she looked over, she saw the same well-dressed man again. He still wore the derby, and he held the golden-tipped cane. He was sitting in the rear seat. He looked an awful lot like Henry Ellis might look had the boy been twenty years older. He nodded to her—then he tipped his hat. He leaned forward and urged his driver to go faster. The driver snapped the lines, and the coach continued on passing the trolley.

Kelly leaned forward and insisted that her driver follow the gentleman's carriage. The trolley driver whipped at the horses, and they broke into a slow gallop.

It wasn't too long before she caught up to the man's carriage, and as she leaned forward again to tell her driver to go a little faster, the horses pulling the gentleman's coach began to gallop. Within moments, the other carriages, buses, and trolleys that girdled them also began moving more rapidly, until all of them appeared to be flying around in a whirlwind. The sounds of galloping hooves on the cobblestone street grew louder and louder; the excited screams and laughter of the people grew louder, too, until there was an explosion of some kind inside her head. She closed her eyes, and when she opened them again, she was sitting on a painted wooden horse on a golden carousel. She looked around her. The carousel was rotating in the middle of a green expanse of lawn—a parklike setting, where there were no other people visible except for the man who was operating the merry-go-round. For an instant, she thought, the carousel began to turn slower, and slower—finally so slow it felt as if she was floating.

That's when she saw the man in the derby hat again. This time he was sitting astride a bright red horse on the golden carousel, directly across from her. Curved mirrors affixed to the carousel's center pole at first obscured the man's face, then there would be his reflection for an instant, staring at her—then a mirror would block her from seeing him once again.

About the third time around, when she was expecting to see the man's face once more, the young Henry Ellis's face appeared instead. The shock of seeing the boy, instead of the man, caused her to let out a muffled shriek.

She sat up straight, only to find that she was covered in perspiration and shivering from a cold wind that had just come up in the darkness of the camp.

It took the outfit just under two days to get back to the border. When they finally reached the sandy bank of the Rio Grande, Colonel Armendariz and Don Sebastian's captain of the guard, Andrés, instructed them to dismount.

As soon as they were standing on solid ground beside their mounts, Andrés ordered one of the guards to return the Americans' weapons.

With help from two other guards, and a couple of Armendariz's men, they pulled a large blanket out of a small wagon they had brought along with them and spread it out on the ground, revealing the pistols and rifles belonging to the outfit.

"Here are your weapons, señors and señoras," said Andrés. "*But* . . . you must not touch them until the colonel's men and my men are out of sight . . . do you understand?"

"We understand," said Charley. "We all understand."

"We will leave the ammunition for your weapons a quarter of a mile up the road from here," said Andrés, "which will give us even more time in case you decide to break your promise to Don Sebastian and come after us."

"Nothing like that will happen," said Charley. "We all gave the Don our word."

"Then we will take our leave," said the captain.

He turned to his men, held up an arm, then motioned for them to move out, following him.

The colonel did the same. His men followed him as he took them up the trail, following the column of guards.

Charley and the members of the outfit stood silently by—watching after the departing guards and the Armendariz gang.

When they were finally out of sight, everyone began talking at once.

"Hold it down . . . all of you," yelled Charley. "Just calm down, will you? . . . Just shut your mouths so I can talk."

The talking dwindled.

"Now listen to me, every one of you," said Charley. "This is where you're all going to have to make a decision. I need to know if you're with me or not . . . whether you want to go home right now and call this whole thing off . . . or ride back to that *hacienda* with me and get my grandson back."

"I can't go home," said Sergeant Stone. "My toolboxes are buried back there."

"I can't go back," said Pennell. "You know what 'back' means for me, Charley."

"I sure do . . . I put you there in the first place, didn't I?"

"I'll go with you, *mi amigo*," said Fuerte.

"Us, too," said Rod and Kelly.

Betty Jean and Kent agreed.

Holliday chimed in with, "You can count on me, Mr. Sunday, that's fer sure."

Feather finally spoke up. "Thank you, Boss," he said. "Here I was just startin' ta dream of fried chicken and mashed potatoes again, and you're sendin' me back fer more tortillas and beans. I'll be goin' back, Boss. Reckon I can wait a little longer fer that chicken an' 'taters."

"Betty Jean," said Charley. "I know you know how to use a gun because I taught you. What about Kent? Can he pull a trigger anything like you can?"

"If there's something you'd like me to do, Charley," said Kent, "I do know how to use a rifle when I have to."

"All right," said Charley. "Go over there and get your guns . . . one at a time. Feather, ride on up the road and find the ammunition. When we've done that, we'll feed ourselves and the horses. Then we'll start heading back to that *hacienda*."

Chapter Twenty-four

Henry Ellis was seated in the *hacienda*'s dining room at the foot of a very long table with chairs for twenty-two people. The table had been set for two—one setting at each end. Several guards, one on either side of the boy, were there to prevent his running off if he felt so inclined.

Occupying the large chair at the other end of the table—across the expanse of burning candles set out on the highly polished wood—was Don Sebastian. He was dressed in fine gentlemanly attire, and he was looking intently at Henry Ellis at the table's other end.

"Why are you staring at me like that?" the boy asked.

"I'm not staring at you, Chico . . . I am merely observing."

"Well, whatever you're doing, it makes me uncomfortable," said the boy. "I just wish you wouldn't do it."

The Don chuckled; he looked beyond the table and snapped his fingers.

Faster than anything the boy had ever seen before, what appeared to be a hoard of waiters entered the room from the large doors to the side of them, then began placing any number of steaming bowls and platters on the table between the two. When the waiters had concluded their delivery of the food, they stood at attention—five on either side of the table, waiting for the Don's command to begin serving.

"Are you expecting more guests, Don Sebastian?" asked Henry Ellis.

"No, Chico," said the Don. "It is just the two of us. I'd like to get to know you a little better, that is why."

"No other reasons?" asked the boy.

"I have reasons, Chico," answered the Don. "I will tell you all about them at a later time. Now . . . shall we eat?"

He nodded to the servants.

With that gesture, the waiters picked up the platters and bowls again and, progressing in a wide, oval rotation, they moved around the table, stopping at Don Sebastian's place—sitting at one end of the table, while at the same time another was halting at the boy's place—sitting at the other end. They presented the platters and bowls to the Don and Henry Ellis before ladling whatever the serving dishes contained onto the proper plate, saucer, cup, or bowl.

When the serving was over, a man with a wine bottle uncorked the container and poured a sample into the Don's silver chalice. He lifted the container to his lips and took some of the liquid into his mouth, swishing it around, then spitting into a special bowl provided by another servant.

"Bring another bottle," the Don said in Spanish.

The waiter took the first bottle away and was met by another server who had uncorked a new bottle. He then went through the same procedure with the Don's wine tasting as the previous waiter had done.

"Ahh, perfection," said the Don as he indicated the boy at the far end of the table. "Will you join me, Chico?"

"Thank you, but no, sir," said the boy. "I'm not old

enough to consume alcoholic beverages just yet. Do you have any milk? . . . I prefer it cold."

The Don threw a look to the headwaiter; the man nodded, then left the room.

"I hope you find everything else agreeable to your palate?" said Don Sebastian.

"It looks like it'll all be really good," said Henry Ellis.

"Then, go ahead, my son . . . please . . . enjoy your meal."

Charley, Fuerte, and the boy's parents sat around the campfire beside the road that would lead them back to the *hacienda*—they were drinking coffee.

Roscoe, Holliday, and Feather were farther down a slight incline, kneeling beside a small creek and washing the tin plates and scrubbing pans. Kelly and Rod were helping them by drying the plates and other utensils.

Sergeant Stone and Mitch Pennell were sitting side by side on their bedrolls, reloading cartridges for everyone.

Pennell yelled across to Charley, "Do you reckon we'll be using more brass than we used before, Charley?"

"Probably not," the ex-Ranger answered. "But you two keep reloading, just in case. Better to have more ammunition than not enough. And that's a fact!"

"When we stop to pick up my toolboxes," said the sergeant, "I'll feel a lot more comfortable."

"I'll be a lot more comfortable, too, when I find out just what's in those toolboxes," said Pennell.

Rod and Kelly were climbing up the steep slope beside the sergeant, coming back from the creek. They were all drying their hands on the same dishtowel.

As they got to the top, Rod said, "Why don't you tell 'em what it is you have in those boxes. At least tell 'em what's in that one box that looked familiar to me. Maybe everyone'll feel more comfortable if they know."

Sergeant Stone turned toward Charley, who was still sitting beside the fire.

"Do you want me to do that, Mr. Sunday?" said the sergeant. "Or do you want me to continue keeping it a secret?"

"Go ahead, Sergeant," said Charley. "It won't hurt anything now if they know."

"All right," said the sergeant. He spoke loud enough for everyone to hear. "I brought some machine guns and automatic pistols with me. Charley thought it might help if we happened to find ourselves outnumbered."

"And now that we know what kind of odds are against us," said Charley, "I want Sergeant Stone to distribute those weapons to you all as soon as we get back to our old campsite where the sergeant buried those toolboxes."

Upon hearing this news, the members of the outfit congratulated the sergeant and their leader.

Charley held up a hand to quiet them.

"I hope that'll give you something to sleep on," he said. "Now, if anybody would like to give Roscoe a hand with the mules, we can all go to sleep early so we can be up before dawn and back on the trail as soon as we've had our breakfast."

Chapter Twenty-five

One of Don Sebastian's servants showed Henry Ellis to his second-floor room. The man lit several candles for him, then he turned down the covers on the feather bed before moving back to the door, where he stopped. He turned toward the boy.

"I must lock the door when I leave, Chico, plus, there are bars on all of the windows," he said. "Since there is no escape, why don't you just go to sleep instead of searching for a way out. At this *hacienda*, tomorrow comes very early."

He left the room, closing, then locking, the door behind him.

Henry Ellis listened as the key was turned in the door's lock, followed by the servant's footsteps as they faded away down the hallway.

At the foot of the bed, Henry Ellis found a neatly pressed robe, nightshirt, and cap laid out, with a pair of slippers on the throw rug in front of them. He gave the nightclothes a good look, then began unbuttoning his shirt and dropping the suspenders from his shoulders.

In no time, the boy had changed, blown out the candles,

and was under the covers with his head resting on a large, comfortable pillow. Minutes later, even though there were still sounds of the guards marching outside in the courtyard, he was sound asleep.

In the vision that surrounded him, Henry Ellis blinked his eyes, and the images in front of him became sharp and easy for him to see. Smells of the Texas countryside, imbedded in his memory over the years, began seeping into his approaching reverie. He could hear the sounds of dogs barking, as if they were just outside the door.

Henry Ellis found himself sitting on the bank of a river with his grampa Charley. They were both eating chicken that had come from a straw basket prepared by Kelly and Miss Elisabeth, who were both sitting on a grassy knoll not far from Charley and the boy. The puppy was there, too, playing at his side, while Buster—the old Buster—romped with the smaller dog, teasing the puppy by keeping a small chicken bone away from him.

When the dogs' little game had gone on long enough, Charley clapped his hands in what appeared to be slow motion. The old Buster dropped the bone and ran to his master's side.

"I sure miss scratching your old butt, Buster," said Charley, in what sounded like a sluggish growl.

The dog stopped by his side while the old man began scratching its backside.

Henry Ellis called his puppy over to his side and began scratching the smaller dog's rear end.

The puppy moved in closer to the boy—the dog appeared to love every precious stroke.

"Look, Grampa, look . . ." said Henry Ellis in an echoing timbre. "The pup likes his behind scratched, too."

"They both like it . . . don't they?" said Charley.

"Like they were one and the same," said the boy.

Both animals got to their feet at the same time. They were both looking at something behind Charley and the boy. They turned their heads around to see.

Don Sebastian and Colonel Armendariz stood several yards away. Both men were surrounded by Don Sebastian's guards and some of the colonel's men. All of them had their weapons drawn and aimed at Charley and his grandson.

The old Buster's hair stood up on his back, and he growled.

The puppy did the same.

"Kill them all!" shouted Don Sebastian.

Twenty guns blazed in unison as both Don Sebastian's and Armendariz's men opened fire.

Henry Ellis sat up straight in his bed. Lightning flashed through the curtains—thunder rolled close by. Perspiration dripped from his forehead. He stared straight ahead into the darkened room.

He could hear the wind blowing outside the windows—he felt the chill leaking in through the fastened sashes. There was another flash of lightning, followed by a loud clap of thunder, and in moments, rain began to fall onto the flat roof above him.

The new storm was also battering the outfit. They were attempting to keep dry some thirty miles east of the *hacienda*.

At the first sign of the approaching storm, Charley ordered everyone to break out their oilskin *ponchos* and attach them together. By doing so, they created a tentlike arrangement with the joined-together *ponchos*, so when draped from overhanging tree branches, and held in place by rocks putting weight on the bottom of the sides, they appeared to do the job just fine. When the makeshift tent was set, they dragged their saddles and bedrolls under the improvised shelter.

Most of them were sleeping when the storm broke, sending buckets of rain down on the slick, oilskin refuge below.

Charley awoke to Roscoe's complaints that a river of mud had joined him inside his sleeping blanket.

"Pipe down, Roscoe, and move your bedroll away from the mud," said Charley.

Then it was Feather who poked his head into the temporary tent, grumbling about how wet he was getting while he watched the horses.

"Didn't you put on your slicker before you started your watch, Feather?" asked Charley.

"No, I didn't," said the pint-size cowboy. "It wasn't rainin' when I started my watch, Boss."

"Well then, come on in here and get your rain gear, and get back out there before those animals realize you're missing."

Feather found his slicker. Someone had "borrowed" it while constructing the tent, and it was now high over his head, and like all the other slickers, an intricate part of the improvised shelter.

"Here, Feather," said Charley, "put this on."

He handed the little guy the *poncho* he'd been wearing.

Feather slipped it on, then went back outside.

"Charley."

The voice belonged to Rod. The young Indian had moved in beside the old ramrod and was hovering over him in the dark.

"Kelly can't sleep," he whispered. "She's worried about her papers . . . you know, the notes she's been taking for the book she intends to write when we get back to Texas."

"Where are they?" asked Charley.

"She says they're in her saddlebags."

"What is she using for a pillow?" Charley wanted to know.

"Her saddle," said Rod.

"Did she take her saddlebags off her saddle, separately, before she bedded down?"

"I don't think so," said Rod. "Let me go check."

He stumbled through the sleeping men, back across the dry ground, to where Kelly was waiting. He felt around near the back of her saddle. Then he whispered loudly in Charley's direction.

"Her saddlebags are right here, Charley."

"That's what I figured," mumbled the old rancher—then he set his head back onto his own saddle and tried to go back to sleep.

The first drip splashed onto Charley's right ear. He sat up. The second drip hit him on the back of the neck, then an icy droplet slithered under his collar and slid down his bare back.

"God-damn-Sam," he said under his breath. He moved his bedroll over a foot or so until he found a dry spot. He crawled back into the warmth of his bedroll.

It wasn't more than a minute later when a bolt of lightning hit a nearby tree and the whole tented structure fell down on top of everyone, causing quite a ruckus.

After a few moments, Roscoe shoved his head through a hole in the top of the downed shelter. The rain was beating him in the face.

"Hey, everyone," he said, "maybe it wasn't such a good idea makin' our shelter under these trees."

"Oh, shut up, will ya?" someone yelled back. "Can't ya see I'm tryin' ta sleep?"

Lightning flashed overhead, and more thunder rolled in the near distance, and the rain kept falling. Nothing was done to repair the temporary refuge.

And all were sleeping peacefully when dawn broke with a cloudless sky.

Henry Ellis tippy-toed down the spiral staircase to the main floor of the *hacienda*. He was all alone. He crossed the tiled floor of the great room, passing between the twin fireplaces. He entered a large, hand-carved, arched, wooden doorway that led into the dining room.

A look of surprise crossed the boy's face upon entering. He had expected to find the room void of human activity. Instead, Don Sebastian was seated in his usual chair at the head of the extensive table. He was eating a rolled tortilla filled with beans, fried eggs, beef, and salsa.

"Sit," said the Don when he saw the boy standing by the door. "You're late. You must have overslept. I unlocked your door."

Henry Ellis nodded to his host, then he moved to the opposite end of the table and took his seat.

"I sleep well when it rains," said the Don. "Don't you?"

"I sleep good when it's not raining, too," said the boy.

Don Sebastian indicated the plate of covered tortillas and the bowl of beans that had been placed beside the boy's table setting. Henry Ellis scooped up several spoonfuls of beans and rolled them in a tortilla. He looked up at the Don, to make sure he had filled the tortilla the proper way, before he took a bite.

The Don was looking right at him. "Salsa?" he offered.

Feeling somewhat embarrassed, the boy found a large

spoon, then helped himself to the salsa beside his plate. He took a bite.

Hot, but not that bad, he thought to himself. *It sure tastes better than that breakfast mush my mother cooks up for me every day at home in Austin.*

"What do you think?" said Don Sebastian.

Henry Ellis threw him a quizzical look.

"Your breakfast," said the Don. "Do you like it?"

"We don't eat much Mexican food where I come from," said Henry Ellis. "And if we do, it's only when we go to my mother's favorite little restaurant outside of Austin . . . or when I'm staying with my grampa at his ranch in Juanita. His friend, Roscoe, knows how to cook Mexican style."

"Your grandfather, Henry Ellis," said the Don, "do you think I can trust that he'll keep his word and not come back for you?"

That's a stupid question, thought the boy. *Of course he'll come back for me.*

Then he continued aloud.

"My grampa is a man of his word, Don Sebastian," said Henry Ellis. "He'd never lie to you."

"So I told this old feller," said Charley as he nudged Dice forward, "I told him I didn't care much whether he had a hundred guns pointed at me, or just the two he had aimed at my belly right then . . . I wasn't about to back down from him, no matter what . . . Well, I must've frightened him a tad with my telling him a whopper like that one, because before you know it, he dropped the barrel on one of those Colts he had pointed my way, which gave me the opening I needed to put his lights out once and for all."

Fuerte, riding beside him, threw Feather, who was riding behind Charley, a look of disbelief.

"Do you mean to tell me, Señor Charley," said Fuerte, "that you drew your *pistola* against a hundred *pistoleros* who had their guns already pointed directly at you?"

"No, Roca," said Charley, "you didn't understand what I said . . . the man only had two guns pointed at me."

"But, Señor Charley," said Fuerte, "I distinctly heard you say there were a hundred guns pointed at you."

"That isn't what I said, Roca," repeated Charley. "When it comes to hearing, you're about as bad a listener as Roscoe back there."

"I heard ya all right, Mr. Smarty Pants," said Roscoe, who was driving the chuckwagon. "I heard you just fine."

"Then maybe we ought to change the subject for a while," said Charley. "Hey . . . this country's starting to look pretty familiar, isn't it?"

Sergeant Stone broke rank and galloped up beside Charley.

"Our old campsite can't be that far ahead of us, Charley," said the sergeant. "Would you mind if I rode on up there and got a head start digging up my tools?"

"Go ahead, Sergeant," said Charley, "and take Rod with you, in case you run into any trouble."

The sergeant reined around and galloped back. He pulled Rod out of the column, then the two of them cantered around the column, moving up the road until they were out of sight.

Elisabeth and Kelly spurred their mounts up the line until they were riding parallel to Charley and Fuerte.

"We can go on ahead, too, Charley," said Kelly. "We could take Roscoe and the chuckwagon with us and have the noon meal ready for the rest of you fellas when you get there."

"That rest of us you're talking about leaves me, Roca, Pennell, Holliday, Kent, Betty Jean, and Feather," said Charley. "So why don't 'everyone' ride on up there with you, then maybe we might all get there about the same time."

There was a smile from the women. They turned their horses and urged them on up the road.

"C'mon, you slackers," shouted Charley to those left behind. "Do you want a couple of females making a fool out of you by getting to the old campsite before we do?"

The remaining four spurred out, following Charley. They caught up with Elisabeth and Kelly in no time at all.

As usual, Roscoe, driving the chuckwagon, trundled on up the road behind them all.

Don Sebastian led Henry Ellis out of the enormous double doors onto the front patio. They walked forward until they reached the steps, then followed them down to the courtyard where they continued their walk.

"I feel it is about time I told you the reason for my interest in you, Chico," said the Don.

"Yes, sir," said Henry Ellis, "I'd like to know that."

"Many years ago," the Don began, "I had a son about your age . . . twelve, is it?"

"No, sir," said the boy, "I'm eleven."

"Eleven, twelve, it really doesn't matter," said Don Sebastian. "Just the fact that I lost my only son when he was close to your age is what concerns me."

"I'm sorry for your loss, Don Sebastian," said Henry Ellis, "I truly am. Can I ask how he died?" added the boy. "Your son?"

"Through my stupidity," said Don Sebastian. "I allowed him to accompany me on a cattle drive."

His voice began to waver.

"We were over halfway to our destination," the Don continued, "which was Matamoros. We were driving the cattle along the Mexican bank of the Rio Bravo, when we were attacked by a band of renegade Comanche warriors. A full-fledged battle broke out between my *vaqueros* and those Comanches . . . bullets were flying one way, arrows the other . . . the cattle stampeded in even another direction. I thought we were all going to be killed, until a small band of Texas Rangers rode into the altercation."

Henry Ellis's mouth turned up into a smile.

"Those three Rangers had the renegade Indians running for their lives before my *vaqueros* and I realized what had happened," said the Don. "All we could do was watch from our position as the Rangers chased those Comanches all the way across the river, where they eventually caught up to them and fought some more, until they surrendered."

"My grampa was a Texas Ranger, Don Sebastian," said the boy.

"I know," said the Don, nodding.

"So what happened after that?" Henry Ellis wanted to know.

The two of them were now stopped at the side of the large fountain in the center of the courtyard.

"I looked around for my son," said Don Sebastian, "but he was nowhere to be seen."

Henry Ellis could only stare at the Don with wide eyes. He had no words.

"Finally," said the Don, "one of my *vaqueros* rode up to my side with the body of my son in his arms. Chico had been killed by a single bullet during the conflict. He was dead."

"Gosh," said Henry Ellis, "I am really, truly sorry."

"It was so long ago, Chico," said Don Sebastian.

"Chico," he said again, "that is what I called him . . . my son . . . Chico."

"Did those Rangers ever come back to talk to you about your son's death?" asked Henry Ellis.

The Don shook his head.

"No, Chico," he said. "Not one of them ever made a move to come over to our side of the river to explain."

"You're sure of that?"

"I am very sure, Chico," said the Don. "But one of my men had seen the man who had fired the bullet that took my son's life . . . It was one of those Texas Rangers who killed my Chico."

"I'm sorry it happened, Don Sebastian, I really am," said the boy.

"Then you know what I am going to say next, don't you, Chico?"

The boy nodded—a tear broke away from the corner of one of his eyes, trickling down his cheek.

"It was your grandfather who killed my son, Chico . . . and that is why you are here."

Henry Ellis felt as if the Don had punched his fist directly into his soul.

"An eye for an eye, Chico . . . a grandson for a son."

All three of Sergeant Stone's weapons boxes were stacked near the campfire. Charley sat beside the sergeant and Roscoe, the three of them slicing pieces of roasted prairie dog from a spit. The rest of the crew were gathered around the threesome, eating and listening to Charley as he finished telling another one of his tales.

"And that's a fact, for sure . . . me, Roscoe, and Feather rode right into that dang shootin' match 'tween them Mexican cowboys and that hunting party of Comanche warriors until we cut every one of 'em out from that herd and chased 'em back across the river into Texas. We finally caught up to 'em and darn near sent the whole bunch to their happy hunting grounds."

"Did you ever go back across the border to see if those Mexican cowboys were all right?" asked Kelly.

"Didn't have the time," said Charley. "Or the manpower. Remember, there was eight of them Comanches left, and only three of us Rangers. Just getting 'em all up to the Laredo Ranger Office was difficult enough for us. Right, boys?"

"You bet it was," said Roscoe.

"Darn right," said Feather at almost the same time.

"Charley," Kelly said, "isn't it about time you let us all in on the rest of your idea on how we're getting Henry Ellis out of that *hacienda*?"

"You don't figger on rushin' the place, do ya, Boss?" said Feather.

"I'm good with a gun," said Holliday, "but not against more'n a hundred men or so at a time."

"No, fellas," said Charley. "We won't be rushing the place."

"If you think we need more help," said Fuerte, "I could go to the *hacienda* workers' village and find out if they might be willing to provide us with some assistance."

"That might work," said Charley, "if those workers feel the Don has done them some kind of an injustice. But the only *hacienda* workers I ever saw looked like they were pretty content doing their jobs, plus they appeared to be pretty well fed, too."

"Just the same," said Fuerte, "the field workers and *vaqueros* could very easily be a little disappointed that Don Sebastian doesn't let them keep any of the crops they grow, or the cattle they raise, and I'll wager he only pays them a pittance to get by on. They're forced to buy their supplies from a Mexican version of an American company store, and most of them are in debt to the Don with no way of ever paying him off.

"Why don't I ride over to that village tomorrow, and at least give it a try?" added Fuerte. "I am one of them . . . I am a Mexican . . . I think like they do . . . I speak more than just their language."

"If you're willing, Roca, I can't stop you. Rod," Charley called out, "go with Roca, if you can . . . make sure that nothing happens to him."

"I will be all right on my own, Señor Charley."

Fuerte broke open his Smith & Wesson revolver and checked the cartridges in the cylinder. He snapped it shut, in the closed, ready-to-fire position, so it was all set for action. "I will talk to them, Charley," he said. "Tomorrow . . . when there is time for me to ride over there."

Henry Ellis's mind was wandering.

He had washed his face and hands upon entering the *hacienda*, and after that he had met Don Sebastian at the long table for supper. Don Sebastian had asked him if he felt ill, to which the boy had answered, no, that he was probably just overly tired.

"Well, eat your supper, Chico," said Don Sebastian, "then we shall take another walk around the courtyard. By then, you may be feeling better."

Henry Ellis toyed with his food when it was served. He found it very difficult to keep his mind on what he was doing.

The recollection unfolded in his anxious brain like a precious treasure map, displaying each piece of its puzzle, one fold at a time, one crease at a time, one panel at a time, until the map was fully opened in front of his mind's eye.

The whole picture ultimately revealed to the boy was a recognizable old dirt road in the Texas Big Bend area where his grampa Charley had taken him hunting on several occasions.

In these semiconscious thoughts, Henry Ellis was riding alongside his grandfather, a borrowed deer rifle resting across the pommel of his saddle. His grandfather was doing the same with his own hunting rifle.

It wasn't too long before Charley spotted an eight-point buck standing proud and erect on a precipice about forty yards in front of them. Charley signaled the boy to rein up and stay perfectly still. Henry Ellis did just that.

Charley raised his rifle and took aim—the boy did the same—he would stand by to render a second shot if it was necessary.

Suddenly a gunshot rang out, coming from somewhere nearby, with the bullet lifting a large chunk of soil from the ground between the two of them and flinging it into the air. Both horses reared back, spoiling Charley's aim and dumping the boy onto the ground at the same time.

"Grab your horse's reins, Henry Ellis," Charley called out. "Don't let him get away."

The boy caught hold of a dangling rein. But before he could gather the second one in his other hand, another shot echoed from the mountains around him, with the bullet slicing the first leather strap into two pieces.

"Forget the horse," yelled Charley. "Just find some cover as fast as you can."

A third bullet slammed into the butt of Charley's rifle, knocking the weapon from his grasp, but at the same moment, allowing him to dismount.

He grabbed his grandson by the jacket collar, then he dove behind a small rock formation with both of them coming out of it no worse for wear.

"Who is it, Grampa?" asked Henry Ellis.

"I don't rightly know just yet," said Charley, who was now snaking his way to the corner of a large boulder, trying to get a view of their attacker.

Henry Ellis watched his grandfather as he slowly edged his way around the rock.

Kaboom—Zingggg!

Another shot was fired; the bullet ricocheted off the rock in front of Charley's face, spraying fine, sandlike granules into his eyes.

Immediately Charley's hands covered his face. He brushed at his eyelids in an attempt to clear away the stinging particles. He turned in the boy's direction.

"I can't see, Henry Ellis," he said. "I can't see for the life of me."

Henry Ellis scooted over beside his grandfather. He had pulled his handkerchief from a back pocket and now held it out to Charley.

The boy quickly saw his error; Charley couldn't see anything at all. Henry Ellis took his grandfather's hands into his own and laid the handkerchief across the palm of the older man's hand.

"Thank you, Henry Ellis," said Charley. "I'll have these old eyes back in seeing order in no time. Right now, it's going to all be up to you to get whoever it is up there that's shooting at us."

The boy pulled his own rifle in closer to his chest. He levered a cartridge into the chamber.

"That's good, son," said Charley, reaching out for his grandson, then patting the boy's knee. "I know you can get her done without me. You're on your own now, Henry Ellis. Do your old grampa justice."

Another shot coming from the higher ground above them dug into the ground behind the two, kicking up a rooster tail of sand that rained down on both of them this time.

"Keep your eyes closed, boy," said Charley, "unless you want to end up like me. Now, my suggestion is—"

"I know what to do, Grampa," said Henry Ellis. "I'm just afraid he'll come down here while I'm circling around and you won't know that he's here."

"That's a chance we'll both have to take," said Charley. "Why don't you just get going . . . Don't waste any more time fretting on it."

Henry Ellis leaned in and gave his grandfather a pat on the shoulder.

Charley managed a small smile. He cocked the old Walker in his boot top before removing it.

"Now get-a-going . . . I'll be safe right here. I'll just fire off a shot or two every other minute or so to make him think both of us are still right here behind these rocks. Now, go on . . . Get," he added.

Henry Ellis surveyed the immediate area. His eyes eventually dropped to a crevasse between two boulders over to the right of where Charley was leaning.

He stayed low on his belly and slithered over to the narrow space. He stopped—took one final look back—then, using his elbows, he crawled his way on his arms and knees into the gap between the boulders, disappearing into some underbrush.

Charley realized he was alone. The first thing he did was to fire off a shot in the direction from which the last bullet had come.

The ambusher returned several bullets, hitting nothing but dirt a few yards away from Charley.

The ex-Ranger cocked his pistol once again and fired another shot.

Meanwhile, Henry Ellis had begun his large circle around the area, hoping he might get a glimpse of the rifleman before the assailant saw him. There was another shot or two exchanged between Charley and the attacker, which gave Henry Ellis a chance to advance further on with his plan.

Back where Henry Ellis had left him, Charley picked up his rifle and levered in another round. He fired off a shot.

When he went to cock the rifle again he could tell by the sound that no brass had been inserted into the proper position—he'd run out of ammunition.

Charley reached into a pocket of the old hunting jacket he was wearing and pulled out some more bullets. With his eyes still blinded, he loaded all seven of them into the rifle, levered in a shell, then fired again.

Another bullet was returned, hitting a rock beside Charley with a heavier velocity than the other bullets that had been fired early on.

This one had come from an entirely different direction—the man was closer than before.

Charley sensed someone was behind him.

"Henry Ellis," he called out. A chill ran up his spine.

"No, Mr. Charley Sunday," said an unfamiliar voice. "Your grandson is still crawling around out there in the tumbleweeds trying to find me. But I decided I'd find you first."

The man slowly cocked his rifle, raising, then aiming it directly at Charley.

"What's your gripe with me, mister?" Charley wanted to know.

"It doesn't really matter, Sunday," said the man. "I'm just one of the many you put behind bars over the years. It didn't matter to you who I was when you killed my brother and wounded me . . . Now I don't care about you, or that kid out there, either."

His gloved finger made a move to pull the trigger.

Blam! Blam!

The man's chest was a bloody mess; his body dropped to the ground—dead.

Charley swung his still sightless eyes around, hoping to see what had happened. Within moments, Henry Ellis threw his arms around his grandfather and pulled him close.

"Sorry I couldn't give you any warning, Grampa," the boy said. "But I saw him moving this way, so I followed as quick as I could.

"Do you recognize him, son?" asked Charley. "My eyesight seems to be coming back to me, but everything's still a little blurry."

"I don't know who he is," said Henry Ellis. "But he sure knew who you were, Grampa."

"I'm just happy to have found out that you have the same instincts as I do, son," said Charley. "It puts me at ease to know that you can handle yourself when I'm not around."

Henry Ellis came out of his reverie to find that Don Sebastian was staring at him from his seat at the other end of the table.

"Did you hear anything I said to you, Chico?" he was asking.

Henry Ellis shook his head.

"Sorry, sir. I wasn't paying attention."

The Don fluffed it off.

"It really doesn't matter, Chico, my son. Just as long as you are here with me."

Several hours later, after the boy had gone to his room to sleep, there was a crash of something falling outside on the balcony, followed by the whistling of heavy wind.

Henry Ellis threw back the covers and got out of bed. He put his feet into his slippers while throwing on his robe. He crossed to a balcony door on the other side of the room and opened it.

The wind whipped in through the open, barred door, blowing out both candles the boy had forgotten to douse before he had gone to bed.

Nearby, he could see that a small table and several chairs had been blown over.

He looked out across the *hacienda* courtyard. A thick dust was being raised by the wind; he could barely see the other structures below. There was light coming from the building where the guards drank and played cards. A softer light came through the windows of the guards' barracks across from that building.

Turning, he could see the regular guards at the gate, hovered over a wind-whipped fire they had built on a flat spot near their lean-to on the top of the wall. The wind was gusting with such ferocity, the flames appeared to go out every so often. They would then burst back to life when the wind let up, just enough to give the fire the oxygen it was gasping for.

Several light drops of rain fell onto the boy's head. He looked up. There was a special sparkle in his eyes. He put his hands together—

"Dear Father in heaven," he began, speaking softly. "Thank You from the bottom of my heart that my mother and father are finally safe . . . and that my grampa Charley is with them. I don't know how I'm going to get out of this mess . . . but like always, I'm sure You'll end up helping me. You've been very good to me, Father . . . Too good. I only ask that You allow me to be with all of my friends again. Also, could I please see my little puppy again, too? I hope he's all right."

By then the wind had started to blow even harder. Henry Ellis realized he was surrounded by the dust, so he turned and closed the door.

He took off his robe and slippers, then combing his hair with his fingers, he climbed back into bed. He put his head on the pillows and closed his eyes. He listened as the wind howled outside. *Whatever lies ahead*, he thought, *I'm ready for it.* Henry Ellis was eternally grateful that he now knew deep within himself that he would be able to handle any situation that might arise, however dangerous it might be.

Chapter Twenty-six

Roscoe awoke to the sun trying to break through the clouds.

Charley, who was sleeping a few feet away, turned to his friend and said, "I think I'll sleep in a few more minutes, Roscoe. Think you can handle it without me for that long?"

"You wanna' sleep in, C.A.," said Roscoe, "you go right on ahead an' sleep in. If anyone deserves to, you do."

By the time Roscoe had breakfast going, he'd been joined by Elisabeth and Kelly. The women chipped right in and started opening several cans of beans and cutting some lengths of jerky, so when the others began to wake up, everyone would have smelled the delicious aroma of hot coffee drifting on the calm morning air.

"Looks like we had a little windstorm last night," said Charley as he joined the others by the campfire.

"I heard it," said Roscoe. "It sure felt good bein' inside my bedroll, thank the Lord. Hey, C.A., I thought you were sleepin' in today."

"I heard it, too," said Elisabeth. "But like Kelly, I was just too tired to take a look."

"The wind stopped about an hour before sunup," said Kelly, who was preparing to dish out some beans from a wooden bowl they had found at the adobe building days earlier.

"Smells real good," said Rod as he joined the group.

"Better'n the coffee my old granny used ta make."

It was Holliday, who had just finished pulling on his boots.

Pennell and Sergeant Stone, who had been guarding not only the camp but the sergeant's three boxes as well, both moved in from opposite sides of the camp. Their mussed-up hair sticking out from under their hats, plus their dusty clothing, showed they had been out in the windstorm during the night, and now they stopped and stood by the rear end of the chuckwagon, staring at the cook's fly where the food was being prepared.

"I'm so hungry I could eat a horse," said the sergeant.

"I sure hope it ain't horse that yer' servin', Roscoe," added Pennell as he watched a still dozing Feather, who appeared to be asleep, walking toward the smells of breakfast.

Rod was at the older man's side.

"I caught ol' Feather here sleep-walking, just like he's doing now, last night when I took the second watch," said Rod. "Instead of carrying the little squirt back to his bedroll, I decided to keep him with me until morning. Unfortunately, I thought he'd be awake by now."

Rod set the still sleeping Feather on someone's bedroll, then walked away.

"All right, you yahoos," said Roscoe, ". . . get a move on, yer breakfast is on the table."

Everyone quickly made up a line, then they began moving past Roscoe and the two women, who served every last one of them. Feather had fallen in at line's end, just in time to get the cooled off dregs from the coffeepot, plus cold beans and jerky.

While everyone was eating, Pennell made a proposal to Charley.

"If you think we could use a few more men," he said, "I'll ride back to that Black-Seminole camp and ask 'em if they might be up ta givin' us a hand."

"If you really want to do that," said Charley, "you had better take Miss Elisabeth along with you."

"I understand," said Pennell, nodding. "That's fine with me."

Elisabeth agreed to accompany Pennell back to the Indian camp. She was delighted she would again be able to see the friends who had rescued her from that creeping desert thirst and eventual starvation, which would have only led to her death.

Within minutes, Mitch Pennell and Elisabeth Rogers were riding away, hoping to reach the Seminole camp before nightfall. To do so, they would be riding hard most of the day.

In the meantime, Charley decided the outfit should remain right where they were, even though Holliday and Feather were raring for a fight.

Across the way, Kelly was playing with the puppy. Sergeant Stone and Rod watched from a distance.

"It's nice to know that I was right when I identified that one toolbox of yours as containing an automatic weapon," said Rod.

"You seem to know quite a bit about them, but have you ever fired one, Mr. Lightfoot?" asked the sergeant.

"Only once," said Rod, "during our Rough Rider training. We never had the chance to lay our hands on any during the Cuban skirmishes. But there were others who cleared a path for us several times using those Colt-Brownings. Even though most of us never got the chance to fire one during battle, we were all prepared to use one."

"Well, you were only wrong about one thing when you guessed at what was in the toolbox," said Sergeant Stone. "I have two of those Colt-Brownings in that box, not one. I was hoping you might manage one of them yourself, if you had to. That is, *if* Charley ever gets around to letting us use them."

"I would be more than happy for you to give me even more lessons in how to operate the weapon," said Rod.

"I will take you away from camp this afternoon, if it's all right with Charley," said the sergeant. "Once we're far enough away, I will reacquaint you in the use of the M1895 Colt-Browning machine gun."

"More than likely, we won't have to go that far," said Rod. I can tell you for sure that Charley won't allow us to use any live ammunition, since we're so close to the *hacienda*."

"Did I ever tell ya about the time me, Charley, and Roscoe got ourselves involved in a Texas family dispute?"

Feather was talking to Holliday, Fuerte, and Rod, who sat across from the little cowboy, waiting for the baloney to unravel.

"Well, sir," Feather went on, "it happened in the late 1870s or '80s when the three of us was rangerin' together. We'd been assigned to ride down into the Big Bend wild country and check on an incident that had taken place down there a week or two before. We was sent down there ta help out the Ranger that was permanently stationed in the Big Bend at that time.

"Ya see, there had been a robbery at the general store at the Hot Springs . . . you know, those old natural hot water baths on the American side of the Rio Grande River there . . . kinda due east from the Study Butte mines on the other side of the Chisos Mountains? Takes about four hours or so by horseback ta get there. It's on the upward swing of the Rio. There's a little Mexican village across the river from it . . . Charley," he said, "do you remember the name of that little Mexican village?"

"*Boquillas*," said Charley, who had just joined the others.

Some of his listeners had heard of it, and they nodded their heads so Feather would go on with his story.

"Well . . . me, Charley, an' Roscoe was sent down there because the three of us had such a good record when it come ta trackin' bank robbers."

"Tell 'em where they put us up while we were there, Feather," said Charley, who had just seated himself.

"Well, uh," said Feather, "well, they put us up in this old one-story hotel, they called it, built out a' rocks and stones . . . same kinda natural materials the general store was built out of.

"Nice thing about it was, they let us have our own rooms. Even though it was the season down there fer those that took the waters fer health reasons, there was still enough rooms left for the three of us ta stay there, too, with each of us in his own private room."

"Tell 'em what them rooms was like inside, why don't you, Feather?" said Roscoe.

Feather shrugged; he hunched his right shoulder.

"Well, them rooms was more like a Huntsville Prison cell than a hotel room. All they was furnished with was one wood an' rope cot. Ya had ta look around outside for weeds and palm leaves to make a mattress fer yerself. Then, on top of that, you had ta use yer own bedroll ta cover up with. Plus, the one outhouse they had favored the general store more'n the sleepin' rooms . . . an' it was one heck of a walk gettin' to the privy at night . . . if you could even find it. An' it was uphill all the way."

"So what about the robbery?" asked Holliday. "Did you ever catch the thief what done it?"

"Darn right we caught who done it . . . but let me go on with my story if you wanna hear how it happened, in the order it happened," said Feather.

He continued.

"The Ranger down there, his name was Quisenberry if I remember correctly, plus a man everyone called Little Sammy No-Thumbs, that run the general store an' livery next door to it, gave us some pretty good ideas about who mighta committed the robbery. Well, thank the Lord they were all names of local folks living in the area, or I don't know what we woulda done."

"Why did they call him Sammy No-Thumbs, Feather?" Holliday wanted to know.

"Oh," said Feather, "Sammy told us he had been a roper most of his life. One time when he was a kid, he took a dally around his saddle horn just after his loop had caught the horns of a big ol' bull. He had somehow put his hand on the saddle horn before he made his dally and when the slack in the rope jerked itself tight, off popped Sammy's left thumb. Ya see, he had dallied over his thumb and didn't realize he'd done it until it was too late."

"What about his other thumb, Feather," asked someone else. "You said they called him Sammy No-Thumbs . . . that sounds like two ta me."

"Well, ya see," said Feather, "after ol' Sammy lost his left thumb, he had ta teach himself to rope left-handed. Wasn't that long after he lost his left thumb that he done the same, exact thing to his right."

"Popped right off like the other one, did it?" said Holliday.

"Like a champagne cork on New Year's Eve," said Feather with a sigh.

Rod got the conversation back on track.

"Since you had a list of names of the potential robbers to go by," he said, "it sounds like all you had to do was find out where the robber lived, then go and arrest him. It was that easy, right?"

"Not quite," answered Feather. "Ya see, they give us several names . . . but no one has addresses down there in the Bend, at least not back then, just post office boxes in the Terlingua general store. Dang near everyone worked at either the Study Butte or the Mercury mines around that area, ya know . . . so they all picked up their mail at the mining company's store there."

"So you didn't have it so easy after all," said Holliday.

Feather answered, "Gosh no, Holliday, we didn't. We checked on them post office boxes in Terlingua, and asked about some men who worked for the mining companies. But no one could give us directions to where any one of them fellers was livin'. We finally went back ta the Hot Springs and that Little Sammy feller told us that the local ranger, Quisenberry, had questioned some of the witnesses again and narrowed our suspects down ta three people . . . and all three just happened to be down at the hot springs right then takin' the water at that particular time."

Roscoe cut in.

"Tell 'em about what I done to help capture them *hombres*, why don't ya, Feather?" he said. "Tell 'em."

"It was Roscoe's idea that he go on down to the hot water baths ahead of me an' Charley and to play like he was one of them bathers. Then he got inta the water with them robber fellers," said Feather.

"An' I done just that," said Roscoe with a big grin.

"But you wasn't grinnin' back then, when one of them robbers recognized that you was a law dog and he drawed down on ya when you was just about ta step inta that hot water wearin' nothin' but yer long johns. You gotta admit, Roscoe, you sure weren't expecting that, now were ya?"

"No, sir, I wasn't," said Roscoe. "But when you an' C.A. stepped out a' the bushes and ordered those men to drop their weapons, I didn't expect that they'd shoot back at us, either."

"I dropped one of 'em with a bullet to the wrist," said Feather. ". . . Then Charley . . . he wounded the other two before they knew what was going on. I had ta pull the three of 'em out a' that hot bath because the water was turnin' red from their blood, an' some of the other folks sittin' in the springs on that day was throwin' up all over the place because of that blood in the water. Anyway," he added, "that's how we captured them Hot Springs robbers."

"We got a re-ward, too, plus our pictures in the paper," said Roscoe.

"Tell them what paper we got our pictures in, why don't you, Feather?" said Charley.

"It was the *Terlingua Star*, a monthly paper they put out fer the locals down there," said Feather. "Wasn't much—but I still got my copy saved away."

Henry Ellis and Don Sebastian were horseback, waiting inside the walls of the *hacienda* for the guards to open the gates. After they'd been allowed through, and the gates were closed behind them, Don Sebastian spurred out into a run while the boy did his best to keep up.

The two of them eventually slowed, then walked their

horses as they rode away from the *hacienda* and into the vast farmlands and cattle holdings belonging to the Don.

Wherever they went, there were guards—in the fields, near the grazing cattle, and even on the one street that stretched between the small dwellings used to house the *hacienda*'s workers.

It was in front of one of these small adobes that the Don dismounted. Then he nodded for the boy to dismount and follow him.

They stepped up onto a porch, knocking at the door. Within moments, the door was answered by a young Mexican girl around Henry Ellis's age.

"Is your father home?" asked Don Sebastian.

The girl shook her head.

"No, sir, Don Sebastian," she answered. "My father is over at the corrals, working with the cattle . . . my mother is at the grocery. She should be back soon."

"Tell your mother not to worry. We will ride out to the cattle corrals . . . I wish to talk with your father."

They turned and stepped off the porch. Mounting their horses, they rode off in the direction of the cattle pens.

"It is oh so good to see you Don Sebastian," said the large, dark-skinned man with chiseled muscles under his dirty, white work shirt. "Can I be of assistance to you, señor?"

"*Si*, Rodolfo," said the Don. "I would like to see the accounting of my cattle for this month."

"If you will wait right here, I will get the books and bring them to you," said Rodolfo.

He turned and entered a small, canvas-covered shepherd's wagon directly behind them. He returned in minutes, carrying several ledgers.

"I have the accounting of your cattle right here," said Rodolfo.

He handed the ledgers to Don Sebastian. The Don immediately began to thumb through the pages of handwritten columns of figures.

"Everything looks fine to me, Rodolfo," he said. "But I would like to take these ledgers back with me to the *hacienda* for the night."

"Whatever pleases you, Don Sebastian," said Rodolfo.

"I will have them delivered back to you before nine tomorrow morning," said the Don. "Oh," he hesitated, "one ledger appears to be missing, Rodolfo. May I accompany you back inside and help you look for it?"

"By all means, Don Sebastian," said the head *vaquero*. "Just follow me."

Once inside the rough-hewn caravan, the Don took Rodolfo by the sleeve and began whispering.

"Tonight, I would like for the cattlemen and the farmers to prepare for a celebration," he began. "A *fiesta* . . . in honor of my son, Chico. Will you be able to prepare for such a *fiesta* in so little time, Rodolfo? I would like to bring my son to the village shortly after seven this evening."

"We can do that, Don Sebastian," said the *vaquero*, smiling.

"All right," the Don continued, "so, if you will excuse us, my son and I must be getting back to the *hacienda*."

They turned to the door and went outside.

"Don Sebastian and his boy must leave us now," said Rodolfo to the other *vaqueros* who had gathered around. They all made sweeping bows in the Don's direction.

"May God be with you, Don Sebastian," said Rodolfo.

The other men did the same.

The Don and Henry Ellis reined their horses around and

nudged them over to the road that would take them back to the *hacienda*.

The others watched them go until they were consumed by their own dust.

One of the other *vaqueros* came from around the side of the wagon. He joined Rodolfo, and they both continued to watch after the departing riders.

"Rodolfo," he began, "I did not know that Don Sebastian had another son."

"He does not have another son, my friend. That boy you just saw riding away with him is a prisoner . . . just as we are."

Roca Fuerte's eyes were following the Don and Henry Ellis as they disappeared behind the curtain of dust they had created themselves. He was observing from his hiding place behind a water tank that sat a few yards away from the shepherd's wagon, where Rodolfo kept the statistics on the cattle. He stood up to his full height before he stepped out to join Rodolfo and the other *vaqueros*.

"I hate that man," said Rodolfo, referring to the Don. "He treats our people as if they were his personal property instead of the keepers of his land and livestock that we are."

"So, you owe no obligation to Don Sebastian?" said Fuerte.

"No, señor," said Rodolfo. "We pay him a percentage of the wages we receive for working the cattle, for the use of his land . . . just as the farmers do with their crops. He means nothing to any of us."

"When we were talking earlier, you said you and the others would not stand in our way if my friends and I attacked the Don's *hacienda*?"

"What if you came for the boy tonight? The Don has ordered a celebration to honor his son."

"That would be all right with us, señor," answered Fuerte.

"Even if you were to kill the Don and drag his body through the manure in the street, he would still mean nothing to us," said Rodolfo.

"Then I have your word that you and the other workers will look the other way when my friends and I try and rescue the American boy?" said Fuerte.

"*Sí*, señor," said Rodolfo, "we will all be looking the other way, as you have asked us to."

Fuerte held out his hand and the two men shook on it.

"And you will also tell the farmers of our agreement?" said Fuerte.

Rodolfo nodded. "The farmers feel the same about Don Sebastian as we *vaqueros* do."

"I will do my best to get you and your people some rifles and ammunition," said Fuerte, "just in case the Don decides to hold you responsible."

"Thank you again, Señor Fuerte. We are very grateful for all you are doing for us," said Rodolfo.

"I will tell Señor Sunday of everything you have agreed to. He will be very pleased."

"Then, we shall see you this evening at the celebration for the boy."

"*Sí*," said Fuerte, "you may not know we are there, but we will be there . . . for sure."

He nodded to Rodolfo. The *vaquero* nodded back.

Finding the Seminole-Negro camp was not that easy for Elisabeth Rogers and Mitch Pennell. They were about to give up their search when a certain, recognizable, Seminole-Negro found them.

It was Billy July, who was once again discovering the

Americans wandering in the desert—only this time they were wandering much closer to his camp than before.

"*Americanos* . . . Up here," yelled Billy July from his perch on a rocky ledge quite near, but somewhat higher up than, the trail on which the pair were riding. "You have returned to the land of the Black-Seminole. Is there something you wish to talk about?"

As before, Mitch Pennell and Elisabeth Rogers were invited to sit near the hut by the pool with Billy July, where they were joined by Chief John Thomas Bodie.

For the first time, the two Seminole-Negro leaders were told of the true motive as to why Pennell and his friends were scouting around in Mexico so many miles away from the international border.

When the two leaders finally understood that a child—a boy of eleven years—was being held hostage by Don Sebastian at his *hacienda* several valleys away, they both showed their dislike for the Don's actions. They asked how the Americans had become involved with someone as immoral as Don Sebastian.

"He used to use our people as we use the burro, when we first arrived in this country," said Billy July. "The Black-Seminole fortified most of the *hacienda* in which he lives."

"That was until the Mexican government advised him not to harass our tribe," added Chief Bodie.

Elisabeth began to repeat the same story that Pennell had told them earlier, about how Armendariz and his men had kidnapped the boy's parents . . . and how Charley and the boy, who was Charley's grandson, had gathered some old friends together and led them all into Mexico with the hope of rescuing the boy's parents.

"So, you came back here to ask us for help. Is that your reason for being here?" said Billy July.

"That was our initial reasoning, gentlemen," said Elisabeth. "If you could possibly do us that favor, I'm sure our leader, Mr. Charles Abner Sunday, would make it worth your while."

"If it is guns and ammunition you need . . ." said Pennell.

"We have plenty of guns and ammunition," answered Billy July. "You must remember that many of our men served in the United States Army before we decided to make our home here in Mexico. But now, our weapons are only used for hunting."

"Then, what I will do before we leave," said Pennell, "is tell you from where, and when, we will begin our attack. And if you choose, it will be entirely up to you to join us in our fight to free the boy."

Roca Fuerte rode his horse into the outfit's camp an hour before sunset. He unsaddled, then tied his mount to the picket line where there was fresh alfalfa and oats—both "borrowed," from the Don's fields nearby.

When Fuerte eventually found, then told, Charley of the good fortune he'd had that day by talking with the leader of the *vaqueros*, and that the farmers would also join the *vaqueros* in their promise not to involve themselves when and if the outfit raided the *hacienda*, it gave Charley a warm feeling inside. He was finally realizing that his choice to leave Henry Ellis behind with Don Sebastian had been a good one—and by doing that, he'd also made it possible for him and the members of his outfit to live, and fight, another day.

Henry Ellis was in the dining room of the *hacienda*. He sat at his end of the long table eating a special Mexican dessert his host had his chefs prepared for them. At the other end of the table, Don Sebastian had chosen a cigar from his humidor and was now puffing on an after-dinner smoke. The Don's eyes were on the boy across the length of the table, and he was thinking about whether this American lad was going to be able to replace the son he'd lost those oh, so many years ago. He liked the boy, he was sure of that, but to ever have a legitimate father/son, loving relationship was something he was beginning to doubt.

So far, Henry Ellis had done nothing to show that he didn't appreciate what Don Sebastian was doing for him. And on a personal side, Henry Ellis had shown him absolute respect since the boy's grandfather, and the other Texans, had been escorted back to the border—which they had promised never to cross again.

"Chico," the Don called out.

The boy looked up.

"I'm sorry, Don Sebastian. My mind was on something else."

"Perhaps in your mind you were with your parents, your grandfather, and your other friends?" said the Don. "Or perhaps you were planning a way to escape again?"

Henry Ellis shook his head. He stood up and walked the span of the table until he stood facing the older man.

"I gave you my word, Don Sebastian," said the boy. "I

gave you my word that I would never try to escape from the *hacienda*, ever again."

"Tonight, my son," said Don Sebastian, "I have decided we will do something different . . . tonight I have requested that the two of us be allowed to join the *hacienda*'s farm and ranch workers. At my insistence, they are putting on a celebration in honor of my new son . . . you . . . who now resides in the *hacienda* with his father."

"Where will this celebration take place, Don Sebastian?" asked Henry Ellis.

"In the people's village, of course," said the Don. "In the village of my workers, in the area in front of the church. After supper, when you have changed your clothing, I will send one of my servants to pick you up. Is that all right with you, Chico?"

"I will be ready, Don Sebastian," said the boy.

"If Roca is right, and the Don is having a *fiesta* celebration for Henry Ellis tonight," said Charley, "then we'll have to change our plans completely, and instead of attacking the *hacienda* like we were going to do before, we'll make an attempt to rescue him tonight, while he is away from the protective walls of the Don's *hacienda*."

"Elisabeth and Pennell are still out there somewhere trying to arrange an agreement with the Black-Seminoles," said Sergeant Stone. "If we make our move tonight, there's no way we can expect any additional help from them."

"I suspect that those special weapons in your toolboxes will have to make up for the Black-Seminoles' absence," said Charley. "You better unpack those cases, Sergeant, and pass out what's inside, while it's still light enough to show the members of this outfit how to use 'em."

"Yes, sir," said the sergeant. "I'll get on that right away." Then he turned and walked over to the chuckwagon, where Fuerte, Holliday, and Feather were sitting with Roscoe.

"We'll need to set these up opposite the outside walls of the *hacienda*," said Fuerte. "Sergeant Stone should be the one to choose the sites. As for the semiautomatic pistols—"

"Semiautomatic pistols?" said Charley, cutting him off, then turning to Sergeant Stone, "you never said you could get semiautomatic pistols. Hell, I didn't know they made such a thing."

"They sure do," said Sergeant Stone. "And I was able to get my hands on five of those little bastards . . . some of the only Borchardt C93 pistols in existence, and some extended magazines plus several cases of the new smokeless-powder ammunition."

He held up one of the semiautomatic pistols for all to see. It was a strange-looking invention. The magazine was contained in the pistol's grip, something never before accomplished until then. Plus there was a large overhang at the rear of the pistol containing a toggle-lock mechanism similar to the recently developed Maxim machine gun, giving the weapon a somewhat unfriendly look.

"Will ya take a look at that," said Feather.

Sergeant Stone went on.

"Both the Borchardt C93 and the M1895 Colt-Browning machine gun use smokeless powder," said the sergeant. "It's non-corrosive. There's no chance of fouling any of the delicate machinery that make these types of weapons work."

"Who will get to use the new pistols?" asked Rod.

"Charley—"

"No," said Charley. "I'll just stick to my Walker Colt, if

you don't mind. I'm also kinda used to all that black powder smoke my Walker spits out . . . it's worked as a good cover for me at times."

The sergeant continued.

"The semiautomatic pistols will go to Fuerte, Rod, and myself."

"I'm happy ta keep my Walker like Charley's doin'," said Roscoe.

"Me too," said Feather.

"I'm so used to my Booger and Ben," said Holliday. He was spinning his matching set of nickel-plated Colt .45s. "I reckon I'll keep 'em at my side instead of one of them new-fangled contraptions."

"I'm very pleased to have been chosen to take one of the semi-autos," said Rod. "My single-action Colt artillery model was good, but it can't fire as fast as the Borchardt C93. Besides, the bandits have it. It was never returned to me."

"I'd like one of the automatic pistols, too," echoed Kelly.

"Sorry, Miss Kelly," said Sergeant Stone, "but I don't have any more available."

"Hey, Roca," said Charley, "what time does that party start tonight?"

"We might want to get there early," said Fuerte.

"But not too early," said Charley. "They know what we look like, you know. There should be a sizable crowd there before we arrive so we can blend in."

"If that's the case," said Fuerte, "I can ride back to the village right now and ask them if we can borrow some of their clothing. We can wear it tonight to disguise ourselves."

"You do that, Roca," said Charley. "And be very careful not to be seen."

* * *

Henry Ellis was washing up at the basin in his room when there was a knock on the door. He found a towel and dried himself before he went over and opened it.

Andrés was standing there, holding a young man's suit of clothes on a hanger.

"This is from Don Sebastian," he said. "These belonged to his son. He wishes for you to wear them tonight."

Henry Ellis took the suit from the captain, holding it out for inspection.

"Did you know him, Andrés?" he asked.

"His son? . . . Yes I did, Chico. His father loved him very much."

"Were you there . . . when he . . . ?"

"*Sí* . . . I was there. I was not the captain of the guard back then, of course, just a friend. There were no guards at all in those days, only *vaqueros*. I was the leader of the *vaqueros*."

"Did you see who shot Don Sebastian's son?" asked Henry Ellis.

Andrés nodded.

"*Sí* . . . I saw the man who shot Chico, the son of Don Sebastian."

"Was it my grandfather?" Henry Ellis wanted to know. "Was it Charley Sunday?"

Andrés hesitated. He lowered his eyes to avoid looking at the boy. The question had made him nervous.

"Did you see my grandfather kill Don Sebastian's son?" said Henry Ellis. "Did you?"

Andrés raised his head. Then he looked the boy directly in the eyes.

"If Don Sebastian says it was your grandfather who

killed his son . . . then it was your grandfather who shot the boy."

"Do you even know what my grampa looked like all those years ago?" said Henry Ellis. "Were you really there at all?"

"Put on the suit, Chico. Make an old man happy."

"That's what you're doing, isn't it, Andrés? Making an old man happy . . . by not telling the truth?"

"Please, Chico," said Andrés. "Do not accuse me of being a liar."

"All I want is the truth. Did you see my grandfather kill Don Sebastian's son or not?"

Andrés took a step back into the hallway.

"I am sorry, Chico. I cannot answer any more of your questions."

He turned, locking the door behind him.

Since noon, the inhabitants of the workers' village—just down the road from Don Sebastian's *hacienda*—had been decorating the area in front of their church with flowers, hanging lamps, hand-painted candleholders, and different colored ribbons. The women had also prepared all kinds of food and desserts, plus a special table had been set up to serve as a bar, not only for the liquor and *cerveza* the working men desired, but also for the tea and other simple drinks enjoyed by the women and children, as well.

A small string quartet played beside the villagers' own homegrown brass band, with both musical groups positioned opposite one another on a large platform that had been set up in the center of the plaza, serving as a stage. This would allow the attendees access to stimulating music for their native dances.

Good times and laughter were being had by all when

the carriage containing Don Sebastian and Henry Ellis pulled out of the *hacienda*'s open front gates, following a group of guards on horseback.

The carriage continued to roll down the slight incline toward the village with the guards leading the way. The music grew louder as they neared the central plaza.

They eventually came to a stop less than a few yards from the center of the festive gathering.

"Remember, Chico," said Don Sebastian, "this *fiesta* is for you, and you alone. These people will treat you like royalty . . . and it is expected that you act as a sovereign toward them in return."

"I will do as you say, Don Sebastian," said the boy. "If you see that I am acting in any way you find displeasing, please tell me at once."

"I will do that, Chico," said the Don. "Now let us go. We do not want to keep our hosts waiting."

With a hand on the boy's shoulder to guide him, Don Sebastian helped the boy out of the carriage, then he set out on the short walk to the crowded area in front of the church with his "son," Henry Ellis Pritchard, at his side.

Charley Sunday stood with his friend, Roca Fuerte, just inside the thick double doors of the plaza church. They were both dressed in *vaquero* clothing. Charley was watching his grandson on the other side of the square. He wasn't surprised to see that Henry Ellis was playing his part very well. The boy was being introduced to several of the town's elders, and instead of shaking their hands or bowing his head, he waited, like a true aristocrat, until they bowed down to him first before acknowledging their presence.

"You see, Roca," said Charley, "my grandson knows how to behave like a person of wealth and breeding."

Sitting under a lattice porch frame, topped with interwoven palm fronds, and attached to one of the many adobe houses that made up the village, Rod and Kelly, dressed as a Mexican farmer and his wife, made a toast to one another as the local band began to play some Mexican fandango dance music.

Castanets in the hands of a beautiful woman began their thrilling rattle. Within moments, they were joined by several guitars being strummed with a vengeance.

Husbands and wives, plus several other couples, took one another into their arms and began dancing. Trumpets and violins mingled together in a moving tribute to the villagers' heritage. A few more couples moved out into the open area to participate in the dance. Music was at the center of the celebration.

Dancers twirled by Sergeant Stone, who was dressed as a farmer. He sat on a hand-carved stool at a table in an outdoor *cantina*, sipping tequila, while at the same time, counting Don Sebastian's guards. By then, every member of the outfit knew the guards were actually soldiers in the private army of Don Sebastian. When he was less than halfway through with his count, Sergeant Stone knew for sure that they were outnumbered by more men than they had ever figured on before.

He kept on counting as more and more guards swarmed through the *hacienda* gates, as if someone had told them Charley Sunday and the Texas Outfit had come to town.

Charley and Roca Fuerte had moved and were now sitting at one of the many outdoor tables surrounding the plaza, hiding behind their *vaquero* facades.

Rodolfo, the head of the estate's *vaqueros*, sat with

them. He was watching to be sure his men, plus the other *vaqueros*, and the farmers, were spread out around the plaza so the presence of the outfit wouldn't appear suspicious to the guards.

"I am very happy this *fiesta* idea came from the Don himself," said Charley.

"It was suggested only this morning," said Rodolfo. "I am glad you had the time to get your men ready."

"Not all of them," said Charley. "We're still waiting for a couple of our friends to get back with word on whether the Black-Seminoles will give us their support."

"The Seminoles will not be of any help, Señor Charley," said Fuerte. "They do not get involved with anyone here in Mexico. We will have to send someone to the Black-Seminole camp to find Elisabeth and Pennell and let them know the battle is going to be fought tonight."

"Can't do that," said Charley. "We can't afford to be without any more members of the outfit than we already are."

"Maybe one of the *vaqueros* could ride to the Seminole-Negro camp with a message for Elisabeth and Pennell," said Fuerte.

"That would be the same as if one of us went," said Charley. "No . . . we need every man . . . and woman . . . we've got."

Sergeant Stone, with his face shadowed by his enormous *sombrero*, stood silently between two buildings. He watched as the Don and Henry Ellis were escorted to the center of the platform in the middle of the plaza.

Don Sebastian and Henry Ellis were then helped up the several steps to the podium, where two matching chairs had been set up, overlooking, and facing, the crowd below.

A cheer went up from the people who were gathered around the platform as the father and "son" took their seats. After a few moments the Don held up a hand to his people.

A moment later, Henry Ellis reluctantly did the same.

As the cheering began to die down, Don Sebastian again raised his hand—only this time it was to get everyone's attention.

"My people," he began, "I have asked that you all come here tonight so I may introduce you to my son."

He turned to Henry Ellis, acknowledging the boy with a sweep of his hand. Then he continued.

"As you all know, many years ago, I lost my son, Chico, during a cattle drive. Through the long and lonely years since that incident occurred, I have cried many rivers of tears over Chico's death, praying every single night and day for my boy's return.

"And now," the Don continued, "he has returned . . . my Chico . . . has returned to live with me in my *hacienda*. Starting tomorrow, my son, Chico, will begin working at your sides . . . first as a *vaquero* . . . then as a farmer. So he can get a feeling for everything that goes on here at my estate. Just as I did with the first Chico, those oh, so many years ago."

Like before, the crowd began to applaud. Before long they were cheering. Don Sebastian stood silently beside Henry Ellis, putting his hand on the boy's shoulder. They both smiled broadly.

All the while, more guards kept spilling out of the *hacienda* gates, heading for the village of the people, down below.

Charley and Fuerte had been listening while the Don spoke, while at the same time they watched as the size of Don Sebastian's small army of guards grew in size. Not only was the entire village surrounded at that point, the guards in the plaza now numbered at least three to one over the villagers in some places.

"The odds," said Fuerte, "are not on our side, Señor Charley. I suggest that we call off our mission at once."

Charley agreed. He made a prearranged signal with his left hand, which was seen by Roscoe and Feather. In turn, they relayed the same message to the rest of the outfit.

Finally, the carriage carrying the Don and Henry Ellis left the village, transporting its occupants back up the road and through the *hacienda* gates. After they had gone, most of the guard followed them up the hill, either on foot or horseback, back through the gates and into the confines of the *hacienda* walls.

That left only a few guards to help close down the *fiesta* and send the villagers into their homes for the rest of the night. By that time, Charley and the members of his outfit were nowhere to be seen. They had removed themselves from the event, one by one, during the confusion that followed the Don's and the boy's departure.

Charley and the others drifted back to their campsite one by one, where they found their own clothing, then slipped into their everyday garments without making a sound.

Once everyone was accounted for, Charley called for a conference to discuss the evening's failure to rescue Henry Ellis, plus he asked if anyone had any ideas or new plans on how to get the boy out of Don Sebastian's *hacienda*.

Chapter Twenty-seven

Don Roberto and his followers rode in a column of twos along the bank of a deep, dry ravine. There were many visible indications that this yawning chasm might possibly fill with runoff during a heavy rain, and take its bubbling waters through the desert some distance before dumping it into a dry lake bed some miles east of where they were riding.

One of Don Roberto's *vaqueros*, Jose Chacon, who had been chosen to replace Luis Hernandez as foreman, had been sent off to scout the trail ahead. Now, as the group of men rounded a bend in the wash, Jose Chacon could be seen, not that far away, dismounted and down on one knee, studying something on the ground before him.

As Don Roberto and the others approached Chacon, he stood up and waved Don Roberto over to where he was waiting.

"What have you found, Jose?" the Don wanted to know.

The man pointed to the dried, once muddy, ground.

"There was some kind of an altercation in this area, Don Roberto," said Chacon.

"How do you know that?" asked the Don.

Chacon stepped over to the edge of the abyss and pointed down the steep embankment.

"What you see down there has its own story to tell," said the *vaquero*.

As the Don edged his horse closer to the brink, he was able to see the remains of two dead bodies sprawled on the side of the gully—both of them wearing crossed bandoliers—plus, two wide-brimmed *sombreros* lay near both bodies.

"Bandits," said Don Roberto.

"There were many horses right here," said Chacon, indicating the dried hoofprints by his feet. "I have surveyed this entire area and also discovered several other places where men were in hiding. Those two dead ones must have started down the side of the gully and were killed for their curiosity."

"I think, maybe," said Don Roberto, "that these dead men, and several others, ran into our ex–Texas Ranger friend, Charles Abner Sunday. Are there any tracks leading away from this spot?" asked the Don.

"There are," said Jose Chacon. "But they do not lead forward. They go back in the direction from which they came."

"There are many members of our tribe who, at one time or another, fought for the white man in his wars against the Comanche."

It was Billy July speaking on the morning following the night of the Don's celebration. July was participating in the ritual of discussion before having his first meal of the day. He sat in a circle that contained, not only Elisabeth and Pennell, but Chief Bodie, himself, and several other members of the chief's council as well.

This dialogue they were having was a continuation of a

debate left over from the night before. Black-Seminole tradition said that any discussion not completed the day before must be resolved prior to the beginning of a new day.

"So, you're implying that there are quite a few members of your tribe who may not want to fight alongside white people in another of our battles," said Elisabeth.

"As we told you last night," said Pennell, "we will not be fighting against other Indian tribes. We will be fighting an evil man who has taken a child away from his parents . . . a man who has demanded that we . . . the child's parents included . . . forget about the boy and leave this country to never come back again."

"All we're asking you for is your help in getting the boy back to his parents," said Elisabeth.

They were finally told by the two men that the entire tribe had voted on this subject earlier that morning, and they did not think it wise to fight white men's battles anymore.

"As evil as this man is," said Chief Bodie, "and we ourselves have lived under his evilness, we must still turn down your request."

"We know of this person," said Billy July. "And we agree that he is indeed a very bad man. But we are very sorry that we cannot be of any help to you."

That afternoon, after the celebration, everyone at the outfit's camp had been surprised by the arrival of Mitch Pennell and Elisabeth. They had made their trek back by following a Black-Seminole shortcut. Their arrival had been made easier by the accompanying sound of a good-size cannon being fired close by. It rattled the water gourds in the trees overhead as the twosome dismounted and tied off their horses. Rod and Sergeant Stone were there within seconds, each quickly finding a horse along the picket line. The two men raced away in the direction from which they figured the sound had come.

Less than a mile and a half away, the two riders found themselves in a clearing. They reined up. From this new vantage, they could see the *hacienda*. Mounted on its front walls, on either side of the double-gated entrance, were two very large brass cannons.

As Rod and the sergeant were beginning to gather their thoughts about what they were seeing, one of the cannons exploded with a ball of fire, sending its missile arcing through the air, then dropping onto one of the worker's adobe houses in the village below. A large blast occurred, sending pieces of adobe and wood chips flying in every direction.

"The Don is attacking his own workers," said Sergeant Stone.

At that point, the other cannon was fired. This time the projectile landed on the tiled roof of the Catholic church. The explosion toppled one of the adobe bell towers, sending its remains crashing down onto the open area in front of the church facade with an echoing dissonance.

"We must go back and tell Charley about this," said Rod. "That Don Sebastian is striking out against his own people."

The two men reined around, then headed back toward the camp as quick as their horses could take them.

Charley and Fuerte, along with Pennell and Elisabeth, plus some of the others who were anxiously standing around the campsite in various degrees of dress, were watching the sky as billowing smoke began to rise above the tree line, blotting out the sun on the western horizon.

Sergeant Stone and Rod Lightfoot galloped into the camp, reining up hard, sliding their mounts to a stop in front of Charley and Fuerte.

As the two men dismounted, they were joined by Kelly and Rod, who were just as curious as everyone else about the deafening explosions rocking the ground around them.

"The Don has ordered his men to fire on his workers' village," said Rod.

Another cannon fired and shook the ground under their feet. Moments later, the sound of the deadly missile exploding was heard, shaking the ground even harder. Another black puff of smoke began rising from the location of the village.

At that moment, Rodolfo and three other *vaqueros* appeared, riding into the camp. They reined up and dismounted near the small crowd.

Charley and the others moved to the new arrivals.

"Rodolfo," yelled Charley, "what is going on over there?"

"Don Sebastian has turned against his own workers," said Rodolfo. "Some of them are already dead or dying."

He moved in closer to Charley who could see the man had been crying.

"My daughter, Señor Sunday," he said, "my daughter is one of the injured. The Don gave us no warning . . . no warning at all."

"Why do you think this is happening, Rodolfo?" asked Fuerte.

"Someone . . . either in your camp or my village, must have told the Don of your presence at the celebration last night. Firing on us with cannons is the Don's way of letting us know he is displeased with us."

Charley shook his head.

"You mean he's done this before?"

Rodolfo answered, "Whenever he wishes to punish us."

"I wonder who could have told him about our being there last night," said Roscoe, who stood nearby.

"Couldn't a' been one of us," said Feather. "At least not on my shift. Absolutely no one came near this camp, or left it, while I was on guard duty last night."

"I can say the same for my shift," said Roscoe. "No one in or out during my four hours."

"Then it must be someone from my village," said Rodolfo. "Though I do not know of anyone who would want to draw the Don's anger to the very place in which they live."

"If you'd like, Rodolfo," said Charley, "we can ride down there and at least stop them from firing those cannons for a while."

"No, no, no, Señor Charley," said Rodolfo. "The cannon fire will die down before you could get there . . . and besides, Don Sebastian is only doing that as a warning to us. What you had better prepare for is an attack on you. I must assume the Don is even angrier with you for breaking your word to him and remaining in Mexico."

Another cannon roared as Henry Ellis started to descend the grand staircase. He held tight to the nearest banister as he made his way down the rest of the steps.

The boy burst into the dining room, stopping in his tracks when he saw Don Sebastian sitting calmly in his usual place at the long table, eating his early supper as if nothing were happening outside.

Another cannon roared, followed by a loud explosion.

As its projectile hit its target, the glass chandeliers in the room jerked and rattled.

Henry Ellis moved closer to the Don.

"What is going on, Don Sebastian? What is all that noise?"

Without looking up, the Don replied, "It appears that your grandfather and his friends were right there at your party last evening, Chico," he said. "I am just letting my workers know that for condoning their presence, I am very unhappy."

"You're having your guards fire cannons at the village," said the boy. "I can see what is going on from my bedroom window. The villagers did nothing to harm you."

"But indeed they did, my Chico," said Don Sebastian. "They allowed your grandfather and his friends to wait in their village when they knew beforehand that I would be bringing you there for the celebration."

"That's not fair," said Henry Ellis.

"What is not fair, Chico? That I am punishing my workers for something I should be punishing your grandfather for?"

He finally looked up, turning slightly to the boy.

"Your grandfather lied to me, Chico. And you, also, lied to me about your grandfather keeping his word. But fear not, my son, I will take care of your grandfather and his friends in due time. No one lies to me and gets away with it. Do you understand, Chico?"

Henry Ellis nodded.

"Now, go to your usual place at the table," said Don Sebastian. "I'll have the servants bring you your supper."

On the day they had returned from escorting Charley Sunday and his outfit back to the international border,

Colonel Armendariz and the members of his gang had been told to make their camp in a far corner of the *hacienda* grounds—near the barracks for the reserve guards. Armendariz had made a handshake deal with Don Sebastian that, for a good sum of money, he and his followers would stay behind the *hacienda*'s walls as a backup for his army of guards. To always be there—to assist the guards, if needed. That was in case the tide turned against the Don and extra soldiers were needed quickly. In return, Don Sebastian would provide, at no cost, food for the bandit leader and his followers, plus forage for their horses, just to have this extra security in case some part of his plan went awry.

As if they were camping alongside a road somewhere, Armendariz's band of outlaws had set up their tents and other portable structures in their usual way. They had been living in this camp for more than a few days, and some of them had become rather fed up with the whole idea.

Sitting around one of the fires in the camp, with several other gang members, Manolito watched as his wife prepared some beans wrapped in tortillas for the two of them, plus the others who were sitting nearby.

"Thank you, Mary Theresa," said Manolito as his wife handed him a bean-filled tortilla.

The others also thanked her as she distributed the rest of the fare she had prepared for them.

She took the last rolled tortilla for herself, then settled back beside her husband to enjoy their evening meal.

"I am getting so tired," said Mary Theresa, "of doing the same things over and over again, day after day. When do you think our colonel will decide to leave this place so we can again get back to our usual way of living?"

"I am afraid," said Manolito, "that if our colonel has

made up his mind to join forces with Don Sebastian, we could be here for a long, long time."

"I just feel so useless," said the woman.

Manolito laughed.

"You are a good cook, Mary Theresa," he told her. "Can't you be satisfied with doing women's work for once in your life?"

A knife sliced through the air, finding a spot near Manolito's left boot to embed itself.

"*Ay caramba*," shouted Manolito. "I was only teasing you when talking about women's work, Mary Theresa. I am your husband. Why would you want to kill me with a knife?"

"Consider it a warning, my dear husband," said the woman. "Never mock me about doing women's work, when I am so much better with a blade and a pistol than you are."

The other bandits chuckled.

Feather came running into the outfit's camp, leaving in his wake pieces of the kindling he'd been gathering. Finally, with just a few feet to go before he would intercept Charley, Fuerte, and Roscoe, he lost the entire load of sticks and small twigs. All the juggling he could muster couldn't save the tinder from scattering every which way, and then some.

"What is it, Feather?" asked Charley. "You look like you've seen a ghost."

Breathing hard, the little cowpoke tried to explain.

"I don't know just who they are, Boss," he said, "but there's a bunch of well-heeled Mexican gunmen ridin' toward our camp, and they look like they mean business."

"Are they soldiers?" asked Fuerte.

"Or more bandits?" said Charley.

"No," said Feather. "They're just a bunch of mean-lookin' Mexicans, and I'll bet my bottom dollar they got business with us."

Charley reached for his Walker Colt, pulling it from his boot.

"Everybody grab a rifle," he called out. "We got some uninvited company on its way."

Everyone scattered to retrieve their weapons, while Charley, Fuerte, Roscoe, and Feather moved out into the middle of the road to await the arrival of the approaching riders.

The rest of the outfit found a tree, a rock, or anything else that could be used for cover, and got behind it.

By the time the galloping horses rounded a nearby bend and came into view, all they could see were the four men standing shoulder to shoulder in the center of the road—and that they were all armed to the teeth.

Don Roberto held up his hand for his men to stop. They all pulled up sharply, reining their horses in behind their leader.

"Who are you, and what do you want from us?" said Charley, furrowing his brow.

"I am Don Roberto Acosta," said the Don. "And these are some of my *vaqueros*. We have been searching for two Americans who were abducted by bandits while they were on their way to my *hacienda*."

Fuerte stepped forward, lowering his rifle.

"It is me, Don Roberto, Roca Fuerte."

"Yes," said the Don. "I recognize you now, Roca."

Charley, Roscoe, and Feather exchanged looks, trying to figure the whole thing out. Now it was Charley who stepped forward.

"One of the Americans you are seeking is my daughter, señor," he offered.

"And her husband would be Kent Pritchard?" said Don Roberto.

Charley nodded. "Yep," he said. "You must be the gentleman they were on their way to visit."

"That is correct," he said. He turned to Fuerte.

"Your friend here, Roca Fuerte, works for me. Only I thought he was going to stay in Brownsville and look for more evidence," said the Don.

"I can explain myself, Don Roberto," said Fuerte.

"I am sure you can," said Don Roberto. "But let me guess. While you were searching for clues in Brownsville, you just happened to run across this gentleman—"

"Charley Sunday," said Charley.

"Charley Sunday," echoed the Don. "And after he told you that he was also searching for Mr. and Mrs. Pritchard, you decided to accompany them in their pursuit of the abductors."

"There is also a young boy, Don Roberto. Mr. Sunday's grandson. We managed to free the Pritchards, but now their son is being held captive . . . by the same man who ordered the Pritchards' abduction in the first place."

"I can only guess who that would be," said Don Roberto.

"It is Don Sebastian de la Vega," said Fuerte.

"Ah yes, my old friend," said Don Roberto. "We were once rivals over who had the largest parcel of land in this part of Mexico. Over the years, Don Sebastian's greed exceeded my wants many times over, so I decided to stay away from him and his acquisitions, as long as he didn't try to steal any of mine."

"Don Sebastian is the one who hired the Armendariz gang to abduct the Pritchards."

"What Don Sebastian has actually done," said Charley,

moving in closer to the others, "is to take my grandson away from his parents and me on the condition that me and my friends get out of Mexico and never come back."

"Which makes it even more obvious that he means to keep the boy for himself, for some particular reason," said Don Roberto. "What have you done to get your grandson back?"

"We thought we had a chance last evening," said Charley, "but we found out we are extremely outnumbered . . . Don Sebastian has a personal private army of close to fifteen hundred guards. There are only nine of us."

"I have eighteen of my *vaqueros* with me," said Don Roberto, "and another hundred and fifty out there somewhere still searching for the boy's parents. If I could only figure out a way to get a message to my other men."

"But you have said that your men are split up all over, still searching for the parents," said Fuerte. "Even if we did have a few men to spare, how would they even know where to start looking?"

"I have no idea," said Charley.

Mary Theresa wandered away from the Armendariz camp after the small squabble she'd had with her husband, Manolito. *The farther I can get from that bandit camp, the better*, she thought to herself, as she walked aimlessly around in the *hacienda*'s walled-in compound.

She strolled through a small fruit orchard, which, from the center, she could not see the perimeter. Then she moved down a gravel-covered path that led her past two very large manmade lakes. Eventually she came across what appeared to be a small collection of buildings that she knew must be the quarters for Don Sebastian's soldiers.

No one was around as she passed through this grouping of barracks buildings. She finally found herself approaching the *hacienda* itself, from the rear.

In all her life, Mary Theresa had never seen such a fine-looking home as the *hacienda* presented to her. This wasn't the first time in her life she had found herself coveting another person's possession—even though she had been taught all her life never to do that.

Mary Theresa had been taught since childhood that the men with riches in her country were her enemy, and that the possessions they held had been earned at the expense of other people—mostly the poor. She knew that it was wrong for her to desire to live in the *hacienda*, as she was thinking. She knew that if she really believed in what her friends and others had taught her over the years, she must destroy buildings like the *hacienda*, and the men who had stolen from the people to obtain such great wealth.

All of these thoughts were running through her head, when she heard a whistle. She stopped where she was and looked around. Everywhere close to her was void of human activity. She was positive she was still alone. Then, from somewhere near, the whistle came again. This time Mary Theresa raised her head, looking up. What she saw made her heart skip a beat or two.

Behind an iron-barred window, on a balcony directly above where she was standing, she saw the face of the boy she and her husband had captured and brought back to the Armendariz camp with two other Americans, some days earlier.

Not knowing what she should do, now that she had been seen by the boy, she raised her hand and waved.

Taking one hand off the bar it had been gripping, and still holding on with the other—the boy waved back.

* * *

The outfit was now sharing its camping space with Don Roberto and his eighteen *vaqueros*. Roscoe had cooked up some of the remaining Mexican-army mess supplies, which made a lean meal because of all who had joined the group.

After supper, Roscoe and Kelly made sure everyone had a cup—then they circled around the campsite, stopping to talk to their friends and the tired Mexican cowboys, pouring coffee for everyone.

Fuerte, Charley, and Don Roberto sat near their bedrolls, sipping coffee and talking, while Charley took out his pipe and filled the bowl with tobacco. He struck a Blue Diamond and sucked the flame into the bowl until he got a good fire going. Then he shook out the flame and tossed the match into the campfire.

"We'll have a better chance next time, with the Don and his men backing us up."

"Eighteen additional guns will not turn the tide in a battle with Don Sebastian's soldiers," said Fuerte.

"At least having eighteen more men who know how to use a weapon will give more confidence to those in the outfit," said Charley.

"I do not think so," said Don Roberto. "It will just take them more time to kill us all . . . and that's what they'll do . . . kill us all."

"Well, I'm about all planned out, Don Roberto," said Charley. "I feel like we've tried everything we know to get Henry Ellis out of that *hacienda*, and nothing's worked."

"Yet," said Fuerte. "Nothing's worked . . . yet."

"Are you saying that you've come up with another plan?" said Charley.

"It's not really a plan, Señor Charley," said Fuerte. "For now, let's just call it . . . a new idea."

Chapter Twenty-eight

Mary Theresa uncoiled her whip. She stepped back, and with a flick of her arm and wrist, she tossed the end of the whip's braided leather tip over the balcony railing. It wound itself tight around the balustrade, allowing the whip to assist her in climbing from the ground to the balcony railing.

Once she was over the barrier and onto the veranda, she stayed low, hoping that no one had seen her. Then she made her way over to the barred window where Henry Ellis was still standing. She checked the strength of the iron. She removed her knife from its scabbard and began picking away at the lock that secured the bars.

Henry Ellis watched as she continued to work at the lock with the knife. Before he knew it, the large padlock broke free and she was inside the room beside him.

"What are you doing?" he asked the woman. "You're one of the Armendariz bandits who captured us in the first place."

"That was when I believed in a cause," she replied. "Now, I am not so sure who is morally on the right side, or on the wrong side. Why is Don Sebastian keeping you here?" she wanted to know.

"He thinks my grampa killed his son many years ago," said Henry Ellis. "And now he wants to keep me here at his *hacienda* to replace that son. You were down there a while ago when Don Sebastian traded my life for those of my parents and some others, were you not?" said the boy.

"*Sí*," she answered. "I was there . . . but I was not paying that much attention."

"Well, anyway," said Henry Ellis, "my grampa, me, and our friends are on the right side, while Don Sebastian and his men, plus your boss—Armendariz—and his followers, are in the wrong."

"For some reason, I am beginning to see it your way . . ."

She hesitated.

"What is your name, son?"

"Henry Ellis," said the boy. "That's my name . . . Henry Ellis."

"Henry Ellis," she said, patting his cheek. "You are a good boy. I could feel the goodness in your heart from the first time I saw you. I am Mary Theresa. I will try to get you back to your grandfather, but you will have to help me."

"I will surely help, Mary Theresa."

"Good," said the woman.

"What would you like me to do?" asked the boy.

"For now, just follow me, and do as I say," was her answer.

Don Sebastian stood on the wall near the main gates, looking out across the green valley from where his *hacienda* was located. Andrés handed him a pair of binoculars. The Don raised them to his eyes.

Over the tops of the low mountains surrounding the green valley, he could see a large cloud of dust being raised.

He turned to Andrés, his captain of the guard who was always at his side. He handed the binoculars back to him.

"What do you think, Andrés? Take a look."

Andrés raised the binoculars to his eyes and focused as best he could.

"Someone is coming, Don Sebastian. It could be several men riding fast, or many men riding slow."

"Alert the guards, Andrés. As fast as you are able, alert the guards."

Andrés ran down the steps to the ground below, then he moved to a bell mounted on a heavy wooden tripod. He pulled on the rope continuously to ring out a warning.

Less than a mile away, at the camp shared by Don Roberto's *vaqueros* and Charley's Texas Outfit, the sound of the clanging bell echoed through the air.

Around the same time, one of Don Roberto's *vaqueros* rode into camp at a full gallop. He was met in front of the Don's tent by Don Roberto, Fuerte, and Charley.

"What is it?" the Don asked his scout.

"Many federal soldiers are coming this way, Don Roberto," said the man. "I was close enough to see that it is your brother who leads them."

"Damn," said Don Roberto. "I did not expect him to be here so soon."

"You contacted the federal army?" said Charley. "I thought—"

"My brother is the ranking general, Señor Sunday,"

said Don Roberto. "I sent him a message two days ago apprising him of our situation. But I so wanted to keep the army, and the federal police, out of this. Now it appears to be too late for that."

"Then we better go for it all while we can," said Charley.

"I will send a messenger back to my brother with an explanation, plus a drawing, showing where Don Sebastian's heaviest troops are concentrated."

He turned to Charley.

"You get your men ready to attack the *hacienda* from the front, Señor Sunday."

"Roca," called out Charley. "Get the outfit together, *now*. On the double!"

"And my *vaqueros*, led by me . . . we will split up and hit them from both sides. My brother will attack Don Sebastian's militia from the rear, taking Don Sebastian's reserve troops full on."

"What about Armendariz and his gang? They are still in there, aren't they?" said Charley.

"If there are others, we will have to hope they get caught in our cross fire."

"Before you go with that plan, Don Roberto," said Charley, "I must tell you that my men are in possession of some very up-to-date weaponry."

The Don looked Charley directly in the eye.

"Just what kind of weapons do you have, Señor Sunday?"

Together, Charley Sunday and Don Roberto decided that one of the two Colt-Browning automatic machine guns would go with eight of Don Roberto's *vaqueros* and cover a side wall. The other machine gun would stay with Charley's outfit and cover the *hacienda*'s front gates.

Sergeant Stone and Mitch Pennell would operate the automatic weapons. Their job would be to strafe the entrance gates and one side of the *hacienda*'s walls. The Don's other eight *vaqueros*, along with Roscoe, Feather, and Holliday, would attack from the opposite side, using their own weapons, plus three of the Borchardt C93 semiautomatic pistols. All of the groups of men would attack on foot, since both Don Roberto and Charley had witnessed cavalry charges in the past where the horses made very cumbersome targets in close-quarter situations like the one at hand. And once on foot, if the riders hadn't been injured too bad, it was agreed that the cavalry troopers did their best fighting.

At that point, the leaders of the federal army troops rode into the camp. Within minutes, Don Roberto was relaying the whole story, plus his battle plan, to his brother and the other officers.

"They are already expecting something," said Don Roberto, in finalizing. "But we will give you time to get your troops around behind the *hacienda* before we attack."

"And, if you're fired upon," added Don Roberto, "don't be afraid to shoot back."

"And just remember," said Charley, "my grandson is somewhere in there . . . so, be careful."

The rest of the federal troops had caught up to their leaders by then. Before they even had a chance for a sip from their canteens, the officers led them away.

Charley took a head count as the men rode by . . . there were at least two hundred fifty soldiers, he figured.

Charley turned to Don Roberto.

"At least the odds are evening up for us," he said.

* * *

Fuerte rode into the camp's center, followed by the rest of the outfit.

"Sergeant Stone . . . Pennell," yelled Charley, "you two get the machine guns and go with Don Roberto and his men. And Sergeant, make sure you take along enough ammunition for a siege, if it turns out that way. Also," he added, "make sure that anyone who has a semiautomatic pistol has enough ammo to get them through the battle, as well."

The sergeant nodded.

"Thanks, Tobias," said Charley, just before the two men rode off to assemble the weapons.

The sergeant threw Charley a wink.

Charley winked back.

"And you, Mitch Pennell," said Charley, "you do a good job for me today and I'll see what I can do about extending your temporary reprieve . . . maybe even making it permanent."

Pennell nodded with a twinkle in his eye, then he turned in his saddle, spurred his horse, and left the area, following the sergeant.

Within the next half hour, Charley's outfit, Don Roberto's *vaqueros*, and Don Roberto's brother's federal army troops had cautiously moved into their positions, surrounding the *hacienda* walls.

Both Colt-Browning machine guns were now mounted on tripods and had been placed where each could do the heaviest damage. Those with semiautomatic pistols had just finished taking up their positions across from the wall to which they had been assigned.

An army messenger brought news that the federal troops had made it to their positions behind the *hacienda* and were surrounding the back wall. The messenger also reported that there was a rear gate to contend with as well. When everyone was in position, Charley and Don Roberto sent word to the others to stand by.

Inside the *hacienda*'s walls, the preparations being taken by the outfit, Don Roberto's *vaqueros*, and the federal troops outside, were being mostly disregarded. Instead, Don Sebastian was having his guards prepare for a frontal attack only. The earlier sight of the rising dust had helped him to realize there was a very large force approaching the *hacienda*, but he had yet to believe the reality that Charley's entire outfit had returned, joined by Don Roberto and his *vaqueros*. Don Sebastian had also figured that if the approaching riders were unsuspecting officers of the law, or government *federales*, he would more than likely be able to talk his way out of a confrontation. And if they happened to be a large gang of *bandidos* looking for a rich man's property to raze, he still had Armendariz and his band camped near the rear entrance. So, one way or the other, Don Sebastian thought he had all his options covered.

The *hacienda*'s two cannons were in position on either side of the arch over the main gates. For about thirty minutes, the guards on the front wall had been aware of movement behind the heavy brush that had been cleared away from the front wall and piled about forty-five meters away, making the semicircle of dry tinder the main obstacle between the *hacienda* and anyone wishing to assault Don Sebastian's holdings. The dry vegetation had been left that way in case there was ever such an attack. It could be ignited by torch within moments and turned into an inferno that would stop the opposition's advance long enough to reset the cannons and add the needed guards.

Don Sebastian climbed to the top of the front wall with Andrés at his side. Once there, they were both able to see the movements behind the brush.

The Don turned to Andrés.

"Have them fire the cannons right over there in the center of the piled brush. I have a feeling it is from there they will begin their assault."

Andrés moved over to one of the cannons, directing his men to fire both weapons into the center of the piled brush.

The cannons were aimed, and their fuses were lit.

All eyes watched as the weapons exploded and the cannon balls arced out over the barren space between the wall and the piled shrubbery.

Chapter Twenty-nine

1961

"I have to go to the bathroom," said Noel, causing her two older brothers to expel several disparaging remarks under their breath.

The girl slid out of her chair and ran inside the house.

"Careful what you say about your sister, boys," said Evie. "Or I'll just have Grampa Hank stop with his storytelling right now, and you can both figure it out for yourself how it all ends."

"Ahhh, Mom," said Josh, raising himself up on one elbow. "Noel always has to go to the bathroom just at the wrong moment."

Caleb agreed, nodding his head.

"He's right, you know. She can be a real spoilsport when she wants to."

"How 'bout the rest of you?" said Hank. "Any of you need to go before I finish up this story?"

Neither boy spoke. They had nothing to say.

"Then, if you'll excuse me," said Hank, "I'd kinda like to go, too. I've been sitting here for a long time without a break. I'll go on with the story when both me and your sister get back."

Chapter Thirty

1900

Both shells hit yards apart and exploded, sending dirt and pieces of undergrowth flying into the sky overhead.

For the briefest of moments, the cannon balls' explosions cleared away just enough brush to expose the barrel of the sergeant's Colt-Browning machine gun before Sergeant Stone began firing back at the cannons and the men standing around them on the top of the wall.

Quite a few bullets found their mark, toppling more than several guards from the fortification. Other projectiles chipped away at the adobe bricks, sending pieces ricocheting through the air, bloodying Don Sebastian's cheek and knocking Andrés off his feet for a short period.

As more shots rang out, Don Sebastian ducked down beside his captain of the guard.

"Are you all right?" he asked.

Again, the cannon beside them roared.

"Just temporarily shaken," said Andrés. "Here," he said, standing again, "I must get you to safety, *mi jefe*. This way."

There was more machine gun fire from the brush pile as Andrés took Don Sebastian by the arm and led him down the steps and into the courtyard. At the bottom of the steps, the two huddled against the wall.

"I am safe here, Andrés," said Don Sebastian. "You must go back . . . I am now putting you in charge of all my troops."

The second machine gun opened up from the other side of the left wall, sending adobe pieces flying every which way. Don Roberto and his eight men opened up with their rifles shortly after.

"They are attacking from the left side, too, Andrés," said Don Sebastian. "You need to move more troops to cover that position."

Once again Andrés got to his feet and started up the steps to the top of the wall.

Charley stood beside Sergeant Stone, who was stationed behind the first Colt-Browning machine gun in the front. Scattered around on either side of the two were Kelly, Roca Fuerte, Mitch Pennell, and Elisabeth—all armed with lever-action rifles and plenty of ammunition. Between blasts from the sergeant's automatic weapon, everyone would pick a target and fire their rifles sporadically, then they would find a new position for their next round. They were hoping to fool their enemies on the wall into thinking they were a much larger force.

Charley could see more guards filling the empty spaces on top of the front wall. Soon guards would spread to the left-hand wall, where Rod Lightfoot and Don Roberto, plus eight of the Don's *vaqueros*, would engage them in battle.

Moments after that, Feather, Roscoe, and Holliday, plus the other eight *vaqueros*, would open fire against the right wall of the *hacienda*, after which even more reserve guards would be needed.

Near Don Sebastian's guards' barracks buildings at the rear of the *hacienda* grounds, the reserve guard units had been notified of the frontal attack on the *hacienda* walls. Most of the men had begun to exit their barracks in full fighting gear—with rifles in hand and pistols and sabers ready at their sides—when a portion of the back wall and gate were blown away by a federal army cannon ball.

The reserve guards were caught by surprise as their officers were still leading them forward toward the front. The new commotion at the back wall and gate pulled their attention around just in time to see the federal troops charge into the open area with all weapons firing.

Reserve guards dropped like flies as the Mexican army soldiers continued their assault from the rear.

Many of the guards were caught in the middle, with their leaders goading them on toward the front of the *hacienda* grounds. Others turned to fight the advancing federal troops behind them, but they were stopped by a wall of lead before they knew what had happened.

Don Sebastian was still standing at the bottom of the steps that led to the top of the front wall, only now he was anxiously searching for Andrés, his captain of the guard, who had not come back down since the battle began. Over to his left he could see several of his guards reinforcing the double gates that were, for now, keeping the attackers from entering the *hacienda* grounds.

He could hear the repetitive sounds of the automatic

weapons firing on the other sides of the front and side walls. Every so often, one of his guards would take a bullet, then tumble off the wall. Don Sebastian wondered what happened to the men if they toppled forward off the wall and into the enemy's path. Were they immediately captured, then dragged off for interrogation before being treated for their wounds? Or were they just shot and their bodies left at the bottom of the wall where they faced their injuries without treatment and would eventually die?

Don Sebastian didn't want to think of these things, but there wasn't much he could do about it while he stood, alone, at the bottom of the steps in the courtyard.

"Don Sebastian."

He turned to see one of his commanding officers who had come up behind him in the chaos.

"Yes, Major Gonzalez," said Don Sebastian.

"They have taken us from the rear and are already inside the walls. It is now hand-to-hand fighting back there."

"I was just going to ask that they send more reinforcements to assist my troops up here—"

"I am afraid that is an impossibility at this time, Don Sebastian," said the officer. "I was told to come here and ask you for reinforcements."

"What are Armendariz and his gang doing to help us?" Don Sebastian wanted to know.

"He is getting ready to counterattack when those who have breached the rear wall advance any farther."

"My God," said Don Sebastian, "how many of them are there?"

"Those at the rear wall are federal troops, Don Sebastian. I am not sure of their numbers, but there are many."

"Go back and tell my men they must hold out; it is imperative that they do."

"Yes, Don Sebastian," said the officer. With a quick salute, he turned and ran back toward the rear wall.

Don Sebastian reflected for a moment. *Federal troops*, he thought. *What have I done to bring the federal troops down on me?*

He turned back to the steps at the side of the wall. Andrés had still not come back down. Finally, Don Sebastian started climbing again to the top.

Charley handed another ammo belt of cartridges to Sergeant Stone, who immediately reloaded the Colt-Browning machine gun.

"Hold off for a minute or two, will you, Sergeant?" said Charley. "I want to get closer and see if we're doing the damage we intended."

Sergeant Stone nodded, stepping back from his weapon.

They were still behind the barricade of piled brush, so Charley started out toward the corner of the left wall. He kept his eyes open all the way, hoping to see something that could possibly give them more advantage.

When Charley had made it closer to the left wall, he could see a small group of *hacienda* guards reinforcing their position on top of the wall with adobe bricks, empty ammo boxes, and the bodies of their dead companions. For a brief moment, one of those guards looked up and saw Charley, who was staring at him from below. It was Andrés—Don Sebastian's captain of the guard. Andrés immediately recognized Charley and ordered the men around him to open fire on the old cowboy. When they did, Andrés turned and started toward the steps behind him.

Andrés was met by Don Sebastian at the top of the steps.

"Where have you been, Andrés?" shouted Don Sebastian over the sounds of battle.

"I have been doing my job," replied Andrés. "But I have some interesting news for you . . . The boy's grandfather did not leave Mexico as you asked him to. He is right here . . . he is the one leading this attack on you."

"Where, exactly, is he?" asked Don Sebastian.

"He is behind the piled brush . . . and that is also where most of the heavy automatic fire is coming from."

"Well," said Don Sebastian, "then don't you think it's about time we took a torch to that pile of brush?"

At the outside base of the right wall, Feather, Roscoe, Holliday, and the other eight *vaqueros* had as much as eliminated the guards sent to defend that barrier. They were moving in closer when Roscoe felt that his boots were getting wet. He looked down and realized he was standing in the middle of a small creek. For a moment, he wondered where the flow was coming from; then he saw it: the small arch at the base of the wall—that inconspicuous entrance to the *hacienda* grounds used by Henry Ellis on the first attempt to get inside the outer fortifications.

"Feather," he called out. "Get over here."

"What's up, Roscoe?" answered the undersized cowboy.

"Do you think you could squeeze through that little ol' hole over there," asked Roscoe, "the one with this creek flowin' through it?"

Feather gave it a look. He shrugged.

"Ain't that the hole in the wall young Henry Ellis first used ta gain access to the *hacienda* grounds?" he said.

"Must be the same one," said Roscoe. "There's only the

one creek. Anyways," he continued, "do you think you could squeeze yourself through that little arch?"

"I probably could . . . and I possibly couldn't," he said. "But I won't know one way or the other until I try. Uh," he hesitated. "What do ya want me ta do if I do get through?"

"Get yerself over to the front gates as fast as you can and open 'em up for us," said Roscoe.

"That's all I'll have ta do?" said Feather.

"However you wanna do it, just do it," said Roscoe. "Just don't get yourself kilt doin' it, though."

"Charley won't get mad at me?"

"He'll probably wanna give you a medal," said Roscoe. "Now, you just go on ahead and see if you can fit."

Feather did fit through the space offered by the arch. He was slightly larger than Henry Ellis so he got more of himself wet than the boy did. When he was all the way through, he turned around and stuck his head back the other way, calling out to Roscoe.

"You an' the others can start headin' around to the front gates now, 'cause I'll have 'em opened up for ya in . . . ah . . . ," he paused, "two shakes of a lamb's tail."

"Just get-a-goin'," said Roscoe, kicking some dirt toward the little cowboy. "We'll be seein' you on the inside before ya know it."

Feather ducked, then he backed himself out of the arch, into the courtyard once again.

At the left wall, Don Roberto held up a hand to keep his men from firing as a blur of a human body came running toward the rock and cactus fortification his men had thrown together while setting up the second machine gun. The Don knew the running man was a friend, and not a foe, by the way he was dressed—in rough American western clothing with leather chaps.

As soon as the man dropped to his knees beside Don Roberto and edged up to him, the Don recognized him to be Charley Sunday.

The first thing Charley did was to throw a nod to Rod Lightfoot, who was sitting behind the smoking machine gun a few feet away.

"How's it going over here?" asked Charley.

Rod nodded, grinned. He made a tipping-the-hat motion to Charley.

Charley turned to Don Roberto. "How about you?" he asked.

"Our opposing fire has gotten lighter," said Don Roberto, "if that is what you mean."

"Same thing out front," Charley told him. "I imagine that's due to the federal army troops preventing any reinforcements from getting through to the front. Have you taken any casualties?"

"One wounded," said Don Roberto. "But he can still fight."

He held up his left arm so Charley could see the bloodied bandage wrapped around his bicep.

"You?" said Charley.

"Me," said Don Roberto. "But as I said before, I can still fight." He raised his right hand, which held a smoking foreign-manufactured revolver. "I only need one hand to use this," he said. "It is double-action."

The Don suddenly raised his gun and fired off two shots at something behind Charley.

The ex-Ranger turned just in time to see a man with a torch lying prone on the ground, the still smoldering flames of the torch mere inches from the brush barrier at the front.

Charley smiled and patted Don Roberto on the back.

"Well," said Charley, "I'd better be getting back to my men."

With that, he did a quick look around, then took off at a run, staying low. Rounding the corner of the wall, he was gone as quick as he had appeared.

Once he was inside the *hacienda* walls, Feather had advanced no farther than a few feet. He hugged the adobe bricks with his body, trying to blend in as much as he could. Most of Don Sebastian's guards—at least the ones he could see—were concentrated on the front wall above him. Every so often, another guard or two would come running up to the front wall from the rear of the *hacienda* grounds and join their comrades by using the one set of steps to the right of the gates. Most of those guards looked as if they had been participating in battle for some length of time before they had been sent as a replacement at the front.

Again, machine gun fire raked the top of the wall, with some of its lead biting into a guard's leg as he got too close to the bullet pattern the automatic weapon was spraying from below.

Feather decided to take a chance. Ducking low, he ran to the double gates beneath the entry arch. No one was near him to guard the gates at that particular moment. Those doing the fighting had need of every guard they could get on top of the wall, defending the *hacienda* from the outside attackers, and they couldn't spare one man to secure the gates.

Now, Feather was there. He stood alone in front of the double gates, holding his Walker Colt in one hand and a Bowie knife in the other. He took a moment to study the locking mechanism that kept the two gates closed. Feather shrugged, raised his pistol, and fired point-blank into the little wooden box that contained the locking device. The box shattered and the gates both began to part.

Fuerte was the first to see the gates swing open wide, so it was he who gave the order to charge.

Sergeant Stone lay down a barrage of fire at the top of the front wall. That caused all the guards to dive for better cover than they were already using.

Charley joined Fuerte, and together they led those who had been trading fire with the guards on the front wall through the piled brush across the small stretch of bare land, then through the open gates, where they were met by Feather.

Behind one of the fortified guard boxes, on one side of the walkway, Andrés led Don Sebastian through a small, hinged trap door, built into the surface of the thickly constructed barrier.

Once inside, the Don found that they were in a crude tunnel of some kind—and it was dark and narrow.

Andrés lit a torch that he found laying on a small ledge.

"Hold on to my belt," he said to Don Sebastian. "And watch your feet."

"Where will this tunnel take us?" the Don asked his captain of the guard.

"To your *hacienda*, of course," answered Andrés.

"Then, let's go there as quickly as possible."

He grabbed hold of Andrés's belt as the captain of the guard stepped out, leading the way.

Don Roberto and his eight *vaqueros* had come around to the front wall where they joined Charley and his group inside the open gates. Charley had just finished thanking Feather for his bravery under fire.

Roscoe, Holliday, and the other eight *vaqueros* came around the right-hand corner of the wall. They saw Charley and the others inside the open gates and joined him and Don Roberto.

"We didn't hear no more shootin', so we figgered Feather had got lucky," said Roscoe.

"And we were right," added Holliday.

"Thanks to Feather," said Charley. "Now, Roscoe, Feather, Holliday," he called out, "go on up there on that wall and settle this thing. Get 'em to surrender, or shoot 'em if they won't. Then bring those you take prisoner down here . . . on the double."

Fuerte called to them.

"Any sign of Don Sebastian?" he asked.

"I seriously doubt that Don Sebastian was ever this close to any of the fighting," said Don Roberto.

"Oh, he was here," said Fuerte. "I questioned a wounded guard who had been up on the wall, and he said that Don Sebastian was right up there with the rest of them until the gates were opened."

"Did anyone up there happen to see where he went?" asked Charley.

"I don't know that yet, Charley," said Fuerte. "But as soon as they are all rounded up and brought down here, I will question every single one of them."

"Charley!" It was Roscoe's voice, coming from the wall. "Y'all better come on up here. There's somethin' you better take a look at."

Armendariz and his gang, plus the remainder of the re-enforcement guards, were being disarmed and lined up single file by the federal soldiers. One of the ranking officers rode over to Don Roberto's brother, the general in command, and relayed a message to him in Spanish. "We have the entire Armendariz gang in custody," he reported. "And the last of the re-enforcement guards are surrendering whenever we can dig them out of their hiding places."

The general nodded. "Very good," he told the officer. "Send a messenger around to the front and let Don Roberto know that we have secured the rear."

On the top of the front wall, behind the fortified guard box, Roscoe was showing the hinged trapdoor opening to Charley, Fuerte, Don Roberto, and the rest of the men.

Fuerte said, "The guards say that their superior, the captain of the guard, led Don Sebastian down those steps into a passageway within the wall."

"Well, find me a torch, someone," said Charley. "I'm goin' in there after 'em."

"Wait a minute," said Fuerte, taking Charley by the elbow. "Why not first try to figure out where they would be going. I will ask any number of these guards and will bet you right now that that tunnel leads right back to the *hacienda* itself."

Chapter Thirty-one

A hidden, sliding panel opened up at the rear of one of the giant fireplaces, allowing Andrés to step out. He was followed by Don Sebastian. The two men walked while bent over until they were out of the fireplace, then they stood to their full height and looked around the great room.

No one was visible except for the two of them.

Don Sebastian grabbed hold of Andrés's sleeve.

"Before we continue with our escape," he said, "I will need to get my son, Chico. He is upstairs, locked securely in his room."

Andrés nodded.

"Let me have the key, Don Sebastian. I will go and get him. Then I will bring him to you," he said.

"Thank you, Andrés," said the Don, "but I prefer that I go and get him."

The key was turned in the lock on the boy's door, and just as quickly, the door was flung wide open. Andrés and Don Sebastian were quite surprised that the boy wasn't there. Andrés stepped inside and did a thorough search of the room, plus he checked the barred windows leading to the veranda outside. He discovered that one of the windows had been tampered with when he spotted a curtain caught between a window frame and a previously secured sash.

Taking a closer look, Andrés could see that the lock on the outside of the window had been picked, with several of the iron obstructions missing entirely. He turned to Don Sebastian.

"Someone, other than the boy, has been in this room, Don Sebastian. Someone else has helped him to escape from you one more time."

He started to step out onto the upstairs landing, but he pulled back. Don Sebastian froze in his tracks behind him.

At that very moment, the front doors downstairs were thrown inward, with the outside sun adding considerable brightness to the great room's interior.

Standing in silhouette in the backlight were Charley, Roscoe, Fuerte, Feather, Holliday, Rod, and Don Roberto—all of them with pistols at the ready.

They began moving forward.

"We must get out of here now!" whispered Don Sebastian to Andrés, as he peeked out the bedroom door.

He could see all the way down the staircase to where Charley and the others were now positioned.

Andrés slowly moved past the Don and out onto the second-floor landing at the top of the stairway. He raised his sidearm, aiming it into the bright light below.

Before he could pull the trigger, seven bullets, one right after the other, bracketed Andrés's heart. The captain of the guard lost his footing and tumbled down the curving stairway, grasping at draperies and wall coverings. He pulled them down on top of himself, until his body came to rest at Charley's feet.

Rod stood beside Charley, in his hand one of the Borchardt C93 semiautomatic pistols. The weapon was proving to be a pretty accurate hand gun, especially when operated by someone with Rod Lightfoot's wartime experience.

"Where is my grandson?" Charley asked the man on the floor.

Even though Andrés's eyes stared straight ahead, his lips were able to utter, "Upstairs."

Charley and the others shifted their look to the top of the stairway.

The landing was clear.

Rod made a move toward the stairs but was stopped by Charley.

"Wait," said the ex-Ranger. "Let me try something."

He put a cupped hand to the right side of his mouth, then he leaned his head back just a little and let out a coyote howl that echoed throughout the entire *hacienda*.

Several silent moments passed before a return coyote call echoed, coming from upstairs.

"Henry Ellis!" Charley yelled out. "It's me . . . Grampa Charley. You should be safe now."

There was another moment, then Henry Ellis, followed by Mary Theresa, stepped out onto the landing, coming from another direction.

"Don't shoot the woman," yelled Henry Ellis. "She is my friend. She helped me to escape this time."

Down below, everyone eased up on their triggers.

Suddenly, a single shot rang out.

The bullet caught Mary Theresa in the neck. She grabbed the wound and fell to her knees.

For a brief moment, the woman and the boy made eye contact. The woman's eyes were desperately trying to tell the boy to turn around.

Finally, he understood.

He slowly turned his head to see Don Sebastian, partially hidden behind the bedroom door, with a smoking pistol now aimed down the stairs in Charley's direction.

The Don nodded to Henry Ellis. He beckoned with his eyes for the boy to join him.

"Chico," he said. "Come along, son. Your father is waiting for you."

There was a long moment.

"Come with me now, my son, or I will shoot your grandfather where he is standing."

The boy's derringer fired its two small-caliber projectiles one after the other, putting two small holes in Don Sebastian's forehead. The man took two steps toward the banister, then Don Sebastian Ortega de la Vega toppled over and fell the eighteen feet to the tiled floor below. He now lay facedown, motionless and silent, as blood slowly began to pool around him.

Chapter Thirty-two

The battle was over.

The soldiers of the federal army were still rounding up Don Sebastian's guards and Armendariz's gang, while Don Roberto and his *vaqueros* faced Charley and the outfit in the center of the *hacienda* grounds, near the fountain.

Henry Ellis's parents had been brought into the yard, and Charley was introducing them to Don Roberto. He stood beside his brother, the commanding general of the federal troops. Everyone was shaking hands and congratulating one another on the victory.

Don Sebastian's covered body was being carried out of the *casa grande* by two of his servants. The body was put into the back of a wagon and driven off toward the rear of the property.

"What about him?" said Henry Ellis.

"Don Sebastian will be buried right here on the *hacienda* grounds, beside his real son, Chico. Armendariz and his gang will be turned over to the local authorities, when they arrive—with the exception of the body of the woman who rescued you, Henry Ellis. She will be taken down to the workers' village and buried with honors in the graveyard beside the church."

One of the federal soldiers walked up to the general holding Henry Ellis's horse by the reins. The cart containing the treasure box was still hitched to the animal.

"My men discovered this box of gold inside the *hacienda*," said the general. "It is filled with sacred objects and gold coins stolen by Spanish soldiers during their conquest of the north. I will make sure the gold gets to the Mexican government. And even if there are those who might dispute this, I am sure the courts in Mexico City will find that the Mexican government is the rightful owner, one way or the other."

Slight grumbling could be heard coming from Feather, Roscoe, and Holliday, as they all exchanged unhappy glances.

"Could ya just make sure the kid gets his horse back?" said Roscoe.

"*Si*, señor," said the general. "If the horse belongs to the boy, I will make sure it is returned to him."

"Riders coming in," shouted Fuerte, who stood on top of the front wall above the open gates. Fuerte moved back down the steps behind them and rejoined the group.

A small cloud of dust and the sounds of galloping ponies swirled through the *hacienda*'s entrance gates. The riders reined up in front of Charley and the others.

It was Billy July, with three other Black-Seminole braves riding along with him.

"It appears that we didn't make it here in time," said Billy July. "It just took the four of us a little longer than we expected to make up our minds."

Mitch Pennell and Elisabeth, followed by Kelly, Rod, and some of the others, moved over to welcome the late arrivals.

"Well," said Elisabeth, putting her hand on Billy July's

hand, "it's the thought that counts, Billy. At least you did decide to help us."

Someone had found the original team of horses and the carriage the Pritchard family had been riding in when they were first attacked. Charley took one of the horses by its harness and led the carriage over to Henry Ellis's parents.

"Go ahead," he said. "Get in. It's a long way back to Don Roberto's *hacienda*."

Sergeant Stone, along with Rod, Kelly, and Holliday, stepped forward.

"We're gonna ride straight on back to Juanita," said Sergeant Tobias Stone. "Probably cross the Rio Grande at Eagle Pass. I have ta get these weapons back to Fort Clark before someone reports 'em missin'."

"And we need to get back to our ranch as soon as we can to do some horse breeding," said Kelly.

"Plus she's got a book to write," added Rod.

"And me," said Holliday, "I don't got much a' nothin' ta get back fer except maybe a few a' my students are probably wonderin' where I run off to."

"What about you, Elisabeth?" asked Charley. "Any ideas of where you might be headed?"

"I'll be going back to my ranch, Mr. Sunday. I know I'll do all right once I'm back there."

"Now, Elisabeth," said Charley, "you know that taking care of a ranch is a full-time job. You can't do it alone. Why, you're going to need—"

"A man?" she said, cutting him off.

"That's right," said Charley, "a man."

"Then I figure that'll be all up to you, Mr. Sunday."

"Me?" said Charley.

"Yes, you," she said. "Mister Pennell has offered his services to come back to my ranch with me and help me get a new start."

Pennell moved in beside Elisabeth and she wrapped her arm around his waist. "All he needs is a new start, too."

Pennell raised his head and both men made eye contact.

"Well," said Charley, "I usually can spot it when two friends of mine take a special shine to one another . . . but I sure missed this one."

Charley hesitated for a long moment.

"I'll send a telegram to the governor when we get back to Juanita . . . and since I was the arresting officer in the first place . . . I don't think that getting you a permanent release will be that difficult."

Pennell took Elisabeth in his arms and swung her around while everyone else applauded.

Now Don Roberto spoke.

"I will be taking Henry Ellis and his parents back to my *rancho* so we can share the time together we were all supposed to have before this all happened.

"And I want to invite you, too, Charley Sunday . . . along with Roscoe, Feather, and our mutual friend, Roca Fuerte. All of you come along and spend a few days, too . . . will you? I have a very large lake on my property, where you men can talk to your hearts' content about the good old days while you sit on the grassy bank of that lake fishing, eating, napping, and drinking tequila by the bottle, until your bellies are full and your bodies are rested."

Epilogue

1961

Hank looked down. Noel had crawled up onto his lap and fallen asleep somewhere during the battle. Evie, the mother, was cleaning up—ferrying dirty dishes and glasses into the house and onto the kitchen sink. She was on her third trip when her two boys, Josh and Caleb, silently joined her, lugging the bigger bowls that still held leftovers into the kitchen behind her.

Josh returned with a broom and started sweeping the patio. Caleb called out that he was tired and going to bed.

Evie returned with two cups of steaming coffee and sat down opposite Hank at the redwood picnic table.

She nodded, indicating Noel, still sleeping in her great-grandfather's lap.

"If she's too much for you, Grampa Hank, I can take her in and put her to bed," said Evie.

"Naw," said the old man. "I've lifted my share of calves, and on some occasions a near full-grown heifer. She's no bother for me."

Evie took a sip of her coffee, then she nodded for Hank to do the same.

"No, thank you, ma'am," said Hank. "I drink that stuff too close to my bedtime, I'll be up half the night."

She leaned in closer with a sly smile on her face.

"Tell me, Grampa Hank," she said, "was all of what you just told your great-grandchildren a true story?"

"Well," said Hank, shifting his weight under the child on his lap, "most of it's true . . . some of it's not . . . and the rest is probably how I wish it had happened. But the one thing I do know is that my parents were kidnapped, and my grampa Charley got 'em back. And these three kids seemed to enjoy it all, didn't they?"

"Sure did," said Evie, yawning, then settling back against the tabletop.

"It took their minds off their own problems for a while . . . and it let them see what goes on in other folks' lives," Hank said.

"Your grampa Charley must have been something, Henry Ellis Pritchard," she told him. "I'll bet he was just like you."

"Not quite," said the old man. "They just don't make 'em like my grampa Charley anymore."

There were a few moments of silence between the two, then:

"Mommy?"

It was Noel, who had just awakened.

"I have to go to the bathroom, again."

Before he lifted the child back down to the ground, Hank looked Evie directly in the eye.

"Me too. And that's a fact," he said with a wink.